Tom Clancy's Op-Centre
State of Siege

D0718400

CREATED BY
TOM CLANCY & STEVE PIECZENIK
WRITTEN BY JEFF ROVIN

I Tom Clancy's Op-Centre
II Tom Clancy's Op-Centre: Mirror Image
III Tom Clancy's Op-Centre: Games of State
IV Tom Clancy's Op-Centre: Acts of War
V Tom Clancy's Op-Centre: Balance of Power
VI Tom Clancy's Op-Centre: State of Siege
VII Tom Clancy's Op-Centre: Divide and Conquer
VIII Tom Clancy's Op-Centre: Line of Control

BY TOM CLANCY

The Hunt for Red October
Red Storm Rising
Patriot Games
The Cardinal of the Kremlin
Clear and Present Danger
The Sum of All Fears
Without Remorse
Debt of Honour
Executive Orders
SSN

BY STEVE PIECZENIK

The Mind Palace
Blood Heat
Maximum Vigilance
Pax Pacifica
State of Emergency

TOM CLANCY'S

Op-Centre

STATE
OF SIEGE

CREATED BY

Tom Clancy
AND
Steve Pieczenik

Written by

JEFF ROVIN

HarperCollins*Publishers*

This novel is entirely a work of fiction.
The names, characters and incidents portrayed in it are
the work of the author's imagination. Any resemblance to
actual persons, living or dead, events or localities is
entirely coincidental.

HarperCollins*Publishers*
77–85 Fulham Palace Road,
Hammersmith, London W6 8JB

www.harpercollins.co.uk

This paperback edition 2005
1

First published in the USA by
Berkley Books 1999

A catalogue record for this book
is available from the British Library

ISBN 9780007810079

Set in Times

Printed and bound in Great Britain by
CPI Bookmarque, Croydon, CR0 4TD

Acknowledgments

We would like to thank Jeff Rovin for his creative ideas and his invaluable contribution to the preparation of the manuscript. We would also like to acknowledge the assistance of Martin H. Greenberg, Larry Segriff, Robert Youdelman, Esq., and the wonderful people at Penguin Putnam Inc., including Phyllis Grann, David Shanks and Tom Colgan. As always, we would like to thank Robert Gottlieb of The William Morris Agency, our agent and friend, without whom this book would never have been conceived. But most important, it is for you, our readers, to determine how successful our collective endeavor has been.

—Tom Clancy and Steve Pieczenik

United Nations—The Security Council put the final touches yesterday on a written demand that Iraq co-operate with international arms inspectors—but threatens no force if Baghdad fails to comply.

—Associated Press,
November 5, 1998

PROLOGUE

Kampong Thom, Cambodia
1993

She died while he held her under a brilliant dawn. Her eyelids closed softly, a faint breath rose from her delicate throat, and then she was gone.

Hang Sary looked down at the pale face of the young woman. He looked at the grass and dirt in her wet hair and the cuts in her forehead and across her nose. He felt revulsion when he saw the red lipstick on her mouth, the rouge that had smeared across her cheek, and the charcoal-gray mascara that had run from her eyes to her ears.

This wasn't how it was supposed to be. Not even here, in a land where the concept of innocence was as foreign as the dream of peace.

Phum Sary should not have died so young, and she should not have died like this. No one should die like this, lying in a windy rice field, the cool water muddy-red with their blood. But at least Phum had died knowing *who* it was that held her in his arms. At least she didn't die as she'd probably lived most of her life, alone and uncherished. And though the search that Hang had never quite abandoned was over, he knew that another was about to begin.

Hang's knees were raised and his sister's head was in

1

his lap. He lightly touched the cold tip of her nose, the fine line of her jaw, her round mouth. A mouth that always used to smile, regardless of what she was doing. The girl felt so small and fragile.

He pulled her arms from the water and laid them on the waist of her tight blue lamé dress. He cuddled her closer. He wondered if anyone had held her like this in ten years. Had she lived this horrible life the entire time? Had she finally had enough and decided that death was preferable?

Hang's long face tightened as he thought about her life. Then it exploded in tears. *How could he have been so near and not have known it?* He and Ty had been in the village, undercover, for nearly a week. Could he ever forgive himself for not having seen her in time to save her?

Poor Ty would be inconsolable when she learned who this was. Ty had been in the camp reconnoitering, trying to find out who was behind this. She had radioed Hang to let him know that one of the women had apparently tried to escape shortly before sunrise, when the watch changed. She'd been chased and shot. Phum had taken the bullet in the side. She'd probably run, then walked until she could no longer move. Then she must have lain down here to look at the waning night sky. Phum used to look at the sky a great deal when she was a little girl. Ty wondered if that sky, the memories of a better time, had given his little sister any peace at the end.

Hang slipped his trembling fingers through his sister's long, black hair. He heard splashing in the distance. That would be Ty. He'd radioed his partner that he'd spotted the girl and saw her go down. She said she'd be there within a half hour. They had been hoping, at least, that she could give them a name, help them break the monstrous union that was destroying so many young lives. But that didn't happen. Seeing him, Phum only had the strength to say his name. She died with her brother's name and the hint of a smile on her bright red lips, not the name of the creature who had done this.

Ty arrived and looked down. Dressed like a local peasant, she stood there with the wind whispering around her. And then she gasped. She knelt beside Hang and put her arms around him. Neither of them moved or spoke for several minutes. Then, slowly, Hang stood with his sister's body in his arms. He carried her back toward the old station wagon that served as his field outpost.

He knew they shouldn't leave Kampong Thom now. Not when they were so close to getting what they needed. But he had to take his sister home. That was where she should be laid to rest.

The sun quickly warmed and then baked his damp back. Ty opened the back of the station wagon and spread a blanket amid the cartons. Inside the boxes were weapons and radio equipment, maps and lists, and a powerful incendiary device. Hang wore the remote trigger hooked around his belt. If they were ever caught, he would destroy everything in the car. Then he would use the .357 Smith & Wesson he carried to take his own life. Ty would do likewise.

With Ty's help, Hang placed the body of his sister on the blanket. Gently, he folded her inside. Before leaving, he looked out across the field. It had been made sacred with her blood. But the land would not be clean until it was washed with the blood of those who had done this.

It would be. However long it took, he vowed that it would be.

3

ONE

Paris, France
Monday, 6:13 A.M.

Seven years ago, during training for service with UN-TAC—the United Nations Transitional Authority in Cambodia—brash, adventuresome Lieutenant Reynold Downer of the 11th/28th Battalion, the Royal Western Australia Regiment, learned that there were three conditions that had to be met before a United Nations peacekeeping operation could be sent to any nation. It wasn't something he'd ever wondered about or wanted to be a part of, but the Commonwealth of Australia felt differently.

First, the fifteen member nations of the UN Security Council had to approve the operation and its parameters in detail. Second, since the United Nations does not have an army, member nations of the General Assembly had to agree to contribute troops as well as a force commander, who was put in charge of deployment and execution of the multinational army. Third, the warring nations had to consent to the presence of the PKO.

Once there, the peacekeepers had three goals. The first was to establish and enforce a cease-fire while the warring parties sought peaceful solutions. The second was to create a buffer zone between the hostile factions. And the third was to maintain the peace. This included military action when necessary, de-mining the terrain so civilians could return to homes and to food and water supplies, and also providing humanitarian assistance.

All of that was carefully explained to the light infantry troops during two weeks of training at Irwin Barracks, Stubbs Terrace, Karrakatta. Two weeks that consisted of learning local customs, politics, language, water purification, and how to drive slowly, with one eye on the dirt roads, so you didn't run over a mine. Also learning not to blush when you caught a glimpse of yourself in a powder blue beret and matching ascot.

When the UN. indoctrination was done—"the gelding," as his commanding officer quite accurately described it—the Australian contingent was spread among the eighty-six cantonment sites in Cambodia. Australia's own Lieutenant General John M. Sanderson was force commander of the entire UNTAC operation, which lasted from March 1992 to September 1993.

The UNTAC mission was carefully designed to avoid armed conflict. UN soldiers weren't supposed to shoot unless fired upon, and only then without escalating the hostilities. The deaths of any enlisted personnel were to be investigated by the local police, not by the military. Human rights were to be encouraged through education, not force. Apart from serving as a buffer, distributing food and offering health care were the PKO's top priorities.

To Downer, being in the field seemed less like a military operation than a carnival. *Come on, you warring or downtrodden Third World peoples. Get your bread here, your penicillin, your clean water.* The circus feeling was enhanced by tents that were topped with colorful banners and local gawkers who weren't sure what to make of it all. Though many of them took what was offered, they looked like they wished it would just go away. Violence was an expected and understood part of their daily lives. Outsiders were not.

There was so little to do in Cambodia that Colonel Ivan Georgiev, a high-ranking officer in the Bulgarian People's Army, organized a prostitution ring. They were protected by officers of Pol Pot's renegade National Army of Democratic Kampuchea, who needed foreign currency to buy arms and supplies and were paid 25 percent of the take. Georgiev ran the ring from tents erected behind his command post. Local girls came for what were supposed to be radio UNTAC language courses and stayed for an infusion of foreign currency. That was where Downer first met both Georgiev and Major Ishiro Sazanka. Georgiev said that the soldiers of Japan and Australia were his best customers, though the Japanese tended to get rough with the girls and had to be watched. "Polite sadists," the Bulgarian had called them. Downer's uncle Thomas, who had fought the Japanese as part of the 7th Australian Division in the Southwest Pacific, would have quarreled with that description. He didn't find the Japanese at all polite.

Downer helped to recruit new "language students" for the tents, while Georgiev's other aides found different ways of getting girls to work for them—including kidnapping. The Khmer Rouge helped gather new girls whenever possible. Except for this sideline, Downer found Cambodia a bore. The United Nations guidelines were too soft, too restrictive. As he'd learned growing up on the docks of Sydney, there was only one guideline that mattered. Did some son of a bitch deserve a bullet in the head? If he did, pull the trigger and go home. If

7

he didn't, what the hell were you doing there?

Downer took a last swallow of coffee and pushed the heavy mug back along the vinyl-covered card table. The coffee was good, black and bitter, the way he drank it in the field. It made him feel energized, ready to act. Maybe that wasn't a good idea, here and now, where there was nothing to act against. But he liked the feeling anyway.

The Australian looked at the watch on his sun-darkened wrist. *Where the hell were they?*

The group was usually back by eight o'clock. How long did it take to make a videotape of something they'd videotaped six times already?

The answer was that it took as long as Captain Vandal needed it to take. Vandal was in charge of this phase of the operation. And if the French officer weren't so efficient, none of them would be here. Vandal was the one who got them all into the country, had acquired the hardware, had supervised the recon, and would get them out of here so they could start phase two of the operation, which would be run by Georgiev.

Downer fished a graham cracker from an open box and snapped at it impatiently. The taste, the crispness, brought him back to his arms training in the outback. The unit lived on these things there.

He looked around the small, dark apartment as he chewed. His soft blue eyes moved from the kitchen on the right to the TV across the room to the front door. Vandal had rented this place over two years before. The Frenchman admitted that luxury was not a consideration. The one-room, first-floor flat was located on a crooked little street just off the Boulevard de la Bastille, not far from the large bureau de poste. Apart from the location,

8

the only thing that was important was that they be on the first floor of the building for a window escape if necessary. As Vandal had promised when the five of them pooled their savings for this operation, he would spend extravagantly only on forged documents, surveillance gear, and weapons.

As the tall, powerfully built Downer brushed crumbs from his faded blue jeans, he glanced at the oversized duffel bags lying in a row between the TV and the window. He was baby-sitting the five lumpy bags filled with weapons. Vandal had done his job there. AK-47s, handguns, tear gas, grenades, a rocket launcher. All of them unmarked and untraceable, bought through Chinese arms dealers the Frenchman had met while the PKO was in Cambodia.

God bless the United Nations, Downer thought.

Tomorrow morning, shortly after dawn, the men would load the bags onto the truck they'd bought. Vandal and Downer would drop Sazanka, Georgiev, and Barone at the factory helipad and then time their departure so everyone could meet again later at the target.

The target, Downer thought. So ordinary yet so vital to the rest of the operation.

The Australian's eyes returned to the table. There was a white ceramic bowl sitting beside the phone. The bowl was filled with black paste—burned diagrams and notes soaked in tap water. The notes contained everything from calculations about approximate tail winds and head winds at one thousand feet up àt eight in the morning to traffic flow to the police presence on the Seine. Ashes could still be deciphered; wet ashes were useless.

Just one more stinking day of this, he told himself.

When the rest of the team returned, there'd be one

more afternoon of studying videotapes, making sure they had everything covered for this phase of the operation. One more night of drawing maps for this part of the operation, then calculating flight times, bus schedules, street names, and the location of arms dealers in New York for the next phase. Just to make sure they'd memorized them all. And then there'd be one more dawn of burning everything they'd written so the police would never find it here or in the trash.

Downer's eyes drifted across the room to the sleeping bags on the floor. They sat in front of a sofa, the only other piece of furniture in the room. There was a big window fan in the room's only window, and it had been running constantly during this heat wave. Vandal assured him that the hundred-plus temperatures were good for the plan. The target was vented, not air-conditioned, and the men inside were going to be a little more sluggish than usual.

Not like us, Downer thought. He and his teammates had a goal.

Downer thought of the four other ex-soldiers who were involved in the project. He'd met them all in Phnom Penh, and each of them had a very different, very personal reason for being here.

A key rattled in the front door. Downer reached for his Type 64 silenced pistol, tucked in a holster hanging from the back of the wooden chair. He gently pushed the graham cracker box aside so he had a clear shot at the door. He remained seated. The only person other than Vandal who had a key was the superintendent. In the three times Downer had stayed at the apartment during the past year, the old man only came by when he was called—and sometimes not even then. If it were anyone else, they didn't belong here, and they'd die. Downer half-hoped it was someone he didn't know. He was in the mood to pull the trigger.

The door opened and Etienne Vandal walked in. His longish brown hair was slicked back and he was wearing sunglasses, a video camera carrying case slung casually over his left shoulder. He was followed by the bald, barrel-chested Georgiev, the short and swarthy Barone, and the tall, broad-shouldered Sazanka. All of the men were wearing touristy T-shirts and blue jeans. They also wore the same, flat expressions.

Sazanka shut the door. He shut it quietly, politely.

Downer sighed. He slipped the firearm back in its holster. "How'd it go?" the Australian asked. Downer's voice was still rich with the tight gutturals of western New South Wales.

"Ewed ih gow?" Barone said, mimicking the Australian's thick accent.

"Stop that," Vandal told him.

"Yes, sir," Barone replied. He threw the officer a casual salute and frowned at Downer.

Downer didn't like Barone. The cocky little man had something none of the other men possessed: an attitude. He acted as though everyone were a potential enemy, even his allies. Barone also had a good ear. He'd worked as a custodian at the American embassy when he was a teenager and had lost most of his accent. The one thing that kept Downer from lashing out at the younger man was they both knew that if the little Uruguayan ever crossed the line too far, the six-foot-four-inch Australian could and would pull him in two.

Vandal put the case on the table and popped the tape from the camera. He walked over to the TV.

"I think the surveillance went fine," Vandal said. "The traffic patterns appear to be the same as they were last week. But we'll compare the tapes, just to make sure."

"For the last time, I hope," Barone said.

"We *all* hope," Downer said.

"Yes, but I'm anxious to *move*," the twenty-nine-year-old officer said. He did not say where he wanted to move. A group of foreigners meeting in a rundown flat never knew who might be eavesdropping.

Sazanka sat silently on the sofa and untied his Nikes. He massaged his thick feet. Barone tossed him a bottled water from the refrigerator in the kitchenette. The Japanese grunted his thanks. Sazanka's command of English was the weakest, and he tended to say very little. Downer shared his uncle's view of the Japanese, and Sazanka's silence made him happy. Ever since Downer was a child, Japanese sailors, tourists, and speculators had been all over the harbor in Sydney. If they didn't act as though they owned it, they acted as though one day they would. Unfortunately, Sazanka could fly a variety of aircraft. The group needed his skills.

Barone handed a bottle to Georgiev, who was standing behind him.

"Thank you," Georgiev said.

They were the first words Downer had heard the Bulgarian speak since dinner the night before—even though he spoke nearly perfect English, having worked for almost ten years as a Central Intelligence Agency contact in Sofia. Georgiev hadn't talked a lot in Cambodia, either. He'd kept an eye out for their Khmer Rouge contacts as well as undercover government police or UN human rights observers. The Bulgarian preferred to listen, even when nothing was being discussed. Downer wished he himself had the patience for that. Good listeners could hear things in casual conversation, when people had their guard down, that often proved valuable.

"Want one?" Barone asked Vandal.

The Frenchman shook his head.

Barone looked at Downer. "I'd offer you a bottle, but I know you'd refuse. You like it hot. Boiling."

"Warm beverages are better for you," Downer replied. "They make you sweat. Cleans the system."

"As if we don't sweat enough," Barone commented.

"I don't," Downer said. "And it's a good sensation. Makes you feel productive. Alive."

"When you're with a lady, sweating is great," Barone said. "In here, it's self-punishment."

"That can be a good feeling, too," Downer said.

"To a psychotic, maybe."

Downer grinned. "And aren't we, mate?"

"Enough," Vandal said as the videotape began to play.

Downer was a talker, too. In his case, the sound of his own voice comforted him. He used to talk himself to sleep when he was a kid, tell himself stories to drown out the sound of his drunken dockworker father slapping around whatever cheap woman he was with in their rickety wooden apartment. Talking was a habit Downer never gave up.

Barone walked into the room. He popped the seal on his own water bottle, chugged it down in a long swallow, then pulled up a chair and sat beside Downer. He snatched a graham cracker and chomped it down as they all watched the nineteen-inch TV set. He leaned toward Downer.

13

"I don't like what you said," Barone whispered. "A psychotic is irrational. I am not."

"If you say so."

"Ah dew," Barone said, imitating Downer, this time with an edge.

Downer let it go. Unlike Barone, he realized that he only needed the man's skills, not his approval.

The men watched the twenty-minute tape through once, then watched it again. Before watching it a third time, Vandal joined Downer and Barone at the rickety table. Barone had gotten himself focused. He was a former revolutionary who had helped found the short-lived Consejo de Seguridad Nacional, which had ousted the corrupt President Bordaberry. His expertise was explosives. Downer's experience was firearms, rockets, and hand-to-hand combat. Sazanka flew. Georgiev had the contacts to obtain whatever they needed through the black market, which was tapped into all the resources of the former Soviet Union, its clients in the Middle and Far East, and in the United States. Georgiev had recently returned from New York, where he spent time arranging for weapons through a Khmer Rouge arms supplier and working with his intelligence contact, going over the target itself. All of that would be needed during the second part of the operation.

But part two was not on their minds right now. First part one had to succeed. Together, the three men single-framed through the tape, making sure that the explosion they planned would get them through the target zone without destroying anything else.

After spending four hours on the tape and the rest of the afternoon meeting in the field with Vandal's local contacts to review the truck, helicopter, and other equipment they'd be using here, the team ate at a sidewalk café. Then they returned to the room to rest.

As anxious as the men were, they all slept. They had to.

Tomorrow, they would begin to inaugurate a new era in international relations. One that would not only change the world by calling attention to a big lie but would also make them rich. As Downer lay on top of his sleeping bag, he enjoyed the gentle breeze of the open window. He pictured himself being somewhere else. His own island, perhaps. Maybe even his own country. And he calmed himself by listening to the voice in his head telling him all the things he could do with his share of two hundred and fifty million dollars.

TWO

Andrews Air Force Base, Maryland
Sunday, 12:10 A.M.

When he'd ended his tenure as the mayor of Los Angeles, Paul Hood decided that cleaning out one's desk was a misnomer. What you were really doing was mourning, just like at a funeral. You were remembering the good and the sad, the bittersweet and the rewards, the accomplishments and the unfinished business, the love and sometimes the hate.

The hate, he thought, his hazel eyes narrowing. He was full of it now, though he wasn't sure at whom or what or why.

Hate wasn't the reason he'd resigned as the first director of Op-Center, the U.S. government's elite crisis management team. He'd done that to spend more time with his wife, his daughter, and his son. To keep his family intact. But he was full of it just the same.

At Sharon? he wondered suddenly, half-ashamed. *Are you mad at your wife for making you choose?*

He tried to sort through that as he cleaned out his desk, dropping declassified memories into a cardboard box—the classified files and even personal letters therein had to stay. He couldn't believe he'd only been here two and one-half years. That wasn't a long time compared to many jobs. But he'd worked cockpit-close with the

17

People here and he was going to miss them. There was also what his intelligence chief Bob Herbert once described as "a pornographic excitement" in the work. Lives, sometimes millions of them, were affected by the wise or instinctive or occasionally desperate decisions he and his team had made here. It was like Herbert had said. Hood never felt like a god making those decisions. He felt like an animal. Every sense hair-trigger alert, nervous energy at a high boil.

He was going to miss those feelings, too.

He opened a small plastic box that held a paper clip General Sergei Orlov had given him. Orlov was the head of the Russian op-center, a facility code-named Mirror Image. Op-Center had helped Mirror Image prevent renegade Russian officers and politicians from throwing Eastern Europe into war. The paper clip had a fiber-thin microphone inside. It had been used by Colonel Leonid Rossky to spy on potential rivals of Minister of the Interior Nikolai Dogin, one of the organizers of the war effort.

Hood put the plastic box in the cardboard carton and looked at a small, black piece of twisted metal. The shard was stiff and light, the ends bubbled and charred. It was part of the skin of a North Korean Nodong missile. It had melted when Op-Center's military unit, Striker, destroyed the weapon before it could be launched at Japan. Hood's second-in-command, General Mike Rodgers, had brought the fragment back for him.

My second-in-command, Hood thought. Technically, Hood would be on vacation for two weeks before his resignation took effect. Mike would be acting director until then. Hood hoped the president would give Mike the job full time after that. It would be a terrible blow to Mike if he didn't.

Hood picked up the Nodong fragment. It was like holding a piece of his life. Japan was spared an attack, one to two million lives saved. Several lives lost. This memento and others like it were passive, but the memories they triggered were anything but.

He put the fragment back in the carton. The hum of air coming from the overhead vents seemed unusually loud. Or maybe the office was just unusually silent? The night crew was on, and the phone wasn't ringing. Footsteps weren't coming to or from his door.

Hood quickly went through the other memories tucked in the top drawer of his desk.

There were postcards from the kids when they vacationed at Grandma's—not like this last time, when his wife took them there while she decided whether or not to leave him. There were books he'd read on airplanes with notes scribbled in the margins, things he had to remember to do when he got where he was going or when he returned. And there was a brass key from the hotel in Hamburg, Germany, where he bumped into Nancy Jo Bosworth, a woman he'd loved and planned to marry. Nancy had walked out of his life over twenty years before without an explanation.

Hood held the brass key in his palm. He resisted the urge to slip it into his pocket, feel like he was back at the hotel, just for a moment. Instead, Hood placed the key in the box. Returning to the girl, even in memory, who'd walked out of his life, wasn't going to help save his family.

Hood shut the top drawer. He'd told Sharon that he would take her on one big last-night-of-having-anexpense-account dinner, and there was no excuse to miss it. He'd already said his last good-byes to the office workers, and the senior staff had thrown him a surprise party that afternoon—even though it wasn't much of a surprise. When intelligence chief Bob Herbert had E-mailed everyone the time and date, he'd forgotten to remove Hood's E-mail address from his list. Paul had pretended to be surprised when he walked into the conference room. He was just glad that Herbert didn't make mistakes like that as a rule.

Hood opened the bottom drawer. He took out his personal address book, the crossword puzzle CD-ROM he'd never gotten to use, and the scrapbook of daughter Harleigh's violin recitals. He'd missed too damn many of those. The four of them would be going to New York at the end of the week so Harleigh could perform with other young Washington virtuosi at a function for United Nations ambassadors. Ironically, they were celebrating a major peace initiative in Spain, where Op-Center had been involved in helping to prevent a civil war. Unfortunately, the public—parents included—were not invited. Hood would have been curious to see how the new secretary-general, Mala Chatterjee, handled her first public affair. She had been chosen after Secretary-General Massimo Marcello Manni had suffered a fatal heart attack. Though the young woman wasn't as experienced as other candidates, she was committed to the struggle for human rights through peaceful means. Influential nations like the United States, Germany, and Japan—which saw her strong stand as a means to tweak China—helped her get the appointment.

Hood left the government phone directory, a monthly terminology bulletin—the latest names of nations and their leaders—and a thick book of military acronyms. Unlike Herbert and General Rodgers, Hood had never served in the military. He'd always felt self-conscious about never having risked his life in the service, especially when he had to send Striker into the field. But, as Op-Center's FBI liaison Darrell McCaskey once pointed out, "That's why we call this a *team*. Everyone brings different skills to the table."

Hood paused when he came to a stack of photos in the bottom of the drawer. He removed the rubber band and looked through them. Among the pictures of barbecues and photo-ops with world leaders were snapshots of Striker's Private Bass Moore, of Striker commander Lieutenant Colonel Charlie Squires, and of Op-Center's political and economic liaison Martha Mackall. Private Moore died in North Korea, Lieutenant Colonel Squires lost his life on a mission in Russia, and Martha had been assassinated just a few days before on the streets of Madrid, Spain. Hood replaced the rubber band and put the stack of pictures in the carton.

He closed the last drawer. He picked up his well-worn City of Los Angeles mousepad and Camp David coffee mug and placed them in the box. As he did, he noticed someone standing to his left, just outside the open office door.

"Need any help?"

Hood smiled lightly. He ran a hand through his wavy black hair. "No, but you can come in. What are you doing here so late?"

"Checking the Far Eastern newspaper headlines for tomorrow," she said. "We've got some disinformation out there."

"About?"

21

"I can't tell you," she said. "You don't work here anymore."

"Touché," he replied, smiling.

Ann Farris smiled back as she walked slowly into the office. The *Washington Times* once described her as one of the twenty-five most eligible young divorcées in the nation's capital. Nearly six years later, she still was. Op-Center's five-foot-seven-inch-tall press liaison was wearing a tight black skirt and white blouse. Her dark rust eyes were large and warm, and they softened the anger Hood was feeling.

"I promised myself I wasn't going to bother you," the tall, slender woman said.

"But here you are."

"Here I am."

"And it's not a bother," he added.

Ann stopped beside the desk and looked down at him. Her long, brown hair fell along her face and over the front of her shoulders. Looking at her eyes and smile, Hood was reminded of all the times during the past two and a half years that she'd encouraged him, helped him, made no secret that she cared for him.

"I didn't want to bother you," she said, "but I also didn't want to say good-bye at a party."

"I understand. I'm glad you're here."

Ann sat on the edge of the desk. "What are you going to do, Paul? Do you think you'll stay in D.C.?"

"I don't know. I was thinking about going back to the financial world," he said. "I've arranged to see a few people after we get back from New York. If that doesn't work out, I don't know. Maybe I'll settle in some small rural town and open an accounting practice.

22

Taxes, money market, a Range Rover, and raking leaves. It wouldn't be a bad life.''

"I know. I lived it."

"And you don't think I can."

"I don't know," she said. "What are you going to do when the children are gone? My own son's scratching on teenagerhood and I'm already thinking about what I'll do when he leaves for college."

"What *will* you do?" Hood asked.

"Unless some wonderful, middle-aged guy with black hair and hazel eyes carries me off to Antigua or Tonga?" she asked.

"Yes," Hood said, flushing. "If that doesn't happen."

"I'll probably buy a house somewhere in the middle of one of those islands and write. Real fiction. Not the stuff I give the Washington Press Corps every day. There are some stories I want to tell."

The former political reporter and one-time press secretary to Connecticut Senator Bob Kaufmann did indeed have stories to tell. Tales of spin-doctoring, affairs, and back-stabbing in the corridors of power.

Hood sighed. He looked at his depersonalized desk. "I don't know what I'll do. I've got some personal things to work on."

"With your wife, you mean."

"With Sharon," he said softly. "If I succeed, then the future will take care of itself."

Hood had made a point of saying his wife's name because it made her seem more real, more present. He did that because Ann was pushing more than usual. This would be her last chance to talk to him here, where the memories of a long, close professional relationship, of

23

triumph and mourning, and of sexual tension were suddenly very vivid.

"Can I ask you something?" Ann said.

"Sure."

Her eyes lowered. So did her voice. "How long will you give it?"

"How long?" Hood said under his breath. He shook his head. "I don't know, Ann. I really don't." He looked at her for a long moment. "Now let me ask you something."

"Sure," she said. "Anything." Her eyes were even softer than before. He didn't understand why he was doing this to himself.

"Why me?" he asked.

She seemed surprised. "Why do I care about you?"

"Is that what this is? Care?"

"No," she admitted quietly.

"Then tell me why," he pressed.

"It isn't obvious?"

"No," he said. "Governor Vegas. Senator Kaufmann. The president of the United States. You've been close to some of the most dynamic men in the nation. I'm not like them. I *ran* from the arena, Ann."

"No. You left it," she said. "There's a difference. You left because you were tired of the smears, of the political correctness, of having to watch every word. Honesty is very appealing, Paul. So is intelligence. So is keeping cool when all those charismatic politicians and generals and foreign leaders are running around swinging their sabres."

"Steady Paul Hood," he said.

"What's wrong with that?" Ann asked.

24

"I don't know," Hood said. He stood and picked up the carton. "What I do know is that something's wrong somewhere in my life, and I need to find out what it is."

Ann also rose. "Well, if you need any help looking for it, I'm available. If you want to talk, have coffee, dinner—just call."

"I will," Hood smiled. "And thanks for stopping by."

"Sure," she said.

He motioned with the carton for Ann to go first. She left the office briskly, without looking back. If there was sadness or temptation in her eyes, Hood was spared both.

He shut the office door behind him. It closed gently but with a solid, final click.

As he walked past the cubicles to the elevator, Hood accepted good wishes from the night team. He rarely saw them, since Bill Abram and Curt Hardaway ran things after seven. There were so many young faces. So many go-getters. Steady Paul Hood was definitely feeling like an antique.

Hopefully, the trip to New York would give him time to think, time to try and fix his relationship with Sharon. He reached the elevator, stepped in, and took a last look at the complex that had taken so much of his time and spirit—but had also given him those adrenaline jolts. There was no point lying to himself: He was going to miss it. All of it.

As the door shut, Hood found himself getting angry again. Whether he was angry at what he was leaving or what he was going to, he just didn't know. Op-Center psychologist Liz Gordon once told him that confusion was a term we'd invented to describe an order of things that was not yet understood.

He hoped so. He truly did.

THREE

Paris, France
Tuesday, 7:32 A.M.

Every section of Paris is rich with something, be it history, hotels, museums, monuments, cafés, shops, markets, or even sunshine. Just northeast of the Seine, beyond the half-kilometer-long Le Port de Plaisance de Paris de l'Arsenal—a canal for recreational boating—is a region rich with something a little different: post offices. There are two of them a few blocks apart on the Boulevard Diderot and a third building between them, just to the north. Other post offices are scattered throughout the district. Most of them derive the bulk of their business from the tourists who come to Paris year round.

Each morning at five-thirty, an armored truck operated by the Banque de Commerce begins its rounds of these post offices. It carries an armed driver and one armed guard up front and another armed guard in back, along with postage stamps, money orders, and postal cards to deliver to the five post offices. When it completes its rounds, the armored truck is carrying canvas sacks loaded with the counted, banded cash collected by each post office the day before. Typically, the cash is international currency equivalent to three-quarters of a million to one million U.S. dollars.

The truck follows the same route every day, making

its way northwest and then turning up the heavily traveled Boulevard de la Bastille. Once the armored car is past the Place de la Bastille, it deposits its cargo at a bank building on the Boulevard Richard Lenoir. The policy of the Banque de Commerce, like many armored car companies, is to adhere to the same path every day. That way, the drivers will know the route and its character and recognize any changes. If there's an electrical team working on a streetlight or a road crew working on a pothole, the driver is informed ahead of time. A two-way radio is always turned on in the cab and is monitored by a dispatcher at the Banque de Commerce office across the river on the Rue Cuvier near the Jardin des Plantes.

The one constant—paradoxically, the one constant that always changes—is traffic. The men watch from behind bulletproof windshields as faster-moving cars and trucks weave around the heavily armored four-ton vehicle. Along Le Port de l'Arsenal, boat traffic is also constant, mostly motorboats from fourteen to forty feet in length. They come here from the river so that crews can dine, rest, take on fuel, or undergo repairs at the docks.

The men in the armored truck did not notice anything unusual on this sunlit morning except for the heat, which was even worse than it had been the day before. And it wasn't even eight A.M. yet. Though their dark gray caps were hot and snug, the men wore them to keep the sweat from dripping into their eyes. The driver wore an MR F1 revolver; the guard in the passenger's seat and the man in the back both carried FAMA assault rifles.

Traffic was heavy at this hour, as trucks made deliveries and small cars maneuvered to get around them.

None of the men in the armored car thought anything was out of the ordinary when a truck in front of them slowed to let a Citroën pass. The truck was an old rig with battered, dirty-white metal siding and a green canvas curtain in the back.

The driver's eyes drifted to the left, toward the canal. "I tell you," he said. "I would like to be out there today on my little Whaler. The sun, the rocking of the waves, the quiet."

The other man's eyes snapped over as the masts and trees rushed by. "I'd be bored."

"That's because you like to hunt. Me? I'd be content to sit in the breeze with my cassette player and fishing—"

The driver swallowed the rest of the sentence and frowned. Neither the caps nor the weapons nor the open radio nor the familiarity of the route mattered when the old truck in front stopped suddenly, and the curtain in back was pulled aside. A man stood in the back. Another man walked around from the passenger's side. Both wore camouflage uniforms, bulletproof vests, gas masks, equipment belts, and thick rubber gloves. Each man held a shoulder-mounted rocket-propelled grenade launcher. The man in the truck leaned to the passenger's side slightly, angling himself so that the back of the RPG was facing away from the cab of their truck. The other man stood on the street, the RPG angled upward slightly.

The guard in the truck reacted immediately. "Emergency!" he said into the open microphone. "Two masked men in truck, license 101763, have stopped in front of us. They are armed with rocket launchers."

A heartbeat later, the men fired.

There was a faint *whoosh* as twin spikes of yellow

orange flame shot from the rear of the grenade launchers. At the same time, a smooth, steel-jacketed, pear-shaped projectile rocketed from the barrel of each tube. The grenades hit the windshield on either side and exploded. The guard in the passenger seat raised his gun.

"The windshield held!" the guard cried triumphantly.

The driver looked into the right and left side mirrors. Then he started to nose to the right, into oncoming traffic. "Attempting evasive maneuver to the north lanes—" he said.

Suddenly, both men screamed.

High-end bulletproof glass, made of plastic laminate, is designed to withstand even close-proximity blasts from hand grenades. It may shatter in a single-hole or web pattern, but it'll hold without fragmentation for one or possibly two assaults. After that, there are no guarantees. Whoever is behind the glass—the driver of an armored car or limousine, the employee at a bank, prison, parking or transit booth, or federal office building—is supposed to call for backup and evacuate the target area if possible. In the case of an armored car, even if the occupants can't drive off, the driver and passenger are both armed. In theory, once the glass is breached, the attackers are equally at risk.

But the grenades that had been fired from the truck were two-chambered. The front chamber contained an explosive. The larger back chamber, which was shattered in the blast, contained disulphuric acid.

The windshield had broken the same way in two spots, a sunburst pattern caused by high-velocity fragmentation: a nearly inch-wide crater at the center with filament-thin cracks radiating from it. Some of the acid had been blown through the hole, splattering the driver and passenger in the face and lap. The rest of the acid ate through the cracks by dissolving the non–chemically inert polymers that were a component of the glass.

Etienne Vandal and Reynold Downer slung the grenade launchers over their shoulders. Downer jumped from the back as the armored car slammed into the right rear corner of the truck. The truck skidded to the right, the armored car to the left, and both came to a stop. Vandal and Downer jumped onto the hood of the armored car. All they had to do was kick the windshield to knock it in. It came apart just as Vandal had said it would. The glass was thicker and heavier than Downer had expected, and the acid residue caused the rubber heel of his boot to smoke. But he only had a moment to think about that. The Australian pulled an automatic from a holster he wore on his right hip. He was standing on the passenger's side. As cars in the other lanes slowed and watched and then sped away, Downer fired a single shot into the forehead of the guard. Vandal did the same on the other side.

The lone guard in the sealed cargo compartment called the dispatcher from his own secure radio in the back. Vandal had known he would do that because, after leaving the military with an impeccable record, the lieutenant had easily landed work as a security guard for the Banque de Commerce armored cars. He had served on an armored vehicle just like this one for nearly seven months. Vandal also knew that at this point in the journey, with traffic as heavy as it was, it would take the police emergency response team at least ten minutes to get there. And that was more than enough time to finish the job.

From studying the videotapes, the men had ascertained that the armor used in the cars hadn't changed in the months since Vandal had left his post. In the military, upgrades of vehicles were ongoing in order to keep up with new ammunition ranging from armor-piercing plasma jets to more powerful land mines, as well as strategic needs such as lighter weight for greater speed and mobility. However, the private sector was slower to make changes.

Careful to avoid the acid that was still burning through the dashboard, Reynold Downer slid into the cab. Between the seats, on the floor, was a deep, narrow well that was used to store extra ammunition. It was accessible from both the front and back of the armored car. Downer pushed the dead guard against the cab door and opened the panel that accessed the ammunition chamber. Then he reached down to his belt and removed a small chunk of C-4 from one of the pouches. He snaked his right hand into the well, fixed the C-4 to the panel that opened into the rear of the van, and plugged in a small timer. He set it for fifteen seconds, then dropped a tear gas canister behind it and shut the door. Climbing over the dead guard, he opened the door and stepped onto the roadway.

While Downer was doing that, Vandal knelt on the hood. He took a pair of tin shears from his equipment belt and pulled back the driver's right-hand sleeve. The key that unlocked the back of the van was on a metal band attached to the driver's wrist. Vandal pulled the man's forearm toward him and snipped through the band. As he did, the C-4 exploded. It not only ripped a hole in the rear panel, it destroyed the container of tear gas. Though some of the gas leaked into the cab, the bulk of it poured into the back.

32

Traffic had stopped well behind the armored car. The road was clear and the backup would slow police even more. When Vandal was finished, he slid from the hood and joined Downer around back.

Neither man spoke. There was always a chance that the open radio would pick up their voices. As Downer stood watch, Vandal unlocked the door. Gas rolled out as he opened it, along with the gasping security guard. He had tried to get the gas mask that was stored in a chest in the back. Unfortunately, the mask had been placed there with the expectation that a gas strike would be made outside the van, not inside. He never reached the chest, let alone the mask. The guard hit the asphalt and Downer stomped hard on the side of his head. The man stopped moving, though he was still breathing.

As Vandal climbed inside, Downer heard the distant hum of an approaching helicopter. The black Hughes 500D swung in from over the river, which was where Sazanka's family owned a waterfront shipping facility. The Japanese pilot had stolen the helicopter so it couldn't be traced to them. He slowed as he flew over the boulevard. The Hughes has exceptional flight stability in slow and hover modes, as well as a tolerable downdraft. It also has room for five people and cargo, which was perhaps the most important consideration.

Barone, who had been driving the truck, ran back. As the Uruguayan pulled on his gas mask, Georgiev opened the aft door of the helicopter. He lowered a line with a hook. Attached to the iron hook was a twelve-by-seven-foot metal platform with large nylon nets along the sides. While Downer made certain that no one interfered, Vandal and Barone stood in the thinning clouds of tear gas and loaded the sacks of money onto the platform. At five minutes into the operation, Georgiev hauled up the first load.

Downer glanced at his watch. They were running slightly behind schedule. "We need to speed things up!" he shouted into the specially built-in mask radio.

"Calm down," Barone said. "We're within the safety net."

"That's not good enough," Downer said. "I want to be dead center, in the sweet spot."

"When you're in charge, *then* you give the orders!" Barone said.

"Same goes for you, mate," Downer snapped.

Barone shot him a look through the faceplate of his gas mask just as the platform came back down. The men threw in a second batch. They heard police sirens in the distance, but Downer wasn't worried. If necessary, they had the unconscious guard as a hostage. Fifty feet above, Sazanka watched the skies. The only event that would cause them to abort the mission and move out was the arrival of a police helicopter. Sazanka was looking out for that with the cockpit radar unit. Downer was watching Sazanka. If there was a blip, Sazanka would signal, and they'd move out.

The second load of bags went up. There was one more to go. Traffic had backed up nearly a quarter mile when people realized what was going on. There was no way to get through. The police would have to respond either with members of *La Brigade Équestre* or by air. The men continued to work quickly but efficiently. There was no sense of panic.

The third load went in. Suddenly, Sazanka raised his finger and moved it around in a quick circle. Then he pointed to the left. There was a police helicopter en route

34

from the west. Georgiev lowered the platform again. As they'd planned, Barone climbed in, followed by Vandal. The Bulgarian didn't reel the net in. Instead, the men all removed their gas masks, hooked them to their equipment belts, and began climbing the line. When the men were respectively twenty and ten feet up, Downer hopped onto the platform. Now Georgiev began reeling it in. While it rose, Downer steadied himself by holding the net siding with one hand while with the other he pulled the grenade launcher from his shoulder. Then he pulled off his gas mask so he could see more clearly, lay on his side, removed a projectile from the grenade pouch on his belt, and loaded the weapon. Above him, Georgiev helped Barone and Vandal climb back into the helicopter.

Sazanka climbed, quickly pushing the chopper to its maximum cruising speed of 160 mph. As he did, Downer made sure that both the barrel and the exhaust of the launcher were poking through the mesh siding. He didn't want to incinerate the net and fall to his death.

Georgiev secured the platform with cables run through two eye hooks on the front and back side nearest the helicopter, but he left it hanging three feet below the open door of the helicopter's aft compartment. From here, Downer could cover pursuit from any direction. Being close to the underbelly would also keep him from being knocked around by the winds and by the down-draft from the rotor. And it would be much more diffi-cult for a sharpshooter on the ground or in the air to notice him in the shadow of the chopper.

While they waited for a possible pursuit, Sazanka held them to one thousand feet and took them northwest along the river. A small plane was waiting for them at

35

a tiny airstrip outside of Saint-Germain. Once the men and money bags had been transferred from the chopper, they would fly south into Spain. There, the chaos of the simmering civil war would make it easy for them to buy their way in and then out of the country.

"There it is!" Georgiev shouted down. The big man was pointing toward the southwest.

Downer didn't have to look up to see where the Bulgarian was pointing. He'd also just spotted the police helicopter. It was about two thousand feet up and a half mile away. As Vandal had expected, it was from the French *Gendarmerie*'s Special Intervention Group.

The white and blue police chopper flew toward them in a sweeping, downward arc. The SIG team would follow their usual operating procedure. They'd attempt to raise the fleeing chopper by radio, which they were probably doing now. When the men didn't respond, the police chopper would stay in constant radio contact with ground forces. Even if they had medium-range weapons, the police wouldn't attempt to shoot the chopper down. Not as long as it was over a populated area and carrying a million dollars in currency. When the Hughes landed, both air and land units would close in on it.

Vandal knew that the Paris police department relied on radar from the two nearby airports to monitor the skies over the city. They used Charles de Gaulle to the northeast in Roissy-en-France and Orly to the south. Vandal also knew that when an aircraft dropped under two hundred and fifty feet, radar was ineffective due to interference from surrounding buildings. He had Sazanka keep the Hughes at one thousand feet.

The police chopper came closer. The hotels of the northern bank of the river passed beneath them in quick succession. To his right, across the river, Downer saw the Eiffel Tower, dark and spidery in the misty morning. They were flying level with the top of the structure.

The pursuing helicopter closed to within a quarter mile. They were still several hundred feet higher than the vehicle they were pursuing. The range of the grenade launcher was one thousand feet. According to the readout on the digital sight, the chopper was just out of range. Downer looked up at Georgiev. Vandal and Georgiev had both agreed that conversation over radios and cellular phones was too easy to intercept. Thus, once their gas masks were off, communication had to be muscular and old-fashioned.

"I need to be closer!" Downer yelled.

The Bulgarian cupped his thick hands around his mouth. "How much closer?" he shouted.

"Two hundred feet higher, three hundred feet back!"

Georgiev nodded. A door separated the cockpit from the aft cabin. The Bulgarian leaned through it and told Sazanka what Downer needed.

The Japanese pilot slowed and climbed. Downer watched the police chopper through his sight. The ascent brought them level with the other helicopter, and the decrease in speed narrowed the distance between them. The platform was jiggling up and down from the force of the rotor while the wind caused it to bump toward the stern. Aiming was difficult.

Downer sighted the cockpit of the police chopper. The optics of the grenade launcher did not magnify the target. Even so, Downer could see that someone was standing in the cockpit, leaning between the pilot and copilot and watching them with binoculars. Now that the two

37

helicopters were level, they would finally be able to see Downer.

There was no time to wait for the police to get closer.

The Australian hunkered down on the platform, curling as tight as possible against the far side brace for the recoil. Again he sighted the cockpit of the pursuing aircraft. The shot didn't have to be pretty; all he had to do was hit the enemy vehicle. He pulled hard on the heavy trigger.

The grenade left the barrel with a rush of air and a very loud pop. The launch knocked the platform backward with a sharp jolt, causing Downer to slide against the mesh siding. He lost the grenade launcher, which hit the platform with a ringing *thunk*. But he kept his eye on the projectile as it cut a thin, off-white contrail through the sky.

The grenade's flight took three seconds. It struck the cockpit on the port side and exploded. There was a bright cotton-ball burst of red and black smoke, with slivers of fire close to the core. The smoke and glass that blew upward were dispersed by the main rotor. A moment later, the helicopter listed to the starboard side and began to roll over. There was no secondary explosion. Then, with the crew dead or disabled, the helicopter simply nosed down and plunged earthward. It reminded Downer of a shuttlecock with busted feathers on one side. The police helicopter spun in a lopsided way as the tail rotor pulled it first to one side and then another. It was almost as though the small propeller were single-handedly trying to keep the crippled chopper aloft.

Meanwhile, Georgiev had reactivated the pulley that raised the cable holding the platform. Downer finished his journey to the open door. He handed the Bulgarian the grenade launcher, and then Barone extended a hand to help him back in. Vandal helped Georgiev pull the platform inside.

Barone continued to hold Downer's hand. The Uruguyan's expression was taut with anger.

"I should have pushed you the other way," Barone said.

Downer glared at him. "What you should have done was say, 'Nice shooting, mate.' "

"You broke my concentration down there with all your *talk*!" Barone cried. He angrily released Downer's hand.

"Didn't take much, did it?" Downer said. "I know soldiers who can do your job in their sleep."

"Then I suggest you work with *them* next time," Barone snarled.

"Enough!" Vandal said over his shoulder.

Georgiev and Vandal had been watching as the police helicopter crashed into a block near the river. There was a small, white explosion. A muffled boom reached them a moment later. They began to shut the door.

"An arrogant ass," Barone muttered. "That's what I'm working with. An arrogant, Australian ass!"

Before Georgiev and Vandal could finish closing the hatch, Reynold Downer suddenly slapped both hands on the front of Barone's uniform. The Australian grabbed it so tightly that his fingertips sank into the meat of the smaller man's chest. Barone screamed in pain as Downer swung him around and pushed him toward the still-open hatchway. He leaned Barone back so that his head and shoulders were hanging over Paris.

"*Jesus!*" Barone yelled.

"I've had enough of this!" the Australian shouted. "You've been riding me for weeks!"

"*Stop it!*" Vandal shouted. He ran over to the men.

"I spoke my mind is all I did!" Downer said. "I also did my job and took down the bloody damn chopper, so climb *off!*"

Vandal forced himself between them. "Get away!" he said as he grabbed Barone's arm with his left hand. At the same time, he used his right shoulder to nudge Downer back.

Downer pulled Barone inside, then stepped away willingly. He turned and faced the bags stacked against the other side of the cabin. Behind him, Georgiev quickly shut the door.

"Everyone calm down," Vandal said quietly. "We're all excitable right now, but we've accomplished what we set out to do. All that should matter now is finishing the job."

"Finishing it without any more *complaints*," Barone said. He was shaking with anger and fear.

"Of course," Vandal said calmly.

"It was a bloody observation," Downer said through his teeth. "That's all it was!"

"All right!" Vandal said. He remained between the men and glanced back at Downer. "I would like to remind you, *both* of you, that in order to complete this part of the mission and move on to the next, we need every member of the team. Now, we all did our jobs here, and did them well. If we take a little extra care in the future, we'll be fine." He looked back at Barone. "Even if anyone heard his voice, I'm confident that we'll be out of the country before anyone can figure out which Australian that accent belongs to."

40

"Which Australian with commando experience to pull off a job like this," Barone shot back.

"They still won't find us in time," Vandal said. *"If* they heard him, the police will still have to go to Interpol, which will check with authorities in Canberra. We'll be long gone before they even have a list of possible suspects." Cautiously, he moved from between the men. He looked at his watch. "We'll be landing in ten minutes, and we'll be airborne again before nine o'clock." He forced a smile. "Nothing can stop us now."

Barone was glaring at Downer. He looked away and angrily smoothed the front of his uniform.

Downer took a long breath and then smiled back at Vandal. The Frenchman was right. They *did* do well. They'd gotten the money they needed to pay for bribes, for the plane, and for the documents they'd need for the next part of the operation. The part that was going to make them wealthy.

The Frenchman relaxed and walked toward the cockpit. Barone turned his back toward Downer and kept it there. Downer sat down on a stack of money bags and ignored Barone—once more. When the Australian reached the combustion stage, he burned hot but fast. He was cool again, no longer angry at Barone or at himself for having screwed up.

Georgiev locked the door and walked over to the cockpit. He didn't make eye contact with Downer as he walked past. It wasn't an intentional snub, just another habit that came from years spent working for the CIA. Always try to remain anonymous.

Vandal was once again in the copilot's seat, monitoring the French police radio communications. Georgiev stood behind him in the open cockpit door. Barone was looking out the window in the sliding cabin door.

Downer shut his eyes. He enjoyed the soothing vibration of the floor. He enjoyed the soft bed of money beneath his head. Even the slamming loud noise of the rotor didn't bother him.

He allowed himself the pleasure of forgetting the details they'd had to remember for this morning. The armored car's route, the timing, alternate plans in case the police got through, an escape by the river in the event the chopper didn't make it. A deep feeling of satisfaction came over him, and he savored it the way he had never enjoyed anything in his life.

FOUR

Chevy Chase, Maryland
Friday, 9:12 A.M.

Under a bright sky, Paul Hood, his wife Sharon, their just-turned-fourteen-year-old daughter Harleigh, and their eleven-year-old son Alexander eased into their new van and set out for New York. The kids were hooked to their respective Discmans. Harleigh was listening to violin concerti to get herself in the mood for the concert; every now and then, she would sigh or mutter a mild oath, awed by the composition or discouraged by the brilliance of the performance. She was like her mother in that respect. Neither woman was ever satisfied with what she'd accomplished, Harleigh on the violin, Sharon with her passion for healthy cooking. For years, Sharon had used her charm and sincerity to lure people away from bacon and doughnuts on a half-hour weekly cable TV show, *The McDonnell Healthy Food Report*. She had left the show several months before to devote more time to putting together a healthy-eating cookbook, which was nearly finished. She had also wanted to spend more time at home. The kids were getting older faster, and she felt they should all spend more time doing things as a family, from having dinner weeknights to taking vacations whenever they could. Dinners that Hood had

43

missed more often than not and vacations that he'd had to cancel.

Alexander was much more like his father. He liked personal challenges. He enjoyed computer games—the more complicated, the better. He liked crossword puzzles and jigsaw puzzles. As they drove, he listened to some flavor-of-the-month singer and worked on an acrostic puzzle. Beneath the puzzle book, on his lap, was a short stack of comic books. To Alexander, there was no outside world right now. There was just what was in front of him. Paul couldn't help but feel proud of the kid. Alexander knew his own mind.

Sharon Hood was sitting quietly by her husband's side. She had left him a week before, taken the children, and gone to stay with her parents in Old Saybrook, Connecticut. She'd returned for the same reason that Hood had resigned from Op-Center: to fight for their family. Hood had no idea what he'd do next in his career, and he wouldn't be putting out feelers until they returned to Washington on Wednesday. He'd cashed in some stock he'd bought during his years as a broker, enough to run the household for two years. Income wasn't as important as satisfaction and banker's hours. But Sharon was right. The wholeness of what he felt in the car, imperfections and all, was something very special.

One of those imperfections—the largest one—was still between Hood and his wife. Though Sharon took his hand and held it as they started the trip, he had the feeling that he was on probation. There was nothing he could pinpoint, nothing that seemed different from any other drive they'd taken. But there was something that stood between them. A resentment? Disappointment?

Whatever, it was the reverse of the sexual tension he felt with Ann Farris.

Paul and Sharon talked a little at first about what they were going to do in the city. Tonight was an official dinner with the families of the other violinists. Maybe a walk through Times Square if they got done early enough. On Saturday morning, they'd drop Harleigh off at the United Nations and then do what Alexander had requested: visit the Statue of Liberty. The boy wanted to see up close how it was "erected," as he put it. At six they'd head for the soiree, leaving the young man in the Sheraton with its built-in video game system.

Paul and Sharon wouldn't be permitted to attend the United Nations reception, which was being held in the lobby of the General Assembly Hall building. Instead, they'd be watching the concert on closed-circuit televisions in the second-floor press room along with the other parents. On Sunday, they'd take in an afternoon performance of the Metropolitan Opera orchestra doing Vivaldi—Sharon's favorite—at Carnegie Hall, after which, at Ann Farris's recommendation, they'd head up to Serendipity III for frozen hot chocolates. Sharon wasn't happy about that, but Hood pointed out that this *was* a vacation, and the kids were looking forward to the dessert stop. Hood was sure she was also unhappy about the fact that Ann had suggested it. On Monday, they'd drive out to Old Saybrook to visit Sharon's parents—this time as a family. That had been Hood's idea. He liked Sharon's folks, and they liked him. He wanted to regain that stability for the family.

Because it was a Friday, traffic thickened going into and out of Baltimore, Philadelphia, and Newark. They finally reached New York at five-thirty and checked into

45

the hotel on Seventh Avenue and Fifty-first Street. The tall, busy hotel was a Sheraton now; Hood remembered when it was the Americana years before. They arrived just in time to join the other families for dinner up the street at the Carnegie Deli. The meal was rich with pastrami, roast beef, and hot dogs. The only couple the Hoods knew was the Mathises, whose daughter Barbara was one of Harleigh's closest friends. Barbara's parents both worked for the Washington police department. There were also a few mothers—two of them attractive, single parents—who recognized Paul from his tenure as mayor of Los Angeles. They treated him with celebrity-worthy smiles and asked what it was like to ''run'' Hollywood. He said he wouldn't know. They'd have to ask the Screen Actors Guild and the other motion picture unions.

All of it, the food and the attention, made Sharon uneasy. Or at least it brought out whatever discomfort she had been feeling since they set out. Hood decided to try to talk to her about it when the kids went to bed.

There was one thing Sharon had been right about, though. Paul had been away from home too much. As he watched Harleigh interact with the other teenagers and their parents, he realized he was observing a young woman and not a girl. He didn't know when the change had happened, but it had. And he was proud of Harleigh in a different way than he was of Alexander. She had her mother's charm along with the acquired poise of a musician.

Alexander was focused on his plate of well-done potato pancakes. He would press the back of his fork on them, wait for the grease to rise from the top, and then watch to see how long it took for the grease to soak back. His mother told him to stop playing with his food.

Hood had reserved a suite on an upper floor. After Alexander had a look around the city with his binoculars—marveling at what he could see on the street and in other windows—the kids went to sleep on cots in the living room, giving him and Sharon some privacy.

Privacy and a hotel room. There was a time when that would automatically have meant lovemaking, not talk or uncomfortable silence. Hood found it disturbing how much time and passion over the last few years went to other things, like guilt or holding their individual ground instead of holding each other. How had things gotten to that point? And how did a couple get them back to where they should be? Hood had an idea, though it would be tough convincing his wife.

Sharon slid into bed. She curled on her side, facing him.

"I'm a mess," she said.

"I know." He touched her cheek and smiled lightly. "But we'll get through this."

"Not when everything is pissing me off," she said.

"Apart from the food, what else bothered you?" Hood asked.

"I was angry at the parents we were with, at the table manners of their kids, at the way the cars raced through red lights or stopped in the crosswalks. Everything got to me. Everything."

"We've all had days like that," he said.

"Paul, I can't remember when I *wasn't* like that," Sharon said. "It's just been building and building, and I don't want to spoil things for Harleigh or Alexander this week."

"You've been through some rough times," Hood

said. "We both have. But the kids aren't stupid. They know what's been happening with us. What I wanted, what I hoped for, was that we not let anything get to us while we're here."

Sharon shook her head sadly. "How?"

"We're not in a rush," Hood said. "The only thing we have to do over the next few days is to build some good memories for ourselves and the kids. Start to pull ourselves out of this funk. Can we focus on that?"

Sharon placed her hand on his. There was a hint of garlic from something she'd cooked the night before. That didn't do a hell of a lot for passion either, Hood had to admit. The routine of life. The smells that became more familiar than that unforgettable first scent of a woman's hair. The chores that turned the tip of your angel's wing back into a hand.

"I want things to change," Sharon said. "I felt something in the van driving up—"

"I know," Hood said. "I felt it, too. It was nice."

Sharon looked at him. Her eyes were moist. "No, Paul," she said. "What I felt was scary."

"Scary?" Hood said. "What do you mean?"

"The whole ride up, I kept remembering the drives we used to take when the kids were small. Out to Palm Springs or Big Bear Lake or up the coast. We were so different then."

"We were younger," Hood said.

"It was more than that."

"We were focused," Hood said. "The kids needed us more than they do now. It's like monkey bars. You've got to stand close together when their reach is small. Otherwise they fall."

"I know," Sharon said. Tears began trickling from

48

her eyes. "But I wanted to feel that togetherness today, and I didn't. I want those good times again, those old feelings."

"We can have them now," Hood promised.

"But there's all this *crap* inside," Sharon said. "All this bitterness, disappointment, resentment. I want to go back and do things over so we can grow together, not apart."

Hood looked at his wife. Sharon had a habit of looking away whenever she was confused and of looking directly at him when she was not. She was looking straight into his eyes.

"We can't do that," Hood remarked. "But we can work on fixing things, one at a time."

He pulled her closer. Sharon moved across the bed, but there was no warmth in their proximity. He didn't understand this at all. He was giving her what she had wanted, what she said she needed, and she was still withdrawing. Maybe she was just venting. She hadn't really had a chance to do that. He held her silently for several minutes.

"Hon," Hood went on, "I know you haven't wanted to do this before, but it might be a good idea if the two of us talked to someone. Liz Gordon said she'd give me some names, if you're interested."

Sharon didn't say anything. Hood held her closer and heard that her breathing had slowed. He craned back slightly. She was staring at nothing and fighting back tears.

"At least the children turned out all right," she said. "At least we did that right."

"Sharon, we did more than just that right," he said. "We've made a life together. Not perfect, but a better

49

life than a lot of people. We've done okay. And we'll do better.''

He pulled her close again as she began to sob openly. Her arms went around his shoulders.

"That isn't what a girl dreams of when she thinks of the future, you know?'' she wept.

"I know.'' He cradled her tighter. "We'll make it better, I promise.''

He didn't say anything else. He just held on as passion sent Sharon's regret into a power dive. She would bottom out and then, in the morning, they'd start the long climb back.

It would be difficult to take things slow and easy, as he'd said. But he owed that to Sharon. Not because he'd let his career dictate his hours but because he'd given his passion to Nancy Bosworth and Ann Farris. Not his body, but his thoughts, his attention, even his dreams. That energy, that focus, should have been saved for his wife and his family.

Sharon fell asleep snuggled in his arms. This wasn't how he wanted to feel closeness, but at least it was something. When he was sure he wouldn't wake her, he released her gently, reached over to the night table, and snapped off the light. Then he lay back, staring at the ceiling and feeling disgusted with himself in the hard, unforgiving way you can only at night. And he tried to figure out if there was a way he could make this weekend a little more special for the three people he'd somehow let down.

FIVE

New York, New York
Saturday, 4:57 A.M.

Standing outside the run-down, two story brick building near the Hudson River made Lieutenant Bernardo Barone think of his native Montevideo.

It wasn't just the dilapidated condition of the body shop that reminded him of the slums where he grew up. For one thing, there were the brisk winds blowing from the south. The smell of the Atlantic Ocean was mixed with the smell of gasoline from cars racing along the nearby West Side Highway. In Montevideo, fuel and the sea wind were ever present. Overhead, a steady flow of air traffic followed the river to the north before turning east to La Guardia Airport. Planes were always criss-crossing the skies over his home.

Yet it was more than that which reminded him of home. Bernardo Barone had found those in every port city he'd visited the world over. What made it different was being out here by himself. Loneliness was something he felt in Montevideo whenever he returned.

No, he thought suddenly. *Don't get into that.* He didn't want to be angry and depressed. Not now. He had to focus.

He backed up against the door. It felt cool on his sweaty back. The door was wood covered with a sheet of steel on both sides. There were three key locks on the outside and two heavy bolts on the inside. The sun-faded sign above the door read *Viks' Body Shop*. The owner was a member of the Russian Mafia named Leonid Ustinoviks. The small, bony, chain-smoker was a former Soviet military leader and an acquaintance of Georgiev's through the Khmer Rouge. Barone had been informed by Ustinoviks that there wasn't a body shop in New York that was exclusively a body shop. By night, when it was quiet and no one could approach the building unseen or unheard, either they were chop shops selling stolen cars, drug or weapon dealerships, or slavery operations. The Russians and Thais were big in this arena, sending kidnapped American children out of the country or bringing young women into the United States. In most cases, the captives were put to work as prostitutes. Some of the girls who had worked for Georgiev in Cambodia had ended up here, moving through Ustinoviks's hands. The size of the crates used to ship "spare parts" and the international nature of the trade made these businesses a perfect front.

Leonid Ustinoviks's business was arms. He had them brought in from former republics of the Soviet Union. The weapons came into Canada or Cuba, usually by freighter. From there, they were slipped into New England and the Middle Atlantic States, or into Florida and the other Gulf Coast states. Typically, they were moved piecemeal from small-town storehouses to places like this body shop. That was to prevent losing everything if the FBI and the NYPD's Intelligence Division caught them in transit. Both groups quietly monitored the communications and activities of persons from nations known to sponsor illicit trade or terrorism: Russia,

Libya, North Korea, and many others. The police regularly changed signs along the riverfront and in the warehouse districts, altering parking restrictions and hours when turns could be made on certain well-traveled corners. This gave them an excuse to stop vehicles and clandestinely photograph the drivers.

Ustinoviks had told him to keep an eye out for anyone who turned off the highway or any of the side streets. If anyone came here, or even slowed down while driving by, he was to rap three times on the body shop's door. Whenever a deal was taking place, operations like this always had someone who would come out and demand that a search warrant be read to him—a right, by New York City law—while anyone inside escaped by the roof onto an adjoining building.

Not that Ustinoviks was expecting trouble. He said there had been a flurry of raids against Russian gangsters two months ago. The city didn't like to give the appearance of targeting an individual ethnic group.

"It's the Vietnamese's turn," he quipped when they arrived here from the hotel.

Barone thought he heard a sound off to the side of the building. Reaching into his windbreaker, he withdrew his automatic. He walked cautiously to the darkened alley to the north. There was a club behind a high chain-link fence. *The Dungeon.* The doors, windows, and brick walls were all painted black. He couldn't imagine what went on there. It was odd. What they had to do in secret in Cambodia, sell girls for money, was probably done openly in places like this.

When a nation stands for freedom, he thought, *it has to tolerate even the extremes.*

The club was closed for the night. A dog was moving

behind the fence. That must have been what he heard. Barone slid the gun back into its shoulder holster and returned to his post.

Barone pulled a hand-rolled cigarette from his breast pocket and lit it. He thought back over the past few days. Things were going well, and they'd continue to go well. He believed that. He and his four teammates had reached Spain without any problem. They split up in the event that any of them had been identified, and over the next two days, flew to the United States from Madrid. They met at a Times Square hotel. Georgiev had been the first to arrive. He had already made the connections necessary to obtain the weapons they needed. The negotiations were going on inside while Barone stood guard.

Barone drew on the cigarette. He tried to concentrate on the plan for tomorrow. He wondered about Georgiev's other ally, the one known only to the Bulgarian. All Georgiev would tell them was that it was an American whom he had known for over ten years. That would be about the time they were in Cambodia together. Barone wondered who he could have met there and what role they could possibly be playing in tomorrow's action.

But it was no use. Barone's mind always went where it wanted to go, and right now, it didn't want to think about Georgiev or the operation. It wanted to go back. It wanted to go home.

To the loneliness, he thought bitterly. A place familiar to him—strangely comfortable.

It wasn't always that way. Though his family had no money, there was a time when Montevideo seemed like paradise. Located on the Atlantic Ocean, it's the capital of Uruguay and home to some of the most spacious and beautiful beaches in the world. Growing up there in the early 1960s, Bernardo Barone couldn't have been happier. When he wasn't in school or doing his chores, he used to go to the beach with his twelve-years-older brother Eduardo. The two young men would stay there long into the night, swimming endlessly or building forts in the sand. They would light campfires when the sun set and often went to sleep beside their forts.

"We'll rest in the stables with the magnificent horses," Eduardo would joke. "Can you smell them?"

Bernardo could not. He could only smell the sea and the fumes from the cars and boats. But he believed that Eduardo could smell them. The young boy wanted to be able to do that when he grew up. He wanted to be like Eduardo. When Bernardo and his mother went to church every weekend, that was what he prayed for. To grow up just like his brother.

Those were Bernardo's happiest memories. Eduardo was so patient with him, so friendly with everyone who came by to watch them build the tall, crenellated walls and moats. Girls loved the handsome young man. And they loved the handsome young man's cute little brother, who loved them right back.

Bernardo's beloved mother was a baker's assistant and their father Martin was a prizefighter. Martin's dream was to save enough to open a gym so his wife could quit her job and live like a lady. From the time Eduardo was fifteen, he spent many days and nights traveling with the elder Barone, working as his corner man. Often they'd be gone for weeks at a time, participating in the Rio de la Plata circuit. Groups of fighters traveled together by bus from Mercedes to Paysandu to Salto, boxing one another or ambitious locals. Pay was a share of the gate, less fees for the doctor who traveled with the fighters. Eduardo learned basic medical skills so they could save the price of the doctor.

It was a difficult life, and it put a terrible strain on the boys' mother. She worked long hours over a hellishly hot brick oven, and one morning, while her husband and eldest son were away, she died in a fire at the bakery. Because the family's credit was bad, the woman's body was brought to the Barone apartment, and Bernardo had to sit with it until his father could be contacted and funeral arrangements could be made and paid for.

Bernardo was nine.

During his travels with their father, Eduardo had learned other things, as well. Quite by chance, in a small tavern in San Javier, he discovered the Marxist Movimiento de Liberacion Nacional-Tupamaros. The guerrilla group had been founded in 1962 by Raul Antonaccio Sendic, leader of the sugarcane workers of northern Uruguay. The government had been unable to control inflation, which went as high as 35 percent, and laborers were particularly hard hit. In the aggressive Sendic movement, Eduardo saw a means by which he could help others like his father who had lost the love of their life and the will to dream. In Eduardo, the group saw someone who could fight and administer medical treatment. It was a good fit. With his father's blessings, Eduardo joined the MLN-T.

In 1972, the despotic Juan Maria Bordaberry Arocena was elected president. Bordaberry had the backing of the well-trained, well-armed military. And one of the first orders of business was to crush the opposition, including the MLN-T, which Eduardo had recently joined. There was a bloody shoot-out in April; by year's end, members were in jail or in exile. Eduardo had ended up in prison, where he died of "unknown" causes. Bernardo's father died less than two years later. He had taken a severe beating in the ring and never recovered. Bernardo always felt that his father wanted to die. He had never been the same after the loss of those who had been so precious to him.

The death of his family turned Bernardo into an angry young firebrand who hated the government of President Bordaberry. Ironically, the military also became disenchanted with the new president and staged its own coup in February 1973. They established the Consejo de Seguridad Nacional. Bernardo enlisted in 1979, hoping to become part of a new order in Uruguay.

But after twelve years of being unable to deal with economic hardship, the military simply returned rule to the people and literally faded from the political scene. The economic situation hadn't changed markedly.

Once again, Bernardo felt betrayed by a cause. The young man remained in the military. As a tribute to his father, he had become skilled in all forms of hand-to-hand combat; he was suited for nothing else. But he never stopped hoping that he would find a way to rekindle the spirit of the MLN-T. To work for the people of Uruguay, not the leaders. Serving with the United Nations in Cambodia, Barone found a way to do just that. To raise money and get attention from the world press, all at the same time.

Barone finished his cigarette. He crushed it on the sidewalk and stood looking at the traffic on the West Side Highway. That was one difference between Montevideo and New York City. In Montevideo, except for the tourist hotels and the bars, everything shut down at sunset. Here, the roads were busy even at this hour. It had to be impossible for authorities to monitor all of it, to keep track of who was coming and going, of what was in the trucks and vans.

Lucky for us, he thought.

It was also impossible for the police to watch every plane that came into the small airstrips that surrounded the city. Airports and even open fields in upstate New York, Connecticut, New Jersey, and Pennsylvania were perfect for small planes to slip in and out unnoticed. Waterways in those states were also ideal spots. A deserted bay or riverbank in the small hours of the morning. Crates quickly and quietly loaded from boat or seaplane to truck. Easy entry, and so close to New York. That, too, was lucky for the team.

An hour passed, then another. Barone had known this was going to take a while, since Downer needed time to examine each of the weapons. Though arms dealers could usually get a client what he wanted, that didn't necessarily mean the weapons would be in perfect working order. Like refugees, a hot weapon never got to travel first class. The wait didn't bother the Uruguayan. What mattered was that the weapon work when he aimed and fired.

Something to the left caught his eye. He turned. Near the mouth of the river, the Statue of Liberty was just catching the first rays of dawn. Barone hadn't realized the monument was out there, and seeing it at first surprised and then angered him. He had no gripe with the United States and her cherished notions of freedom and equality. But there, in the harbor, was a giant idol celebrating a spiritual concept. It seemed sacrilegious. The way he was raised, these things were very personal. They were celebrated in the heart, not in the harbor.

Finally, shortly before seven A.M., the door behind him opened. Downer leaned out.

"You're to come around back," the Australian said, then shut the door.

Barone didn't feel like making fun of Downer's accent. Since the incident in the helicopter over Paris, he hadn't felt like talking to the unrepentent mercenary Downer at all.

Barone turned to his left and walked around the side of the building. His new boots had deeply treaded rubber soles that squeaked on the asphalt as he made his way along the driveway. To his right was a tire shop surrounded by a high chain-link fence. A guard dog slept in the shadows. Earlier in the evening, the soldier had tossed him some of his hamburger—American meat tasted funny to the Uruguayan—and the animal became his best friend.

Barone walked past a pair of green trash bins to where the rented van was parked. There were seventeen weapons—three guns for each man and a pair of rocket launchers—plus ammunition and bulletproof vests. Each weapon was swaddled in bubble wrap. Sazanka and Vandal were already carrying them from the body shop as Barone hopped into the open side door of the van. As the men handed the weapons up, Barone carefully placed them in six plain cardboard boxes. Downer watched from the back door of the body shop, making sure none of the weapons were dropped. It was the first time Barone had ever seen the Australian so quiet and professional.

As he worked, the sense of loneliness left the Uruguayan. Not because he was with his teammates but because he was moving again. They were close to their goal now. Barone had always believed in the plan, but now he believed they might actually pull this off. Just a few small steps remained.

Months before, Georgiev had obtained a counterfeit New York State driver's license. Since rental car companies routinely checked police records before letting cars off the lot, the Bulgarian had to pay extra to have it entered into the motor vehicle department computer system. He even gave himself a traffic ticket a year before, not just to show residency but because people who drove in big cities usually got one. A clean record might arouse suspicions.

All the team had to do now was make certain they didn't run any lights or have an accident before reaching the hotel. They'd drawn straws earlier, and Vandal would be sleeping in the van while the others went up to the room to rest. Georgiev didn't want to risk the van being stolen by Ustinoviks.

Then, at seven P.M., they'd leave the hotel garage and head to Forty-second Street. They'd drive east, across town, and at First Avenue they'd turn north. Once again, Georgiev would drive carefully.

Then, suddenly, he would speed up. He would approach the target at between sixty and seventy miles an hour, and in less than ten minutes, the target would fall.

The United Nations would be theirs. And then the third and final part of their plan could commence.

SIX

New York, New York
Saturday, 6:45 P.M.

The League of Nations was formed after World War I, conceived, in the words of its covenant, "to promote international cooperation and to achieve international peace and security." Though President Woodrow Wilson was a fierce advocate of the League, the American Senate wanted no part of it. Their key objections involved the potential use of United States troops to help preserve the territorial integrity or political independence of other countries, and acknowledging the jurisdiction of the League in matters pertaining to North, Central, or South America. President Wilson collapsed and suffered a stroke as a result of his ceaseless efforts to promote American acceptance of the League and its mandate.

Housed in a spectacular, six-million-dollar palace built for it in Geneva, the League and its noble intentions proved ineffectual. They were unable to prevent the Japanese occupation of Manchuria in 1931, Italy's taking of Ethiopia in 1935, and the German conquest of Austria in 1938. It was also notably ineffective in preventing World War II. It's a matter of ongoing debate whether an American presence in the League would have changed the unfolding of any of these events.

The United Nations was formed in 1945 to try to accomplish what the League of Nations had failed to do. This time, however, things were different. The United States had a reason to be actively involved with the sovereignty of other nations. Communism was perceived as the greatest threat to the American way of life, and each nation that fell gave the enemy another foothold.

The United Nations chose the United States as the home of its international headquarters. Not only had the United States emerged from World War II as the world's dominant military and economic force, but it had agreed to provide one-quarter of the United Nations's annual operating budget. Moreover, because of the despotic tradition of many European nations, the Old World was deemed unacceptable as a site for a world body promoting a new era of peace and understanding. New York was selected because it had become the hub of international communications and finance and was also the traditional link between the Old World and the New. Two other potential sites in America were rejected for very different reasons. San Francisco, which was favored by the Australians and Asians, was vetoed because the Soviet Union did not want to make travel more convenient for the hated Chinese or Japanese. And rustic Fairfield County, on the Long Island Sound in Connecticut, was disqualified when New Englanders, opposed to what they perceived as the onset of "world government," stoned United Nations prospectors who were looking at possible locations.

A large parcel of land for the new United Nations headquarters—the site of an abattoir on the East River—was bought with $8.5 million donated by the Rockefellers. The family was granted a tax exemption for their gift. The Rockefellers also benefited from the development of land they still owned all around the new complex. Offices, housing, restaurants, shopping, and entertainment came to the once-dilapidated neighborhood in order to service the thousands of delegates and workers who staffed the United Nations.

The limited acreage made available for the project caused two things to happen. First, the headquarters had to be designed in skyscraper form. The skyscraper was a uniquely American invention created to maximize space on the small island of Manhattan, and the look of the complex would make the United Nations even more American. However, this limitation suited the founders of the United Nations. It gave them an excuse to decentralize key functions of the organization, from the World Court to the International Labor Organization. These were located in other world capitals. The UN's principal ancillary headquarters was established at the old League of Nations palace in Geneva. This was a pointed reminder to the United States that a world peace group had been tried once before and failed because not every nation was committed.

Paul Hood remembered some of that from junior high school. He also remembered something else from junior high school. Something that had permanently shaped his view of the building itself. He had come to New York from Los Angeles for a week during the Christmas vacation with other honor students. As they drove to the city from Kennedy International Airport, he looked across the East River and saw the United Nations at dusk. All the other skyscrapers he saw were facing north and south: the Empire State Building, the Chrysler Building, the Pan Am Building. But the thirty-nine-story glass-and-marble United Nations Secretariat Building was facing east and west. He happened to mention that to James LaVigne who was in the seat next to him.

The thin, bespectacled, very intense LaVigne looked up from *The Mighty Thor* comic book he was reading. The magazine was hidden inside a copy of *Scientific American.*

"You know what that reminds me of?" LaVigne said. Hood said he had no idea.

"It's like the symbol on Batman's chest."

"What do you mean?" Hood asked. He had never read a Batman comic book and had only seen the popular TV show once, just to see what everyone was talking about.

"Batman wears a bright gold-and-black bat symbol on his chest," LaVigne said. "Do you know why?"

Hood said that he did not.

"Because Batman wears a bulletproof vest *under* his costume," LaVigne said. "If a criminal starts shooting at him, that's where Batman wants him to aim. At his chest."

LaVigne returned to his comic book. The twelve-year-old Hood turned back to the United Nations building. LaVigne often made bizarre observations, his favorite being that Superman was a retelling of the New Testament. But this one made sense. Hood wondered if New York had built it that way on purpose. If someone wanted to attack the United Nations from the river or airport, it was a big, fat target for a Cuban or Chinese secret agent.

Because of that vivid childhood impression, Paul Hood always thought of the United Nations as New York's bull's-eye. And now that he was here, he felt surprisingly vulnerable. Intellectually, he knew that made no sense. The United Nations was on international territory. If terrorists wanted to strike at America, they would attack the infrastructure—the railroads, bridges, or tunnels—like the terrorists who blew up the Queens-Midtown Tunnel and forced Op-Center to work with its Russian counterpart. Or monuments like the Statue of Liberty. When he was on Liberty Island that morning, Hood was surprised how accessible the island was from the air and sea. Coming over on the ferry, he was disturbed to see how easy it would be for a pair of suicide pilots in planes loaded with explosives to reduce the statue to slag. There was a radar system located in the administration complex, but Hood knew that the NYPD harbor patrol had only one gunship stationed on nearby Governor's Island. Two planes coming from opposite directions, with the statue itself blocking the gunship's fire, would enable at least one terrorist to reach the target.

You stayed at Op-Center too long, he told himself. Here he was on vacation, running crisis scenarios.

He shook his head and looked around. He and Sharon had arrived early and gone down to the gift shop to get Alexander a T-shirt. Then they went up to the vast public lobby of the General Assembly Building, near the bronze statue of Zeus, to wait for the UN Youth Arts representative. The lobby had been closed to the public since four o'clock so employees could set up for the annual peace reception. Because it was a clear, beautiful night, guests would be able to eat inside and chat outside. They could roam the north-side courtyard, admiring the sculptures and gardens, or walk along the East River promenade. At 7:30, the new Indian United Nations Secretary-General Mala Chatterjee would go to the Security Council chambers with representatives of member nations of the Security Council. There, Ms. Chatterjee and the Spanish ambassador would congratulate the members for the massive United Nations peacekeeping effort being mounted to prevent further ethnic unrest in Spain. Then Harleigh and her fellow violinists would play "A Song of Peace." The composition had been written by a Spanish composer to honor those who died over sixty years before in the Spanish Civil War. Musicians from Washington had been selected to perform, which turned out to be fitting because an American, Op-Center's Martha Mackall, had been the first victim of the recent unrest. It was a coincidence that Paul Hood's daughter was among the eight violinists chosen.

The twelve other parents had all arrived, and Sharon had scooted off downstairs to find the rest room. The musicians had come down to say a brief hello a few minutes before she left. Harleigh had looked so mature in her white satin gown and pearls. Young Barbara Mathis, who was standing beside Harleigh, was also calm and poised, a diva in the making. Hood knew that Harleigh's appearance was the reason Sharon excused herself. She didn't like to cry in public. Harleigh had been studying violin since she was four and wearing overalls. He was used to seeing her that way, or in her track and field clothes when she was earning all her ribbons. To see her walk upstairs from the dressing room, an accomplished musician and a woman, was overwhelming. Hood had asked his daughter if she were nervous. She said no. The composer had done the hard part. Harleigh was poised and she was smart, too.

Now that Hood thought about it, the old bull's-eye image of the United Nations probably wasn't what made him feel vulnerable. It was now. This moment, this point in his life.

Standing in the open four-story-tall lobby, Hood felt very much alone. He felt detached from so many things. His kids were growing, he'd ended a career, he felt estranged from his wife in so many ways, and Hood would no longer be seeing the people he'd worked with so closely for over two years. Is that what he was supposed to feel halfway through his life? Vulnerable and adrift?

He didn't know. Everyone he'd associated with at Op-Center—Bob Herbert, Mike Rodgers, Darrell McCaskey, computer genius Matt Stoll, and even the late Martha Mackall—were single. Their job was their life. The same was true of Colonel Brett August, head of the Striker team. Had being with them made him like this? Or was he drawn to them because he wanted that life?

If the latter were true, he was going to have a very difficult time making his new life work. Maybe he should talk to psychologist Liz Gordon about this while he was still eligible for office perks. Although she was single, too, and worked about sixty hours a week.

Hood saw Sharon come up the winding staircase on the other side of the lobby. She was dressed in a smart beige pantsuit and she looked terrific. He'd told her so back at the hotel, and that had put a little bounce in her step. The bounce was still there. She smiled at him, and he smiled back as she approached. Suddenly, he didn't feel quite so alone.

A young Japanese woman walked toward them. She was wearing a navy blue blazer, a laminated ID badge on her breast pocket, and a big, welcoming smile. She came from a small lobby located on the eastern side of the General Assembly Building. Unlike the main lobby,

67

which was located on the far northern end of the building, the smaller lobby adjoined the main plaza in front of the towering Secretariat Building. In addition to the offices of the member nations, the Secretariat Building housed the halls of the Security Council, the Economic and Social Council, and the Trusteeship Council. That was where they were headed. The three magnificent auditoriums were situated side by side, overlooking the East River. The United Nations Correspondents Club, which was where the parents would be taken, was located across the hall from the Security Council.

The young guide introduced herself as Kako Nogami. As the visting parents followed her, the young lady went into an abbreviated version of her tour-guide speech.

"How many of you have been to the United Nations before?" she asked, walking backward.

Several parents raised their hands. Hood didn't. He was afraid Kako would ask what he remembered about it, and he'd have to tell her about James LaVigne and Batman.

"To refresh your memories," she went on, "and for the benefit of our new guests, I'd like to tell you a little about the area of the United Nations we'll be visiting."

The guide explained that the Security Council is the United Nations's most powerful body, primarily responsible for maintaining international peace and security.

"Five influential countries including the United States sit as permanent members," she said, "along with ten others, elected for two-year terms. Tonight, your children will be playing for the ambassadors of these nations along with their executive staffs.

"The Economic and Social Council, as the name implies, serves as a forum for the discussion of international economic and social issues,'' the young woman went on. ''The council also promotes human rights and basic freedoms. The Trusteeship Council, which suspended operations in 1994, helped territories around the world attain self-government or independence, either as sovereign states or as part of other nations.''

For just a moment, Hood thought it would be fascinating to run this place. Keeping the peace inside, among the delegates, had to be as challenging as keeping the peace outside. As though sensing his thoughts, Sharon slipped her fingers between his and squeezed tightly. He let the idea go.

The group passed a large, ground-floor window that looked out onto the main plaza. Outside was the Shinto-style shrine that housed the Japanese Peace Bell. It was cast from coins and metal donated by people from sixty nations. Just past the window, the lobby fed into a wide corridor. Straight ahead were elevators used by UN delegates and their staff. To the right was a series of display cases. The guide led them over. The cases contained relics of the atom bomb blast that razed Hiroshima: fused cans, charred school clothes and roof tiles, melted bottles, and a pocked stone statue of Saint Agnes. The Japanese guide described the destructive force and intensity of the blast.

The exhibit wasn't moving Hood or Barbara's father Hal Mathis, whose father had died on Okinawa. Hood wished that Bob Herbert and Mike Rodgers were here. Rodgers would have asked the guide to show them the Pearl Harbor exhibit next. The one about the attack that happened when the two nations *weren't* at war. At twenty-two or twenty-three years old, Hood wondered if the young woman would have understood the context of the question. Herbert would have raised a stink even before they got this far. The intelligence chief had lost his wife and the use of his legs in the terrorist bombing of the United States embassy in Beirut in 1983. He had gotten on with his life, but he did not forgive easily. In this case, Hood wouldn't have blamed him. One of the UN publications Hood had browsed through at the gift shop described Pearl Harbor as "the Hirohito attack," tacitly absolving the Japanese people of guilt in the crime. Even the more politically correct Hood found the revisionist history disturbing.

After finishing at the Hiroshima exhibit, the group went up two flights of escalators to the upstairs lobby. To their left were the three auditoriums with the Security Council chambers located on the far end. The parents were led to the old press bull pen across the hall. There was a guard outside, a member of the United Nations Security Forces. The African-American man was dressed in a powder blue short-sleeve shirt, blue gray trousers with a black stripe down each leg, and a navy blue cap. His name tag read Dillon. When they arrived, Mr. Dillon unlocked the bull pen door and let them in.

Today, reporters generally work in the high-tech television press rooms situated in long, glass booths on either side of the Security Council auditorium. These booths are accessible by a common corridor between the Security Council and the Economic and Social Council. But in the 1940s, this spacious, windowless L-shaped room was the heart of the United Nations's media center. The first part of the room was lined with old desks, telephones, a few banged-up computer terminals, and hand-me-down fax machines. In the larger second half of the room—the base of the L—were vinyl couches, a rest room, a supply closet, and four TV monitors mounted on the wall. Ordinarily, the monitors displayed whatever discussion was going on in the Security Council or Economic and Social Council. By putting on headsets and switching channels, observers could listen in whatever language they wished. Tonight they'd be watching Ms. Chatterjee's speech followed by the recital. A pair of card tables at the end of the room held sandwiches and a coffeemaker. There were soft drinks in a small refrigerator.

After thanking the parents for their cooperation, Kako very politely reminded them what they'd been told by letter and by the United Nations representative who had met them at the hotel the night before. For security reasons, they must remain in this room for the duration of the event. She said she would be returning with their children at eight-thirty. Hood wondered if the guard had been posted to keep tourists out of the press room or to keep them in.

Hood and Sharon walked over to the sandwich table.

One of the men pointed to the plastic plates and utensils. "See what happens when the U.S. doesn't pay its dues?" he cracked.

The veteran Washington police officer was referring to the nation's billion-dollar debt, a result of the Senate's unhappiness with what it characterized as chronic waste, fraud, and financial abuses at the United Nations. Key among these charges was that money allocated for UN peacekeeping forces was being used to bolster the military resources of participating nations.

Hood smiled politely. He didn't want to think about big budgets and big government and greenback diplomacy. He and his wife had had a good day today. After

71

their tense first night in New York, Sharon tried to relax. She savored the pleasant fall sunshine at Liberty Island and didn't let the crowds get to her. She enjoyed Alexander's excitement at learning all the technical facts about the statue and at being left alone with his video games and less-than-nutritious takeout from a salad bar on Seventh Avenue. Hood wasn't going to let imprisonment or America-bashing or cheap utensils ruin that.

Harleigh may have been the catalyst for all these good feelings, but neither their daughter nor Alexander was the glue.

There's something here, Hood told himself as they filled their plates and then sat on one of the old vinyl couches to await their daughter's New York City debut. He wanted to hold onto that feeling in the same way that he had held Sharon's hand.

Tightly.

SEVEN

New York, New York
Saturday, 7:27 P.M.

Traffic in Times Square is extremely dense after seven
P.M. on Saturday night as theatergoers arrive from out
of town. Limousines clog the side streets, garages have
cars lined up waiting to get in, and cabs and buses inch
through the center of the theater district.

Georgiev had allowed for the delay when he planned
this part of the operation. When he finally turned east
on Forty-second Street and rolled toward Bryant Park,
he was relaxed and confident. So were the other members of the team. But then, if he hadn't served with them,
seen that they were cool under pressure, he never would
have recruited them for this mission.

Apart from Reynold Downer, the forty-eight-year-old
former colonel of the Bulgarian People's Army was the
only truly mercenary man on the team. Barone wanted
money to help his people back home. Sazanka and Vandal had issues of honor dating back to World War II.
Issues that money would clear away. Georgiev had a
different problem. He'd spent nearly ten years as part of
the CIA-financed underground in Bulgaria. He'd fought
the Communists for so long that he couldn't adapt to an
era that had no enemy. He had no trade apart from soldiering, the army was not paying its people with regu-

larity, and he was much poorer now than he'd been taking American dollars and living under the shadow of the Soviet empire. He wanted to open a new business: financing petroleum and natural gas exploitation. He would do that with his share of the take from today's mission.

Because of Georgiev's familiarity with CIA tactics and his fluency in American English, the others had no trouble with him leading this half of the operation. Besides, as he'd proven when he organized the prostitution ring in Cambodia, he was a natural leader.

Georgiev drove slowly, carefully. He watched out for jaywalking pedestrians. He didn't tailgate. He didn't shout at taxi drivers who cut him off. He didn't do anything that would cause him to be stopped by the police. It was ironic. He was about to commit an act of destruction and murder that the world would not soon forget. Yet here he was, the model of tranquil, lawful motoring. There was a time, growing up, when Georgiev wanted to be a philosopher. Maybe when all of this was over, he would finally get to take that up. Contrasts fascinated him.

When he had driven this route the day before, he noticed a traffic camera on a streetlight at the southwest corner of Forty-second Street and Fifth Avenue. The camera faced north. There was another on Forty-second Street and Third Avenue facing south. Vandal, who was sitting in the passenger's seat, and Georgiev both adjusted their sun visors to cover those windows. They'd be wearing ski masks when they went into the UN. The NYPD would probably review all the cameras in the area, and he didn't want anyone to have a photographic record of who was in the van. The traffic cameras would tell them nothing. And while police might find a few tourists who had videotaped the van, Georgiev had intentionally approached the target from the setting sun. All any videotape would see was glare off the windshield. God bless the things he'd learned from the CIA.

They passed the New York Public Library, Grand Central Station, and the Chrysler Building. They reached First Avenue without incident. Georgiev timed his approach so they'd stop at the light. He'd made sure he was in the right-hand lane. When they made the left turn, he would be on the same side of the street as the United Nations, on the right. He glanced toward the north. The target area was just two blocks away. Almost straight ahead was the Secretariat Building, set back behind a circular courtyard and a fountain. A seven-foot-high iron fence fronted the complex for its four-block length. There were three guard booths spaced along the gates, behind them. NYPD officers patrolled the street. Across First Avenue, on the corner of Forty-fifth Street, was an NYPD command booth.

He had reconnoitered all of this the day before. And he'd studied photographs and videotape he'd taken months before that. He knew this area completely, from the location of every streetlight to every fire hydrant.

Georgiev waited until the DON'T WALK sign began flashing to his left. That meant they had six seconds until the light changed. Georgiev's black ski mask was tucked between his legs. He pulled it out and slipped it on. The other men did likewise. They were already wearing thin white gloves so they wouldn't leave fingerprints but could still handle their weapons.

The light turned.

So did Georgiev.

EIGHT

New York, New York
Saturday, 7:30 P.M.

Etienne Vandal pulled on his ski mask. Then he turned to receive his weapons from Sazanka, who was in the back of the van along with Barone and Downer. The seats had been removed and piled in a corner of the hotel garage. The windows had been painted over. The men were able to prepare in total secrecy. Barone holstered his own two automatics and picked up the Uzi. He would also be wearing the backpack containing tear gas and gas masks. If it became necessary to fight their way out, they'd have the gas as well as hostages.

It was difficult to twist very far because of the bulletproof vest, but Vandal preferred discomfort to vulnerability. The Japanese officer handed him two automatics and an Uzi.

Downer was kneeling beside the door on the driver's side of the van. He placed his own weapons on the floor. A Swiss-made B-77 missile launcher lay across his shoulder. He had requested an American M47 Dragon, but this was the closest Ustinoviks could come. Downer had examined the short-range, lightweight antitank missile and had assured the team it would do the job. Vandal and the others hoped so. Without it, they'd be dead in the street. Barone was crouched beside the side door, ready to pull it open.

Vandal had already checked his weapons at the hotel. Now he sat and waited as the van continued to accelerate. It was here at last. The countdown they'd been working for, going over again and again for more than a year. In Vandal's case, it was a moment he'd been awaiting for even longer than that. He was calm, even relieved, as the target area came into view.

The other men also seemed calm, especially Georgiev. Yet he always came across as a big, cold machine. Vandal knew very little about the man, but what he did know, he didn't like or respect. Until Bulgaria drafted a new constitution in 1991, it was among the most repressive nations in the Soviet bloc. Georgiev helped the CIA recruit informants inside the government. Vandal would have understood if the man had struggled to overthrow the regime for principle. But Georgiev had worked for the CIA simply because they paid well. Though the goals were the same, that was the difference between a patriot and a traitor. As far as Vandal was concerned, a man who would betray his country would certainly betray his partners in crime. That was something Etienne Vandal knew about. His grandfather was a former Nazi collaborator who died in a French prison. It wasn't only that Charles Vandal had betrayed his country. He'd been a member of the Mulot resistance group, which had been responsible for stealing and hiding art and treasures before the Germans could plunder them from French museums. Charles Vandal not only turned over Mulot and his team, but he led the Germans to a cache of French art.

They had less than one block to go. A few tourists

who were still out at this hour turned to look at the speeding van. The vehicle shot past the UN library building on the south side of the plaza. Then Georgiev raced past the first guard booth with its green-tinted bulletproof glass and bored-looking officers. The booth was located behind the black iron fence, which was separated from the avenue by twenty feet of sidewalk. There were extra guards for tonight's soiree and the gate was closed, but that didn't matter. The target area was less than fifty feet to the north.

Georgiev passed the second guard booth. Then, clearing a fire hydrant just beyond, he swung the van to the right and floored the gas pedal. The vehicle shot across the sidewalk, hitting one pedestrian and running him under the driver's-side wheel. Several others were knocked to the side. A moment later, the van ripped through a yard-high chain-link fence. The sound of the metal scraping the sides of the van drowned out the screams of injured pedestrians. The vehicle plowed through a small garden filled with trees and shrubs, Georgiev steering clear of the large tree on the south side of the garden. A few low-hanging branches from other trees smashed against the windshield and roof. Some branches snapped, others whipped back as the van pushed ahead.

To the north and south, UN police, members of the NYPD, and a handful of white-shirted State Department police were just beginning to respond to the breach. Guns drawn, radios in hand, they ran from the three guard booths along First Avenue, from the booth inside the courtyard to the north, and from the police outpost across the street.

It took just over two seconds for the van to drill through the garden and the row of hedges at the far end.

The men in the back of the van braced themselves as Georgiev crushed down on the brake. The garden was separated from the circular plaza by a concrete barrier just over three feet high and nearly one foot thick. The flagpoles, which flew the flags of the 185 member nations, stood in a row beyond the barrier.

Georgiev and Vandal ducked low. They were expecting to lose the windshield. Barone slid the van door open. Sazanka lay down, prepared to spray covering fire if necessary. Downer leaned out over him and pointed his missile launcher at the thick wall. He aimed low to make sure he didn't leave anything close to the ground. Then he fired.

There was an ear-ringing roar, and then a seven-foot-wide section of the concrete barrier was gone. Several large chunks flew across the plaza like cannonballs, some landing in the fountain, others bouncing across the drive. But most of the wall rose in a wide, fifty-foot-high plume of jagged white shards, then rained down like hail. Behind the wall, five of the tall white flagpoles snapped near the bases. They fell straight and hard and landed on the asphalt with a loud *clang*. Vandal could hear it even though his ears were still clogged from the explosion.

Even as the bits of concrete were still falling, Georgiev gunned the engine and pushed the van ahead. Timing was critical. They had to keep moving. He roared through the breach in the barrier, clipping the driver's side on an outthrust of concrete, but didn't stop. Downer had ducked back into the van, but Sazanka continued to lie in the open side door, ready to fire at anyone who shot at them. No one did. While they were part of the PKO and first conceived of this idea, the men had easily

80

obtained a copy of the United Nations police guidelines. They were very explicit: No one was to act individually against a group. The threat was to be contained, if possible, by whatever personnel were on hand, but not challenged until sufficient units were made available. It was pure United Nations philosophy. It didn't work in the international arena, and it wasn't going to work here.

Georgiev headed northeast across the plaza. Though the windshield had shattered, it was still in the frame. Fortunately, there wasn't much the Bulgarian needed to see. The van shot across the exit lane of the courtyard and hopped onto the lawn that led to the General Assembly Building. Georgiev sped east around the Japanese Peace Bell. As Vandal ducked again, the van crashed through the large plate glass windows that opened onto the courtyard from the small lobby. The van slammed into the statue of El Abrazo de Paz, a stylized human figure "embracing peace" that stood just inside. The statue fell over, and the van rode up on it; that was as far as the van was going. But that was also as far as they needed the van to go. By the time guards and attendees at the delegates' soiree first became aware of the disturbance, the five men were already out of the van. Georgiev fired a short burst at the guard who was posted outside the corridor that led to the staff elevators. The young man spun and fell, the first UN casualty. Vandal wondered whether he'd get a peace statue in his honor as well.

The five men ran down the corridor and swung onto the escalators. The escalators had been shut down by security personnel. That was something they hadn't anticipated, not that it mattered. They quickly ran up the two flights, then turned to their left. The stalled escalator

81

was the only form of resistance they met. What Germany had proved in Poland in 1939, what Saddam Hussein had proved in Kuwait in 1990, is that there is no effective defense against a well-planned lightning strike. There's only recovery and then a counterattack. And in this case, neither would be of any use.

Less than ninety seconds after turning off First Avenue, the five men were inside the heart of the Secretariat Building. They ran alongside the tall windows that overlooked the courtyard. The fountain had been shut down to allow clear visbility into the Secretariat windows. Traffic had been stopped, and tourists were being herded onto side streets. Police and security forces were everywhere now.

Seal off the building, contain the problem, Vandal thought. They were so damned predictable.

There were also several guards running toward them. The three men and one woman were wearing bulletproof vests and listening to their radios. They had their guns drawn and were obviously headed toward the Security Council chamber, which was on their right. They had probably been sent to evacuate the delegates in case that was the target.

The young guards never made it. Upon seeing the intruders, they stopped. Then, like any soldier or police officer who had never been in combat, they snapped into the only thing they knew: training mode. From the United Nations security force manual, Vandal knew that in a showdown situation, they would attempt to spread out and present a less concentrated target, take cover if possible, and attempt to disable the enemy.

Georgiev and Sazanka didn't give them the chance. Firing their Uzis from the hip, they sliced across the guards' thighs and dropped them virtually where they stood. Guns and radios clattered on the tile floor. As the wounded guards moaned, the two men walked on, firing a second burst into the head of each one. They stopped a few yards from the bodies. Georgiev picked up two of the radios that had skidded across the floor.

"Come on," Vandal said and hurried on.

Barone and Downer joined him, and the five men continued forward. Now the only things that stood between them and the Security Council chambers were four dead guards and a blood-slicked floor.

NINE

New York, New York
Saturday, 7:34 P.M.

All the parents in the correspondents' area heard and felt the crash downstairs. Since there were no windows in the room, they couldn't be sure exactly where or what it was.

Paul Hood's first thought was that there had been an explosion. That was also the conclusion of several parents who wanted to go and make sure the children were all right. But Mr. Dillon walked in then. The guard asked everyone to stay where they were and to remain calm.

"I just went across the hall to the Security Council," Dillon said. "The children are fine. Most of the delegates are also there waiting for the secretary-general. Security personnel are on the way to evacuate the kids, the delegates, and then you folks. If you stay calm, everyone will be fine."

"Do you have any idea what happened?" one of the parents asked.

"I'm not sure," Mr. Dillon said. "It looks like a van ran through the barrier and into the courtyard. I could see it out the window. But no one knows—"

He was interrupted by several pops from below. It sounded like gunfire. Dillon got on his radio.

"Station Freedom-Seven to base," he said.

There was a lot of yelling and noise. Then someone on the other end said, "There's been a breach, Freedom-Seven. Intruders unknown. Go to Everest-Six, Code Red. Do you have that?"

"Everest-Six, Code Red," Dillon said. "I'm on my way." He clicked off the radio and headed toward the door. "I'm going back to the Security Council chambers to wait for the other guards. Please, all of you—just stay here."

"How long until the other guards arrive?" one of the fathers shouted.

"A few minutes," Mr. Dillon replied.

He left. The door shut with a solid click. Except for shouts from somewhere outside the building, everything was quiet.

Suddenly, one of the fathers started toward the door. "I'm going to get my daughter," he said.

Hood stepped between the larger man and the door.

"Don't," Hood said.

"Why?" the man demanded.

"Because the last thing security, medics, and fire personnel need is people getting in the way," Hood said. "Besides, they called this a code red situation. That probably means there's been a major security breach."

"All the more reason to get our kids out!" one of the other fathers said.

"No," Hood replied. "This is international soil. American laws and niceties don't apply. The guards will probably shoot unidentified personnel."

"How do you know that?"

"I worked for a federal intelligence agency after I left Los Angeles," Hood told them. "I've seen people gunned down for being in the wrong place at the wrong time.''

The man's wife came over and took his arm. "Charlie, please. Mr. Hood is right. Let the authorities handle this.''

"But our daughter is out there," Charlie said.

"So is mine," Hood said. "And getting myself killed isn't going to help her." It hit him just then that Harleigh *was* out there, and she really was in danger. He looked at Sharon, who was standing to the right, in the corner. He walked over and hugged her.

"Paul," she whispered. "I—I think we should be with Harleigh.''

"We will be, soon," he said.

There were footsteps in the hall followed by the distinctive *phup-phup-phup* of an automatic. The shots were followed by clattering, cries, shouts, and more footsteps. Then the hall was silent.

"Whose side was that?" Charlie asked no one in particular.

Hood didn't know. He left Sharon and walked toward the door. He crouched low in case someone fired and motioned for everyone in the room to stand back, clear of the door. Then he reached up and slowly turned the silver knob. He eased the door open.

There were four bodies lying in the corridor between the correspondents' room and the Security Council. They belonged to UN security personnel. Whoever had shot them was gone, though they'd left bloody tracks in their wake. Tracks that led to the Security Council.

Hood experienced a strange flashback. He felt like Thomas Davies, a firefighter he used to play softball with in Los Angeles. One afternoon, Davies had gotten

87

a call that his own home was burning. The man knew what to do, he knew what was happening, yet he couldn't react.

Hood shut the door and walked toward the desks.

"What is it?" Charlie asked.

Hood didn't answer him. He was trying to get himself moving.

"Dammit, what happened?" Charlie shouted.

Hood said, "Four guards are dead, and whoever shot them has gone into the Security Council chambers."

"My baby," one of the mothers sobbed.

"I'm sure they're all right for now," Hood said.

"Yeah, and you were sure they'd be all right if we stayed in here!" Charlie yelled.

Charlie's rage brought Hood out of his shock. "If you'd been outside, you'd be dead now," Hood said. "Mr. Dillon wouldn't have let you into the chambers, and you'd've been killed with the guards." He took a breath to calm himself. Then he slipped his cell phone from the pocket of his blazer. He punched in a number.

"Who are you calling?" Sharon asked.

Her husband finished entering the number. He looked at her and touched her cheek. "Someone who won't give a shit that this is international territory," he replied. "Someone who can help us."

TEN

Bethesda, Maryland
Saturday, 7:46 P.M.

Mike Rodgers was going through a Gary Cooper phase. Not in his real life but in his movie life—though at the moment, the two lives were entirely codependent.

Op-Center's forty-five-year-old former deputy director, now acting director, had never been confused or insecure. He had his nose broken four times playing college basketball because he saw the basket and went for it, damning the Torpedoes—as well as the Badgers, the Ironmen, the Thrashers, and the other teams he played. When he'd served two tours of duty in Vietnam and commanded a mechanized brigade in the Gulf War, he was given objectives and had met them all. Every damn one of them. On his first mission with Striker, to North Korea, he'd kept a fanatical officer from nuking Japan. When he returned from Vietnam, he'd even found time to get a Ph.D. in world history. But now—

It wasn't just Paul Hood resigning that depressed him, though that was part of the problem. It was ironic. Two and a half years ago, Rodgers had found it difficult to report to the man—a civilian who had been attending fund-raisers with movie stars while Rodgers was chasing Iraq out of Kuwait. But Hood had proven himself a steady, politically savvy manager. Rodgers was going to miss the man and his leadership.

Dressed in a loose-fitting gray sweat suit and Nikes, Rodgers shifted carefully on the leather sofa. He slumped back slowly. Just two weeks before, he'd been captured by terrorists in the Bekaa Valley in Lebanon. The second- and third-degree burns he'd suffered during torture were still not completely healed. Neither were the internal wounds.

Rodgers's gaze had wandered. He looked back at the TV, profound sadness in his light brown eyes. He was watching *Vera Cruz*, one of Cooper's last films. He was playing a former Civil War officer who went south of the border to work as a mercenary and ended up embracing the cause of local revolutionaries. Strength, dignity, and honor—that was Coop.

That used to be Mike Rodgers, he reflected sadly.

He'd lost more than some flesh and his freedom in Lebanon. Being strung up in a cave and burned with a blowtorch had cost him his confidence. And not because he'd been afraid to die. He believed passionately in the Viking code, that the process of death began with the moment of birth, and that death in combat was the most honorable way of reaching one's inevitable end. But he was nearly denied that. Extreme pain, like a high fever, robs the mind of orderliness. The calm and collected torturer becomes the voice of reason and tells the mind where to touch down. And Rodgers was perilously close to that point, to telling the terrorists how to operate the Regional Op-Center they'd captured.

That's why Rodgers needed Gary Cooper. Not to heal his soul—he didn't think that was possible. He'd seen his breaking point, and he could never lose that knowledge, that awareness of his own limitations. It reminded him of the first time he twisted his ankle playing basketball and it didn't heal overnight. The sense of invulnerability was gone forever.

A broken spirit was worse.

What Mike Rodgers needed now was to try to prop up the confidence his captors had taken from him. Fortify himself enough to run Op-Center until the president decided on a replacement for Paul Hood. Then he could make decisions about his own future.

Rodgers looked back at the TV screen. Movies had always been a haven for him, a source of nourishment. When his alcoholic father used to punch the hell out of him—not just hit but punch, with his Yale class ring—young Mike Rodgers would get on his bicycle, go to the local movie theater, pay his twenty-five cents, and crawl into a Western or war film or historical epic. Over the years, he modeled his morality, his life, his career after the characters played by John Wayne and Charlton Heston and Burt Lancaster.

He couldn't remember a time when any of them came close to breaking under torture, though. He felt very alone.

Coop had just rescued a Mexican girl who was being abused by renegade soldiers when the cordless phone rang. Rodgers picked it up.

"Hello?"

"Mike, thank God you're in—"

"Paul?"

"Yeah. Listen," Hood said. "I'm inside the United Nations Correspondents' room across from the Security Council chambers. Four guards have just been gunned down in the corridor."

91

Rodgers sat up. "By whom?"

"I don't know," Hood said. "But it looks like the people who did it went inside."

"Where's Harleigh?" Rodgers asked.

"She's in there," Hood said. "Most of the members of the Security Council and the entire string ensemble were in the chambers."

Rodgers grabbed the remote, switched off the DVD, and turned on CNN. Reporters were live at the United Nations. It didn't sound as if they knew much about what was going on.

"Mike, you know what the security setup is here," Hood said. "If this is a multinational hostage situation, depending on who the perpetrators are, the UN could argue about jurisdiction for hours before they even address the issue of getting the people out."

"Understood," Rodgers said. "I'll call Bob and put him on this. Are you on your cell phone?"

"Yes."

"Keep me apprised when you can," Rodgers said.

"All right," Hood replied. "Mike—"

"Paul, we're going to take care of this," Rodgers assured him. "You know there's usually some kind of cooling-down period immediately after a takeover. Demands stated, attempts to negotiate. We won't waste any of that time. You and Sharon just have to try and stay calm."

Hood thanked him and hung up. Rodgers turned up the volume on the TV, listening as he rose slowly. The newscaster had no idea who had driven the van or why they'd attacked the United Nations. There had been no official announcement, and no communication from the five people who'd apparently gone into the Security Council chambers.

Rodgers shut off the television. While the general headed to his bedroom to dress, he punched in Bob Herbert's mobile phone number. Op-Center's intelligence chief was at dinner with Andrea Fortelni, a deputy assistant secretary of state. Herbert hadn't dated much in the years since his wife was killed in Beirut, but he was a chronic intel collector. Foreign governments, his own government, it didn't matter. As in the Japanese movie *Rashomon*—which was the only thing besides sushi and *The Seven Samurai* that Rodgers enjoyed from Japan—there was rarely any truth in government affairs. Just different perspectives. And professional that Herbert was, he liked having as many perspectives as possible.

Herbert was also a man who was devoted to his friends and coworkers. When Rodgers called to tell him what had happened, Herbert said he'd be at Op-Center within the half hour. Rodgers told him to have Matt Stoll come in as well. They might need to get into UN computers, and Matt was a peerless hacker. Meanwhile, Rodgers said that he'd call Striker and put them on yellow alert, in case they were needed. Along with the rest of Op-Center, the elite, twenty-one-person rapid-deployment force was based at the FBI Academy in Quantico. They could get to the United Nations in well under an hour if necessary.

Rodgers hoped the precautions would not be necessary. Unfortunately, terrorists who started out with murder had nothing to lose by killing again. Besides, for nearly half a century, terrorism had proven impervious to conciliatory, United Nations–style diplomacy.

Hope, he thought bitterly. *What was it some play-*

wright or scholar had once written? That hope is the feeling you have that the feeling you have isn't permanent.

Rodgers finished dressing, then hurried into the fading light and climbed into his car. His own concerns were forgotten as he headed south along the George Washington Memorial Parkway to Op-Center.

To help rescue a girl from renegades.

ELEVEN

Andrews Air Force Base, Maryland Saturday, 8:37 P.M.

Forty years ago, at the peak of the Cold War, the nondescript, two-story building in the northeast corner of Andrews Air Force Base was a ready room. It was the staging area for elite flight crews known as the Ravens. In the event of a nuclear attack, it would have been the job of the Ravens to evacuate key government and military officials from Washington, D.C., and relocate them in an underground facility in the Blue Ridge Mountains.

But the ivory-colored building was not a monument to another era. There were gardens in the dirt patches where soldiers used to drill, and the seventy-eight people who worked here were not all in uniform.

They were handpicked tacticians, generals, diplomats, intellience analysts, computer specialists, psychologists, reconnaissance experts, environmentalists, attorneys, and press liaisons who worked for the National Crisis Management Center.

After a two-year tooling-up period overseen by interim director Bob Herbert, the former ready room became a high-tech Operations Center designed to interface with and assist the White House, the National Reconnaissance Office, the Central Intelligence Agency, the National Security Agency, the State Department, the Department of Defense, the Defense Intelligence Agency, the Federal Bureau of Investigation, Interpol, and numerous foreign intelligence agencies in the management of domestic and international crises. However, after single-handedly defusing the crises in North Korea and Russia, Op-Center proved itself uniquely qualified to monitor, initiate, or manage operations worldwide.

All of that had happened during Paul Hood's watch.

General Mike Rodgers stopped his Jeep at the security gate. An Air Force guard stepped from the booth. Though Rodgers was not in uniform, the young sergeant saluted and raised the iron bar. Rodgers drove through.

Although it was Paul Hood who had run the show, Rodgers had been a hands-on participant in every decision and in several of the military actions. He was eager to handle the crisis at hand, especially if they could work this in the way he knew best: independently and covertly.

Rodgers parked and jogged as quickly as his tight bandages would allow. He passed through the keypad entry on the ground floor of Op-Center. After greeting the armed guards seated behind the bulletproof Lexan, Rodgers hurried through the first-floor administrative level. The real activity of Op-Center took place in the secure, below-ground facility.

Emerging in the heart of Op-Center, known as the bullpen, Rodgers moved quickly through the checkerboard of cubicles to the executive wing. The offices were arrayed in a semicircle on the north side of the facility. He bypassed his own office and went directly to the conference room, which attorney Lowell Coffey III had dubbed "the Tank."

The walls, floor, door, and ceiling of the Tank were all covered with sound-absorbing strips of mottled gray and black Acoustix; behind the strips were several layers of cork, a foot of concrete, and more Acoustix. In the midst of the concrete, on all six sides of the room, was a pair of wire grids that generated vacillating audio waves. Electronically, nothing could enter or leave the room. In order to receive calls from his cell phone, Rodgers had to stop and program the phone to forward calls to his office and then to here.

Bob Herbert was already there, along with Coffey, Ann Farris, Liz Gordon, and Matt Stoll. All had been off duty but came in so that the weekend night crew could continue to attend to regular Op-Center business. The concern everyone felt was palpable.

"Thanks for coming," Rodgers said as he swung into the room. He shut the door behind him and took his seat at the head of the oblong mahogany table. There were computer stations at either end of the table and telephones at each of the twelve chairs.

"Mike, you spoke with Paul?" Ann asked.

"Yes."

"How is he?" she asked.

"Paul and Sharon are both worried," Rodgers said curtly.

The general kept his conversations with Ann as short as possible with as little eye contact as possible. He didn't care for the press, and he didn't like spinning it. His idea of press relations was to tell the truth or to say nothing. But above all, he didn't approve of Ann's fascination with Paul Hood. It was partly a moral issue— Hood was married—and partly a practical one. They all had to work together. Sexual chemistry was unavoidable, but "Dr." Farris never took off her lab coat when she was around Hood.

If Ann noticed, she didn't react.

"I told Paul we'd let him know when we have something," Rodgers said. "But I don't want to call unless it's absolutely necessary. If Paul doesn't get evacuated, he may try to get closer to the situation. I don't want the phone beeping while he's got his ear to a closed door."

"Besides which," Stoll said, "that line's not exactly secure."

Rodgers nodded. He looked over at Herbert. "I phoned Colonel August on the way over. He's got Striker on yellow alert and is checking the DOD database for everything they've got on the United Nations complex."

"The CIA did a pretty thorough job of mapping the place while it was going up," Herbert said. "I'm sure there'll be a lot on file."

Well-dressed attorney Lowell Coffey III was seated to Rodgers's left. "You understand, Mike, that the United States has absolutely no jurisdiction anywhere on the grounds of the United Nations," he pointed out. "Not even the NYPD can go in there without being asked."

"I understand," Rodgers said.

"Do you care?" Liz Gordon asked.

Rodgers looked at the husky staff psychologist who was seated next to Coffey. "Only about Harleigh Hood and the other kids in the Security Council chamber," he replied.

Liz looked like she wanted to say something. She didn't. She didn't have to. Rodgers could see the disapproval in her expression. When he came back from the Middle East, she'd talked to him about not taking out his anger and despair on other targets. He didn't think he was. These people, whoever they were, had earned his anger on their own.

Rodgers turned to Herbert, who was sitting to his right. "Is there any intel on whoever did this?"

Herbert sat forward in his wheelchair. "Nothing," said the balding intelligence chief. "The perps came in with a van. We got the license number off the TV and chased it down to the rental car agency. The guy it was rented to, Ilya Gaft, is a fake."

"He had to show a driver's license to the clerk," Rodgers said.

Herbert nodded. "And it checked out with the Department of Motor Vehicles until we asked for his file. There wasn't one. A counterfeit license is pretty easy to get."

Rodgers nodded.

"There was triple security on board for this soiree," Herbert said. "I had a look at the comparable figures from last year's bash. The problem is, they were all concentrated pretty much at the three drive-through checkpoints and in the square north of the United Nations. These perps apparently blew their way through the concrete barrier using a rocket launcher, then drove across the countyard and right into the damned building. Shot everyone they came up against before holing up inside the Security Council."

"And there's been no word from them?" Rodgers asked.

"Not a whisper," Herbert said. "I called Darrell over in Spain. He called someone at Interpol in Madrid who is close to people at UN security. They got in touch immediately. As soon as they hear anything about what's inside the van or the kind of weapons these guys used, we'll know."

"What about the UN? Have they said anything about this publicly?" Rodgers asked Ann.

"Nothing," she told him. "No spokesperson has come out."

"No statement to the press?"

Ann shook her head. "The UN Information Service is not a rapid-response force."

"The United Nations's not a rapid-response anything," Herbert said disgustedly. "The guy Darrell's friend at Interpol called—he's a personal aide to a Colonel Rick Mott, who's the head of United Nations security. The aide said that they hadn't even collected the spent shells from outside the Security Council chamber yet, let alone checked them for fingerprints or provenance. And that was about thirty-five minutes after this whole thing started. They were just getting themselves organized to look at tapes from the security cameras and then go into a meeting with the secretary-general."

"They're good at meetings," Rodgers said. "What about other tapes?" he asked Ann. "The news services must've gone after every tourist on the street, trying to get video of the attack."

"Good idea," she said. "I'll have Mary make some calls, though at that hour, there probably weren't very many tourists out."

Ann picked up the phone and asked her assistant to run a check of what the networks and cable news services might have collected.

"You know," Coffey said, "I'm pretty sure the police have surveillance cameras on some streets in New

York. I'll call the city's district attorney and find out." The attorney reached inside his blue blazer and slipped out his digital pocket address book.

Rodgers was staring at the table. Both Ann and Coffey were on the phone. But not enough was happening. They needed to do more.

"Matt," Rodgers said, "the attackers had to have accessed the DMV computer at some point to put the fake license in."

"That's a pretty easy hack," Stoll said.

"Fine. But is there any way we can track the hack backward to whoever did it?" Rodgers asked.

"No," said the portly Stoll. "A trace like that is something you have to set up. You wait until they strike and then follow the signal back. Even then, a good hacker can run the signal through terminals in other cities. Hell, he can bounce it off a couple of satellites if he wants. Besides, for all we know, these people had someone on the inside."

"That's true," Herbert said.

Rodgers continued to stare. He needed a history, a pattern, anything they could use to start building a profile. And he needed it fast.

"They've held these parties every year for five years," Herbert said. "Maybe someone cased the thing last year. We should probably have a look at the guest list, see if anyone—"

Just then Rodgers's phone beeped. He grabbed it, wincing as he strained the bandages around his right side. "Rodgers here."

"It's Paul," said the caller.

Rodgers motioned for everyone to be quiet, then

punched the speaker button. "We're here," he said. "In the Tank."

"What are you hearing?"

"Nothing," Rodgers told him. "No statements, no demands. How are you doing?"

"The phone rang a minute ago," Hood said. "They're sending up an evac team. Before they do, I want to try and see what's going on."

Rodgers didn't like the idea of Paul moving around unannounced. Skittish security forces just arriving on the scene could mistake him for a terrorist. But Paul knew that. Paul also knew that if Striker were going to do anything to help get Harleigh and the other kids out, they needed intel.

"I'm at the door," he said. "I hear footsteps outside. Opening—"

There was a long silence. Rodgers looked at the faces of the other people in the room. Everyone was somber and staring down; Ann was flushed. She had to know everyone was thinking about how she was reacting to all this. Everyone but Rodgers. He was wishing that he were there with Hood, in the thick of this. How did the world turn upside down like this? The manager was in the field, and the soldier was at a desk.

"Hold on," Hood said quietly. "Something's happening."

There was another silence, this one short.

"Mike, there's someone coming out of the Security Council chamber," Hood said. "Oh, Christ," he said a moment later. "Christ."

TWELVE

New York, New York
Saturday, 9:01 P.M.

Reynold Downer stood in one of the two Security Council chamber doorways that opened into the corridor. The double oak doors were in the far northern corner of the long, back wall of the council. Outside and just beyond the doors, a second wall jutted into the corridor perpendicular to the Security Council wall. Downer had opened only the far side door. The Australian was still wearing his ski mask.

In front of Downer was a slender, middle-aged man in a black suit. He was Swedish delegate Leif Johanson. There was a single sheet of legal-sized paper in his trembling hands. Downer was holding a handful of the man's blond hair and pulling backward slightly. His automatic was pressed to the base of the man's skull. The Australian turned the man so that he was facing away from the corner formed by the two walls.

Ahead of them were a dozen United Nations security guards. The men and women were wearing bulletproof vests and helmets with thick visors. Their guns were drawn. Several of the guards were shaking slightly. That wasn't surprising. Though the bodies of their dead comrades had been removed, their blood was still on the floor.

"Speak," Downer said into the captive's ear.

The man looked down at the legal-sized paper. He was trembling hard as he read from it.

"I've been ordered to inform you of the following," he said softly in a Swedish accent.

"Louder!" Downer hissed.

The man spoke up. "You have ninety minutes to deliver 250 million dollars U.S. to the Zurich Confederated Finance account VEB-9167681-EPB. The name on the account is false, and any attempts to access it will result in additional deaths. You will also deliver a helicopter with ten-person capacity, running and fully fueled, in the courtyard. We will be taking passengers with us to ensure your continued cooperation. You will notify us by radio on the regular United Nations security channel when both are there. No other communications will be acknowledged. If you fail, one hostage will be killed then and every hour thereafter starting with—with myself." The man stopped. He had to wait until the paper stopped shaking before continuing. "Any attempt to liberate the hostages will result in the release of poison gas which will kill everyone in the room."

Downer quickly pulled the man back toward the open door. He told him to drop the paper so the officials would have the bank number, then ordered him to shut the door as they stepped inside. When it closed, Downer released the man's hair. The Swede stood there unsteadily.

"I—I should have tried to run," the Swede muttered. He looked at the door. He was obviously weighing his chances of getting back outside.

"Hands on your head, and move," Downer growled. The Swede looked at Downer. "Why? You're going to shoot me in an hour whether I cooperate or not!''

"Not if they deliver," Downer said.

"They can't!" he cried. "They won't simply turn over a quarter of a *billion* dollars!''

Downer raised the gun. "It would be a shame if they do, and I've already killed you," he said. "Or if I kill you and then have to shoot your companion ninety minutes from now.''

His defiance faded quickly. Reluctantly, the Swede put his hands on top of his head. He started down the staircase, which ran along the southern side of the gallery.

Downer walked several paces behind the delegate. To the left were green-velvet seats grouped in two tiers of five rows each. Before the era of heightened security, these seats were used by the public to watch the activities of the Security Council. A waist-high wooden wall separated the bottom row of seats from the main floor. There was a single row of chairs in front of that wall. These seats were reserved for delegates who were not members of the Security Council. Beyond the viewing area was the main section of the Security Council chamber. This section was dominated by a large table shaped like a rounded horseshoe. Inside this table was a narrow, rectangular table facing east and west. When the Security Council was in session, the delegates sat at the outer table and the translators sat at the center table. Tonight, the children were sitting at the far side of the circular table and the guests of the delegates were seated at the circular table and at the rectangular one in the center. The delegates themselves were sitting on the floor inside the circular table. As the Swede rejoined the other delegates, his companion, a striking young woman, looked at him from where she was seated at the table. He nodded that he was all right.

Beyond the table, on either end of the chamber, two tall floor-to-ceiling windows allowed the members of the Security Council to look out on the East River. The glass was bulletproof, and the green drapes were drawn now. Between them was a large painting that depicted the phoenix soaring from the ashes, the world symbolically rising from the destruction of World War II. On either side of the room, one floor up, were the glass-enclosed media rooms, which had replaced the correspondents' room.

Barone and Vandal were standing in either corner of the chamber, by the windows. Sazanka was positioned by the north side door, and Georgiev was a floater, moving around and keeping an eye on the five additional doors on the main floor. Right now, he was standing in the opening of the horseshoe table. Like Downer, the men were all still wearing their ski masks.

As soon as the Swede was seated, Downer walked over to Georgiev.

"Who was out there?" Georgiev asked.

"They had about a dozen ladies in the corridor," Downer said.

The ladies were the general-purpose UN security guards, so-called because they usually stood around talking. The guards they had shot on the way in were all ladies.

"There were no special forces personnel," Downer said. "They can't even act decisively when their own bacon is burning."

"That is something they will learn to do this evening," Georgiev said.

Georgiev nodded toward the Swede. "He delivered the message exactly as I wrote it?"

Downer nodded.

The Bulgarian looked at his watch. "Then they have eighty-four minutes left before we start sending out bodies."

"You really think they'll comply?" Downer asked quietly.

"Not at first," Georgiev said. "I've said that all along." He glanced over at the tables. His voice was matter-of-fact as he said, "But they will. When the bodies pile up and we come closer and closer to the children, they will."

THIRTEEN

New York, New York
Saturday, 9:33 P.M.

Paul Hood did a quick, schizophrenic two-step.

Hood hadn't breathed while he listened to the terrorists' demands. The crisis manager in him hadn't wanted to miss a word or inflection, anything that might tell him if they had any of that wiggle room Mike had spoken about. They did not. The demands were specific and time-sensitive. Now that the terrorists were finished addressing the guards, Hood couldn't breathe. The crisis manager had been replaced by the father, one who had just learned the improbable price of his daughter's freedom.

What was improbable was not the amount of the demand. Hood knew from his banking days that up to a billion dollars was liquid in banks and in the local federal reserve institutions in New York and Boston. Even the time frame was manageable if the United Nations and the federal government put their minds to it. But they wouldn't. In order to get cooperation from local banks and the federal reserve, the United States government would have to guarantee the loan. The federal government might do that if the secretary-general asked and agreed to cover the loan with UN assets. However, the secretary-general might be afraid to do so for fear of offending nations that already resented American influence over the United Nations. And even if the United States wanted to pay the money as a means of settling part of its outstanding debt, Congress would be required to okay the expenditure. Even an emergency session could not be organized in time. And, of course, once the money was transferred, the terrorists would execute electronic transfers, scattering it in different accounts throughout the system and into linked accounts in other banks or investment groups. There would be no way to mark the funds or to stop the transfer. And there would be no way to stop the terrorists. They'd asked for a ten-seat helicopter because they intended to take hostages with them. One hostage per person, excluding the pilot. That meant there were probably four or five terrorists.

All of this shot through Hood's mind in the time it took him to shut the door. He turned back into the room and managed to draw a low, shallow breath. The other parents had heard the demands and were still processing what had happened. Sharon was standing beside her husband. She was looking at him, tears trickling down her cheeks. Suddenly he was someone else: the husband. A husband who had to stay steady for his wife.

The door opened, and Hood turned. A guard leaned into the room while another guard covered the corridor.

"Come with me!" the young man barked. "Quickly and quietly," he added as he waved them on.

Hood stepped aside as the parents filed by. Sharon stepped with him. He took her hand in his left hand and just now remembered the phone in his right. He put it to his mouth.

"Mike?" he said. "Are you still there?"

"I'm here, Paul," Rodgers said. "We heard."

"We're being moved," Hood said. "I'll call back."

"We'll be here," Rodgers assured him.

Hood closed the phone and slipped it back into his pocket. As the last parent left the room, Hood gave his wife's hand a gentle tug. She went along, and he followed her out.

The parents were hurried past the Security Council chamber, back toward the escalators. There were a few sobs and shouted pleas for their children's return, but the guards kept the group moving.

Hood was still holding Sharon's hand. She was squeezing his fingers tightly, probably without being aware of how hard she was gripping them.

As they filed onto the escalators, Hood could see more guards coming up with six-foot-high, transparent blast shields, audio equipment, and what looked like fiber-optic gear. They were obviously going to try to get a look at how the hostages were being held and also listen for snippets of conversation that might tell them who the terrorists were. But Hood knew that this wasn't going to get their kids back. The United Nations didn't have the tactical know-how or the personnel to do that. They were an organization of consensus, not action.

"Tell me you have a plan," Sharon said softly as they rode the escalators down. She was weeping openly. So were several other parents.

"We're going to think of something," Hood replied.

"I need more than that," Sharon said. "Harleigh's my girl, and I'm leaving her alone and scared up there. I have to know I'm doing the right thing."

"You are," Hood said. "We'll get her out of there, I promise."

As soon as the group reached the main lobby, they

111

were taken downstairs. A temporary command center was being set up in the lobby outside the gift shops and restaurant. That made sense. If the terrorists had accomplices, it would be difficult for them to monitor activities down here. The press would also have trouble getting down here, which was probably good. Given the international scope of what was happening, press coverage was inevitable. Since the UN would want to keep the number of people down here to a minimum, they would probably select a small pool of journalists.

The parents were taken to the public cafeteria, where they were seated at tables far from the lobby. They were offered sandwiches, bottled water, and coffee. One of the fathers lit a cigarette. He was not asked to put it out. Moments later, senior security personnel arrived to debrief the parents about things they might have seen or heard while they were in the press room. A psychologist and doctor also came down to help them get through the crisis.

Hood did not need their assistance.

Catching the eye of the security head, Hood said that he was going out to the rest room. Rising, he managed to smile for Sharon and then walked around the tables into the lobby. He went to the rest room, entered the rearmost stall, and got Mike Rodgers back on the phone. He stood there, leaning against the tile wall. His shirt was cold with perspiration.

"Mike?" he said.

"Here."

"The UN people are moving in with AV gear," Hood said. "We've been relocated downstairs for debriefing and psych support."

"Classic response," Rodgers said. "They're setting up for a siege."

"That isn't going to be an option," Hood said. "The terrorists don't want to negotiate, they don't want anyone freed from prison. They want money. Doesn't the UN have a special response unit?"

"Yes," Rodgers said. "The UNS-Ops is a nine-person division of the security force. Established in 1977, trained by the NYPD in SWAT tactics and hostage situations, and never field-tested."

"Jesus."

"Yeah," Rodgers said. "Why would anyone go after the United Nations? They're harmless. We've got Darrell on another line. He says that NYPD policy is to contain and negotiate, to keep things from exploding. And if things do blow, to keep them localized. It sounds like the security team's setting up to do that where you are."

Hood felt like he'd been kicked in the gut. *This was his daughter's death they were talking about "localizing"!*

"Darrell's also in touch with a contact in the secretary-general's office," Rodgers went on. "Chatterjee is getting together with representatives of the affected nations."

"To do what?" Hood asked.

"At the moment, nothing. There doesn't appear to be any inclination to accommodate the terrorists's demands. They're still trying to figure out who these people are. They have the paper with the Swede's script, but it was obviously dictated and written by the delegate. No help in tracing the terrorists."

"So they just intend to sit this out."

"For now," Rodgers said. "That's what the UN does."

Hood's sadness shaded to anger. He felt like going into the Security Council chamber himself and shooting the terrorists one after another. Instead, he turned and punched the bottom of his fist into the wall.

"Paul," Rodgers said.

Hood had never felt so helpless in his life.

"Paul, I have Striker on yellow alert."

Hood leaned the top of his head against the wall. "If you send them in here, the world—not just the federal government—the *world* is going to chew you up and crap you out."

"I have one word for you," Rodgers said. "Entebbe. Publicly, the world condemned Israeli commandos for going into Uganda and rescuing those Air France hostages from Palistinian terrorists. But privately, every right-thinking individual slept a little prouder that night. Paul, I don't give a damn what China or Albania or the secretary-general or even the president of the United States thinks of me. I want to get those kids out."

Hood didn't know what to say. The jump from yellow to red alert wasn't even his decision to make, yet Rodgers wanted his approval. Something about that touched him deeply.

"I'm with you, Mike," Hood said. "I'm with you, and God bless."

"Go back to Sharon and sit tight," Rodgers said. "I promise, we'll get Harleigh out of there."

Hood thanked him, shut the phone, and slipped it into his pocket. Mike's gesture triggered tears he'd been fighting since this whole thing started. He stood there sobbing with his cheek pressed against the cold tile. After a minute, the bathroom door opened. Hood sniffed back his tears, stood, and unspooled some bathroom tissue. He wiped his eyes.

It was odd. Hood had told Sharon what she'd wanted to hear, that they'd save Harleigh, even though he didn't entirely believe it. Yet when Mike said the same thing, Hood believed him. He wondered if all faith was so easily manipulated. A need to believe given a firm push.

He blew his nose and flushed the tissue down the toilet. There was one difference, he thought as he left the stall. Faith was faith, but Mike Rodgers was Mike Rodgers. And one of them had never let him down.

FOURTEEN

Quantico, Virginia
Saturday, 9:57 P.M.

The Marine Corps base at Quantico is a sprawling, rustic facility that is the home to diverse military units. These range from the MarCorSysCom—Marine Corps Systems Command—to the secretive Commandant's Warfighting Laboratory, a military think tank. Quantico is regarded as the intellectual crossroads of the Marine Corps, where teams of neologistic "warfighters" are able to devise and study tactics and then put them into operation in realistic combat simulations. Quantico also boasts some of the finest small-caliber weapons and grenade ranges, ground maneuver sites, light armor assault facilities, and physical challenge courses in the United States military.

Many of the base's key functions actually take place at Camp Upshur, a training encampment located twenty-five miles northwest of the base inside Training Area 17. There, Delta Company, 4th Light Armored Reconnaissance Battalion, 4th Marine Division, Op-Center's Striker division, and the Marine Reserve Support Units refine the techniques they learned when they were recruits. Comprised of twenty-one buildings that range from classrooms to Quonset hut–style squad bays, Camp Upshur can billet up to 500 troops.

117

Colonel Brett August liked Quantico, and he really liked Upshur. He spent his time equally between drilling his Striker squad and giving classroom lectures in military history, strategy, and theory. He also liked to put his people through rigorous sports competitions. To him, those were as much a psychological as a physiological workout. It was interesting. He had set it up so that the winners pulled extra duty. Garbage, kitchen, and latrine. Yet no one had ever tried to lose a basketball or football game, or even a weekend piggyback fight in the pool with their kids. Not once. In fact, August had never seen soldiers so happy to be doing drudge work. Liz Gordon was planning to write a paper on the phenomenon, which she'd dubbed ''The Masochism of Victory.''

Right now, though, it was August who was suffering. Upon returning from action in Spain, promotions and long-in-the-works transfers had cost him some key Strikers. In the few days following the depletion, he'd been working hard with four new warfighters. They'd been concentrating on night targeting with 105mm Howitzers when the call came from General Rodgers to put the team on yellow alert. August had wanted to give the new members more time to integrate with the old, but it didn't matter. August was satisfied that the new people were ready to see action if it became necessary. Marine Second Lieutenants John Friendly and Judy Quinn were as tough as August had ever seen, and Delta's Privates First Class Tim Lucas and Moe Longwood were their new communications expert and hand-to-hand combat specialist. There was natural competitiveness between the two branches, but that was good. Under fire, the barriers vanished, and they were all on the same team. Skill-wise, the new people would fit in nicely with seasoned Strikers Sargeant Chick Grey, Corporal Pat Prementine—the boy-genius of infantry tactics—Private First Class Sondra DeVonne, burly Private Walter Pupshaw, Private Jason Scott, and Private Terrence Newmeyer.

A yellow alert meant gearing up and waiting in the ready room to see if the team was going to take the next step. The ready room consisted of a gunmetal desk by the door, which was manned round the clock by a desk sergeant; hard wooden chairs arranged classroom style—the brass didn't want anyone getting too comfortable and going to sleep; an old blackboard; and a computer terminal on a table in front of the blackboard. In the event that they were needed, a Bell LongRanger fifteen-seat Model 205A-1 was being fired up on a nearby landing strip for the half-hour ride to Andrews Air Force Base. From there, the team would be flown by C-130 to the Marine Air Terminal at New York's La Guardia Airport. Rodgers had said that Striker's potential target was the United Nations building. The C-130 didn't need a lot of runway, and La Guardia, though not a regular stop for military traffic, was the field closest to the United Nations.

The one thing the tall, lean, thin-faced colonel hated above all was waiting. A holdover from Vietnam, it gave him a sense of being out of control. When August was a prisoner of war, he had to wait for the next middle-of-the-night interrogation, the next beating, the next death of someone he served with. He had to wait for news, passed along in careful whispers, by new arrivals in the camp. But the worst wait of all came when August tried to escape. He had to turn back when his partner was wounded and needed medical care. He never got

119

another chance to break out. His captors saw to that. He had to wait for the long-winded, heel-dragging, face-saving diplomats in Paris to negotiate his release. None of that taught him patience. It taught him that waiting was for people who had no other options. He'd once told Liz Gordon that waiting was the real definition of masochism.

The United Nations was on the water's edge, so Colonel August had the Strikers bring their wet gear. And since they were going to Manhattan, they were dressed like civilians. While the ten team members checked their suits and equipment, August used the ready room computer to visit the United Nations home page. He had never been to the building and wanted to get an idea of the layout. As he navigated to the web site, the on-line news of the day talked about the breaking story in New York, the hostage situation at the United Nations. August was surprised—not just that a nonpartisan facility would be attacked by terrorists but that U.S. troops would be on call to assist. He couldn't think of a single scenario in which American armed forces would be invited to help out in a situation like that.

As he studied the web site options, Sondra DeVonne and Chick Grey came up behind him. There were icons for Peace and Security, Humanitarian Affairs, Human Rights, and other feel-good topics. He went to the icon for Databases to try and find a map of the damn place. Not only had he never been there, he had no desire to go. For all their tub-thumping about peace and rights, they'd left him and his comrades from Air Force Intelligence in a Vietnamese prison for over two years.

There were other reference materials in the databases. Video records of Security Council and General Assembly meetings. Social indicators. International treaties. Land mines. Peacekeeping Training Course database. There was even a site for a glossary of United Nations Document Symbols, which was itself an acronym: UN-I-QUE for UN Info Quest.

"I hope Bob Herbert is having better luck," August said. "There isn't a single map of the compound."

"Maybe publishing it is considered a security risk," DeVonne suggested. Since joining Striker, the pretty African-American had been training for Geo-Intel—geographic intelligence—which, in addition to planning reconnaissance, was being used more and more to target smart missiles. "I mean," she said, "if you posted a detailed blueprint, you could plan and even run a missile attack without ever leaving your post."

"You know, that's the problem with security today," Grey said. "You can set up all the fancy antiterrorist protection you want, they can still get through the old-fashioned way. A jerk with a meal knife or a hat pin can still grab a flight attendant and take over an airplane."

"That doesn't mean you have to make it easy," DeVonne said.

"No," Grey agreed. "But don't kid yourself that any of it's really going to work. Terrorists will still get anywhere they want to go, just as a determined assassin can still get to a world leader."

The phone beeped, and the desk sergeant answered the call. It was for August. The colonel hurried over. If and when they left this room, the squad would instantly switch to the secure, mobile TAC-SAT phone. While they were here, they still used the secure base lines.

"Colonel August here," he said.

"Brett, it's Mike." In public, the officers observed

formal protocol. In private conversation, they were two men who had known each other since childhood. "You've got a go."

"A go is understood," August replied. He glanced over at his team. They were already beginning to gather their gear.

"I'll give you the mission profile when you arrive," Rodgers said.

"See you in thirty minutes," August replied, then hung up.

Less than three minutes later, the Striker squad was buckling themselves into the helicopter seats for the ride to Andrews. As the noisy chopper rose into the night and arced to the northeast, Colonel August was puzzled by something Rodgers had said. Typically, mission parameters were downloaded to the aircraft via secure ground-to-air modem. It saved time and allowed the process to continue even after the team was airborne.

Rodgers had said he was going to give them the mission parameters when they arrived. If that meant what he thought it meant, then this was going to be a more interesting and unusual evening than he had expected.

FIFTEEN

New York, New York
Saturday, 10:08 P.M.

When the violinists had first arrived in the Security Council chambers, they assembled behind the horseshoe-shaped table on the main floor. Their musical director, Ms. Dorn, had just arrived. The twenty-six-year-old had given a recital in Washington the night before and had flown in that day. While Ms. Dorn reviewed the score, Harleigh Hood stood by the curtains in front of one of the windows. She peeked outside at the darkening river and smiled at the jiggling lights reflected on the surface. The bright, colorful spots reminded her of musical notes, and she found herself wondering why sheet music was never printed in color—a different color for each octave.

Harleigh had just released the edge of the curtain when they heard pops in the hallway. Moments later, the double doors on the north side of the chamber slammed open, and the masked men ran in.

Neither the delegates nor their guests moved, and the young musicians remained where they were, in two tight rows. Only Ms. Dorn moved, protectively positioning herself between the children and the intruders. The masked men were too busy to notice her. They were running down the sides of the chamber, surrounding the delegates. None of the intruders said anything until one of the men grabbed a delegate and pulled him off to the side. The intruder spoke to the man quietly, as though he were afraid of being overheard. The delegate, who had been introduced to the violinists earlier in a receiving line—he was from Sweden, though she forgot his name—then told the group that no one would be harmed as long as they stayed quiet and did exactly as they were told. Harleigh didn't find him convincing. His collar was already sweaty, and the whole time his eyes were moving all over the place like he was looking for a place to run.

The intruder resumed talking to the delegate. They sat down at the horseshoe-shaped table. The delegate was handed paper and a pencil.

Two of the intruders checked the windows, opened the doors to see what was behind them, then took up other positions. When one of them had been standing beside her window, practically at her shoulder, Harleigh had had to fight the urge to say something. She'd wanted to ask this person what he was doing. Her father had always told her that a reasonable question, reasonably asked, rarely provoked an angry response.

But Harleigh could smell the tartness of the gunpowder—or whatever the smell was—wafting from the man's gun. And she thought she saw blood spots on his glove. Fear froze her throat and loosened her insides. Her legs really did go weak, though at the thighs, not the knees. She didn't say anything and then got angry at herself for having been afraid. Talking could have gotten her shot, but it also might have made the intruders sympathetic toward her. Or maybe they would have made her a spokesperson or a group leader or something that would have taken her mind off her fear. And what if they all got shot later? Not necessarily by these people but by whoever came to save them. Her dying thought would be that she should have said something before. As she watched him go, she almost said something again, but her mouth wouldn't let her.

Shortly thereafter one of the men—again speaking very quietly, with an accent that sounded Australian—began collecting people around the table. The children were first. He told them to leave their instruments where they were, on the floor, and come over.

Harleigh's violin case was already open, and she took the time to lay the instrument inside. It wasn't a small, belated act of defiance. She wasn't even testing the man to see what she could get away with. Her parents had given the violin to her, and she wasn't going to let anything happen to it. Fortunately, the man either didn't notice or decided to let it go.

As Harleigh sat at the circular table, she felt very exposed. She'd liked it better by the drapes, in the corner.

The fear, which had been liquid, began to solidify. Harleigh began trembling as she sat there and was almost glad when one of the girls beside her began to shake. Poor Laura Sabia. Laura was her best friend, but she was a skittish girl to begin with. She looked like she wanted to scream.

Harleigh touched her hand and caught her eye and smiled at her. *It's going to be okay,* her smile said.

The girl didn't respond to that. She did respond when the masked man began walking toward them. He didn't have to say a thing, didn't even have to walk all the way over. Just coming over scared her to silence.

Harleigh patted the girl's fingers and then withdrew

her hand. She folded her hands in front of her. Harleigh drew a deep breath through her nose and stopped herself from trembling. A girl across the table saw her and did likewise. After a moment, the girl smiled. Harleigh smiled back. She discovered that fear was like being cold. If you relaxed, it wasn't as bad.

The cavernous room became quiet. There was a feeling of tense resignation at the table, an awareness that the quiet was thin and could be broken at any moment. Inside the table, the diplomats seemed a little more restless than the musicians, probably because they were the most vulnerable. The intruders seemed very angry about somebody not being there, but Harleigh didn't know who. Perhaps the secretary-general, who had been late.

Ms. Dorn was sitting at the head of the table. She made eye contact with each of her violinists, making sure they were all right. Each girl responded in turn with a little nod. It was all bravery, Harleigh knew; no one was really okay. But in the absence of anything else, the sense of *we're all in this together* was something to hold onto.

Harleigh thought she heard footsteps outside the door. Security people were bound to show up. She looked around for places to hide if something did happen, if people began shooting. Behind the horseshoe table looked like the safest spot. She could run over, slide across, and be on the other side in a matter of moments. She lifted her knees very slowly against the bottom of this table, like she did to her desk at school when she was bored—make it seem to float. The table rose slightly, which meant it wasn't bolted to the floor. They could turn it over and duck behind it if they had to.

As Harleigh thought about defending themselves, she experienced a flash of terror. She wondered if this might have something to do with her father and Op-Center. He had never talked about work at home, 'not even when he and her mother had argued. Could it be that Op-Center had wronged these people in some way? She had learned in civics class that except for Israel, the United States was the largest target of terrorism in the world. The violinists were the only Americans here. Were they after *her*? What if they didn't know her father had resigned? What if they wanted to control her to control him?

The flesh of her neck and shoulders grew warm. Harleigh began to perspire along her sides. The gown that had felt so new, so elegant, clung to her like a bathing suit.

This isn't happening, she thought. It was the kind of thing you saw on the news happening to other people. There were supposed to be safeguards here, weren't there? Metal detectors, guards at the doors, security cameras.

Suddenly, the man who'd been talking to the delegate from Sweden called the Australian man over. After a short discussion, the Australian man grabbed the delegate by the collar, hoisted him up and, at gunpoint, walked him up the stairs toward the door.

Harleigh wished she had her violin to hug close. She wished she could be held by her mother. Her mom was probably frantic—unless she was trying to be Ms. Calm to other frantic mothers. She probably was. That had to be where Harleigh got it from. Then she thought of her father. When Harleigh's mother had taken her and Alexander to visit their grandparents and figure out their future, her father decided to give up his career rather

127

than lose them. She wondered if he'd be able to look at this as another crisis and think calmly, even though his daughter was involved.

The Australian man returned. After exchanging a few rough words with the delegate, he took the paper from him and shoved the man along the stairs. Harleigh assumed that their captors had just given someone a list of demands. She no longer thought that she might be the target. She felt her neck cool. They were *going* to get through this.

The Swedish delegate was seated with the other delegates, back on the floor with his hands on his head. Harleigh assumed it was time to wait. That would be all right. Her father had once said that as long as people were talking, they weren't shooting. She hoped so.

She decided not to think about it. Instead, quietly, very quietly, she did what she came here for.

She hummed "A Song of Peace."

SIXTEEN

Andrews Air Force Base, Maryland
Saturday, 10:09 P.M.

After hanging up with Colonel August, Mike Rodgers looked at the clock on his computer screen. The LongRanger would be at Andrews in about twenty-five minutes. The C-130 would be ready to go by then.

Bob Herbert looked over at the general. The intelligence chief scowled. "Mike? Are you listening?"

"Yes," Rodgers said. "You've got a team working on Mala Chatterjee's past to see who might want to humiliate the new secretary-general. Possibly fellow Hindus who oppose her public stand on behalf of women's rights. You're also checking the whereabouts of the people Paul helped to stop in Russia and Spain, in case this is about him."

"Right," Herbert said.

Rodgers nodded and rose slowly; the damn bandages were constricting. "Bob, I'm going to need you to run the show here for a while."

Herbert seemed surprised. "Why? Aren't you feeling okay?"

"I'm feeling fine," Rodgers said. "I'll be going to New York with Striker. I'm also going to need a base of operations once we get there. Something near the United Nations that could also serve as a staging area.

The CIA must have a shell in that neighborhood."

"There's one right across the street, I believe," Herbert said. "Eastern tower of the twin skyscrapers, UN Plaza. The Doyle Shipping Agency, I think it's called. They keep an eye on the comings and goings of spooks pretending to be diplomats, probably gather ELINT as well."

"Can you get us in?"

"Probably." Herbert's mouth twisted unhappily. He glanced across the table at Lowell Coffey.

Rodgers caught the look. "What's wrong?" he asked.

"Mike," Herbert said, "we're on pretty shaky ground as far as Striker is concerned."

"Shaky in what way?" Rodgers asked.

Herbert raised and lowered a shoulder. "In a lot of ways—"

"Spell them out. Morally? Legally? Logistically?"

"All of the above," Herbert said.

"Maybe I'm being a little naive here," Rodgers said, "but what I see is a strike force with extensive antiterrorist training moving into position to deal with terrorists. Where's the moral, legal, or logistical shakiness?"

Attorney Coffey spoke up. "For one thing, Mike, we haven't been asked to help the United Nations with this situation. That in itself weighs pretty heavily against you."

"Granted," Rodgers said. "Hopefully, I can arrange that when I get there, especially if the terrorists start sending bodies out. Darrell McCaskey's communicating with Chatterjee's security staff through Interpol—"

"At a very low level," Herbert reminded him. "The UN security commander isn't going to put a lot of stock in what an aide tells him secondhand through an Interpol guy in Madrid.''

''We don't know that,'' Rodgers said. ''Hell, we don't know anything about the commander, do we?''

''My staff is reviewing his file,'' Herbert said. ''He's not someone we've had any dealings with.''

''Regardless,'' Rodgers said. ''He's in a situation where he's probably going to have to look outside for help. For real, solid, *immediate* help, wherever it's coming from.''

''But Mike, that's not the only problem,'' Coffey said.

Rodgers looked down at the computer clock. The chopper would be here in less than twenty minutes. He didn't have time for this.

''Countries that have no interest in the outcome of this situation will absolutely *not* want a covert team of elite, United States forces moving through the Secretariat building.''

''Since when are we worried about hurting the feelings of Iraqis and the French?'' Rodgers asked.

''It isn't a matter of feelings,'' Coffey pointed out. ''It's a question of international law.''

''Christ, Lowell—the terrorists broke that law!'' Rodgers said.

''That doesn't mean we can, too,'' Coffey said. ''Even if we're willing to break international law, every Striker action to date has been executed according to Op-Center's charter—U.S. law. Specifically, we've gotten the permission of the Congressional Intelligence Oversight Committee—''

''I'm not worried about a goddamn court-martial, Lowell,'' Rodgers interrupted sharply.

"This isn't about personal culpability," Coffey said. "It's about Op-Center's survival."

"I agree," Rodgers said. "Its about our survival as an effective, counterterrorist force—"

"No," Coffey said, "as a division of the United States government. We were chartered to act, and I quote, 'when the threat to federal institutions or any constituents thereof, or to American lives in the service of those institutions, is clear-cut and immediate.' I don't see that here. What I *do* see is that if you go in, whether you succeed or fail is irrelevant—"

"Not to Paul and the other parents."

"This isn't about them!" Coffey snapped. "It's about the larger picture. The American public will applaud. Hell, *I'll* applaud. But France or Iraq or *some* member nation will pressure the administration to take us to task for overstepping our mandate."

"Especially if the terrorists turn out to be foreigners and any of them are killed," Herbert said. "American soldiers effectively executing foreign nationals on international territory with every media outlet in the world covering the event will destroy us."

"And they'll do it with American law, not international law," Coffey added. "Congress will have no choice but to pull everyone in this room in front of the CIOC. Never mind our careers. If they vote to dissolve Op-Center or even just Striker, how many future lives will be lost? How many battles won't we be able to fight that have a direct influence on the security of the United States?"

"I can't believe this," Rodgers said. "We're talking about children being held hostage!"

"Unfortunately," Herbert said, "as angry as it makes

us all, the threat to the delegates and to Paul's daughter doesn't fall under those parameters. Saving her is a luxury we may not be able to afford.''

"A *luxury?*" Rodgers said. "Jesus, Bob, you're talking like a goddamned Camp Fire girl!''

Herbert glared at Rodgers. "That was my late wife. *She* was the Camp Fire girl.''

Rodgers looked at Herbert and then looked down. The ventilators in the ceiling sounded very loud.

"Since the subject has been raised,'' Herbert continued, "my wife was also a victim of terrorists. I know what you're feeling, Mike. The frustration. I know what Paul and Sharon are feeling. And I also know that Lowell is right. The place for Op-Center in this fight is on the sidelines.''

"Doing nothing.''

"Surveillance, tactical assistance, moral support—if we can contribute those, they aren't nothing,'' Herbert said.

" 'They also serve who only stand and wait,' '' Rodgers said solemnly.

"Sometimes, yes.'' Herbert patted the arms of his wheelchair. "Otherwise, you could end up sitting and waiting. Or worse.''

Rodgers glanced at his watch. Lowell Coffey had made valid legal points. And Rodgers's stumble about Yvonne Herbert had given her husband the right to sermonize. But that didn't make either man right.

"I've got about fifteen minutes to meet the plane,'' Rodgers said quietly. "Bob, I've already put you in charge. If you want to stop me, you can.'' He looked at Liz Gordon. "Liz, you can have me declared mentally unfit, suffering from post-traumatic stress disorder,

133

whatever the hell you want. If you do, I won't fight either of you. But barring that, I won't stand and wait. I *can't*. Not while a band of murderers is holding kids hostage."

Herbert shook his head slowly. "This one's not that black and white, Mike."

"That's no longer the issue," Rodgers said to him. "Are you going to stop me?"

Herbert stopped shaking his head. "No," he said. "I'm not."

"May I ask why?" Coffey asked indignantly.

Herbert sighed. "Yeah. In the CIA, we used to call it respect."

Coffey made a face.

"If a superior wanted to bend the rules, you bent them," Herbert went on. "All you could do was try not to bend 'em so far that they came around and bit you in the ass."

Coffey sat back. "I expect that from the Cosa Nostra, not the lawful government of the United States," he said unhappily.

"If we were all so damn virtuous, lawful government wouldn't be necessary," Herbert said.

Rodgers looked at Liz. She was not happy either.

"Well?" Rodgers said.

"Well what?" Liz said. "I'm not a brick in Bob's wall of silence, but I'm not going to stop you. Right now, you're being headstrong, impatient, and you're probably acting out, looking to hit someone hard for what your captors did in the Bekaa Valley. But unfit? From a psychological standpoint, not a legal one, I can't say you're unfit."

Rodgers looked back at Herbert. "Bob, will you try to get me into the CIA shell?"

Herbert nodded.

Rodgers looked at Coffey. "Lowell, will you go to the CIOC? See if they'll call an emergency meeting?"

Coffey's thin mouth was tight, and his polished fingernails were tapping the table. But above all, the attorney was a professional. He hooked back his sleeve and looked at his watch.

"I'll call Senator Warren on his mobile phone," Coffey said. "He's our most sympathetic ear over there. But those people are tough enough to reach on a weekday. On a weekend, at night—"

"I understand," Rodgers said. "Thanks. You, too, Bob."

"Sure thing," Herbert replied.

Coffey was already looking up the phone number on his electronic pocket directory as Rodgers looked over at Matt Stoll and Ann Farris. The technical genius was staring intently at his folded hands, and the press liaison was quiet, her expression noncommittal. He thought he might get her approval since he was trying to help Paul Hood, but he wasn't going to ask. He turned toward the door.

"Mike?" Herbert said.

Rodgers looked back at him. "Yes?"

"Whatever you need, you know you've got our support back here," Herbert said.

"I know."

"Just try not to destroy the Secretariat Building, okay?" Herbert said. "And one more thing."

"What's that?" Rodgers asked.

"I don't want to find myself running this goddamned

135

place," Herbert said with the hint of a smile. "So make sure you get your headstrong, impatient, acting-out self back here."

"I'll try," Rodgers said, smiling slightly himself as he opened the door.

It wasn't exactly the endorsement Rodgers had hoped for but, as he hurried through the cubicles toward the elevator, at least he didn't feel like Gary Cooper in *High Noon*—alone. And right now, that was something.

SEVENTEEN

New York, New York
Saturday, 10:11 P.M.

The short-lived but legendary Office of Strategic Services was formed in June of 1942. Under the leadership of World War I hero William Joseph "Wild Bill" Donovan, the OSS was responsible for collecting military intelligence. After the war, in 1946, President Truman established the Central Intelligence Group, which was chartered to gather foreign intelligence pertaining to national security. A year later, the National Security Act renamed the CIG the Central Intelligence Agency. The act also broadened the scope of the CIA charter to allow it to conduct counterintelligence activities.

Thirty-two-year-old Annabelle "Ani" Hampton had always enjoyed being a spy. There were so many mental and emotional levels to it, so many sensations. There was danger and there was reward proportionate to the danger. There was a sense of being invisible or, if you were caught, of being more naked than naked. There was a feeling of having power over others, of risking punishment and death. There was also a great deal of planning involved, of positioning yourself just so, of patience, of catching someone in the right frame of mind, of seducing emotionally and sometimes physically.

It was, in fact, a lot like sex only better, she thought. *In spying, if you grew tired of someone you could have them killed.* Not that she ever had. Not yet, anyway.

Ani had enjoyed being a spy because she'd always been a loner. Other children had no curiosity. She did. As a child, she liked to find out where squirrels made their homes or watch birds as they laid their eggs or, depending on her mood, help wild rabbits escape from red foxes or help red foxes snare the hares. She liked to eavesdrop on her father's pinochle games or on her grandmother's teas or on her older brother's dates. She even made a journal of the news she picked up while spying on her family. Which neighbor was "a prick." Which aunt was "a bitch on wheels." Which mother-in-law "should learn to keep her mouth shut." Ani's mother once found the journal and took it away, but that was all right. Ani had been smart enough to keep a duplicate book.

Ani's parents, Al and Ginny, had owned a women's clothing store in Roanoke, Virginia. Ani used to work at Hampton's Fashions after school and on weekends. Whenever possible, she would study everything about the people who came in to browse. She attempted to hear what they were saying, tried to guess what they were going to look at based on how they were dressed or how well they spoke. And then she moved in to make the sale. If she'd been careful and smart, she got it. Usually, she was.

The spying ended when her parents's store went bankrupt, driven out of business by larger discount chains. Her parents were forced to go to work for one of those chains. But Ani's fascination with understanding and then carefully manipulating people did not die. She won a full scholarship to Georgetown University in Washington. She majored in political science and minored in Asian affairs since, at the time, it looked like Japan and the Pacific Rim were going to be *the* hot spots of the twenty-first century. Though her parents' own hopes had died, Ani never saw them prouder than when she graduated from college summa cum laude. That was when she set herself a goal to make them prouder still. Ani resolved that she would not only become a CIA agent, but before she was forty years old, she would be running the agency.

Upon graduating, the slender, five-foot-ten-inch-tall blonde applied to the CIA. She was hired—partly because of her exemplary academic record and partly, she later learned, because equal opportunity guidelines found the notoriously chauvinistic agency short on women. The reasons didn't matter then. Ani was in. Officially, she served as a visa consultant in a succession of U.S. embassies in Asia. Unofficially, she used her downtime to develop contacts in the government and military. Dissatisfied officials and officers. Men and women who were hurt by the Asian financial collapse of the mid-1990s. People who might be persuaded to provide information for money.

Ani was singularly effective as a CIA recruiter. Ironically, she found that her greatest asset was not her knowledge of Asian culture or government. It wasn't even the fact that she'd seen her parents lose their slice of the American Dream and knew how to talk to people who felt disconnected. Her greatest asset was her ability to remain emotionally uninvolved with her recruits. There had been times when it was necessary to sacrifice people for information, and she had not hesitated to do so. She understood from school, from life, from reading history, that people were the coin of governments and armies and that you couldn't be afraid to spend them. In a way, it was no different from telling women they'd looked good in coats or slacks or blouses when she knew they didn't. The store needed their money, and she was determined to get it.

Unfortunately, Ani found that talent and drive weren't enough. When she accomplished what she'd been sent abroad to do, the young woman wasn't given a promotion or higher security clearance. Now the antifemale bias mattered: The good jobs went to her male colleagues. Ani was sent to Seoul to collect data submitted by the contacts she'd established. Most of it was transmitted electronically, and she was not even involved in interpreting what came in. That was done by ELINT teams back at Company headquarters. After six months of sitting at a computer, working as an intel shuffler, she asked to be transferred to Washington. Instead, she was transferred to New York. As an intel shuffler.

Because of her overseas experience, Ani had been sent to work at the Doyle Shipping Agency. The CIA front operated from the shell office on the fourth floor of 866 United Nations Plaza. Their mission was to spy on key United Nations officials. The DSA consisted of a small reception area with a secretary—who was off today, since it was Saturday—an office for field office director David Battat, and another office for Ani. There was also a small office for the two floaters who were shared by this office and another in the financial district. The floaters trailed diplomats who were suspected of trying to meet with spies or prospective spies in this country. The office also stocked arms, from guns to C-4, which could

140

be used by the floaters or carried to agents abroad in diplomatic pouches. Ani's small, East River–view office was really the heart of the operation. It was filled with fake DSA files, books of shipping schedules and tax regulations, along with a computer linked to high-tech equipment locked in a broom closet at the end of the small corridor.

Ani's job was to monitor the activities of key United Nations personnel. She did this by using bugs developed by the CIA's research and sciences group and being field-tested in the UN for the first time—"to work the bugs out," as Battat had put it. The bugs were literally mechanical bugs the size of a large beetle. Made of titanium and extremely lightweight piezoelectric ceramics—materials that caused very little drain on the batteries, allowing them to run for years without being recalled—the bugs are electronically attuned to the voice of a subject. After being set loose inside a building, they required no further maintenance. The fleet, six-legged devices could reach any point in the building within twenty minutes and followed their individual targets by moving behind walls and through air ducts; hooklike feet allowed them to travel vertically along most surfaces. The voices were transmitted from the bugs to the receiver attachment to Ani's computer, which was nicknamed "the hive." Ani typically listened to the broadcast with headphones to keep out extraneous office and street noises.

Seven mobile bugs inside the United Nations complex enabled the CIA to eavesdrop on influential ambassadors as well as on the secretary-general. Because all the bugs operated on the same very narrow audio frequency, Ani could only access one at a time. She was able to shuttle between them using the computer. The bugs also contained sound generators that emitted an ultrasonic *ping* once every few seconds. The pulse was designed to frighten potential predators. At two million dollars apiece, the CIA did not want the bugs to be eaten by hungry bats or other insect eaters.

Though Ani deeply resented the transfer and the grunt work she was doing, there were three bright spots. First, though the work tended to be uneventful, she was spying as clandestinely as possible. The voyeur in her enjoyed that. Second, her superior spent most of his time in Washington or at the CIA office at the American embassy in Moscow—which was where he was now—so she effectively ran this small office. And finally, being held back by the "Chauvinists Institute of America" had reminded her that whether you're selling women's clothes or selling information, you have to find ways of making yourself happy. Since coming to New York, she had developed an appreciation for art and music, for fine restaurants and elegant clothes, for good living and pampering herself. For the first time in her life, she had been setting goals that had nothing to do with her career or making someone proud. It felt good.

Very good.

Ani listened closely to the meeting. Disappointments aside, this situation required very close monitoring. And though the bugged conversation was being recorded, her superior would want a concise but comprehensive summary of what was being said.

It was interesting to know people only from their voices. Ani had come to listen for inflection, pauses, speed much more than she did in face-to-face conversation. Finding out about the different people had been fun, especially Mala Chatterjee, who was one of only two women on Ani's roster. More than half of Ani's time was spent with the secretary-general. The New Delhi native was the forty-three-year-old daughter of Sujit Chatterjee, one of the most successful motion picture producers in India. An attorney who had achieved dazzling victories in the cause of human rights, Mala Chatterjee had worked as a consultant with the Centre for International Peacebuilding in London before accepting a post as deputy special representative of the secretary-general on human rights in Geneva. She moved to New York in 1997 to serve as undersecretary-general for Humanitarian Affairs. Her appointment as secretary-general was motivated as much by politics and a TV-friendly appearance as by her credentials. It came at a time when nuclear tensions between India and Pakistan were rising. The Indians were so proud of the appointment that even when the freshly appointed Ms. Chatterjee went to Islamabad and made overtures to Pakistan regarding disarmament, Indians supported her. This, despite a front-page editorial in Pakistan's English-language newspaper, *Dawn*, which chided New Delhi for "blinking cravenly in the face of annihilation."

Secretary-General Chatterjee's brief United Nations career had been one of confronting problems personally, head-on, relying on her intelligence and charismatic personality to defuse situations. That was what made this moment so exciting. Ani was not unaware of the lives at stake or unmoved by their plight. But over the past few months, she'd gotten to feel as though Chatterjee was a close friend and respected colleague. Ani was extremely curious to see how the secretary-general was going to handle this. As soon as the CIA had been

143

alerted to the hostage situation, Ani ascertained that none of the delegates with bugs had been present in the Security Council chambers.

Chatterjee was meeting with Deputy Secretary-General Takahara of Japan, two undersecretary-generals, and her security chief in the large conference room off her private office. The deputy secretary-general of administration and head of personnel was also present. He and his staff were on the phones, updating governments whose delegates were among the hostages. Chatterjee's aide, Enzo Donati, was there as well.

There had been very little talk about actually paying the ransom. Even if the sum could be collected, which was doubtful, the secretary-general would be powerless to deliver it. In 1973, the United Nations had established a policy for dealing with ransom demands if UN personnel were kidnapped. The Security Council had proposed, and the General Assembly had agreed by the requisite two-thirds vote, that in the event of an abduction, the affected nation or nations would be responsible for pursuing their own national policy. The United Nations would become involved only as negotiators.

So far, only one of the nations involved, France, had agreed to contribute to the ransom demand. The other countries either couldn't commit without formal authorization or had a policy of not negotiating with terrorists. The United States, whose delegate, Flora Meriwether, was among the hostages, refused to pay the ransom but agreed to participate if a dialogue were opened with the terrorists. Chatterjee and her staff agreed to check in again with the affected nations when the deadline had passed.

The immediate problem that needed a quick resolution

was who would be responsible for making decisions in the crisis. If only tourists were being held, then the Military Staff Committee of Colonel Rick Mott would have had sole jurisdiction. But that wasn't the case. According to the charter, decisions affecting the Security Council could only be made by the Security Council or the General Assembly. Since Security Council President Stanislaw Zintel of Poland was among the hostages, and since the General Assembly could not be convened, Chatterjee decided that as the leader of the General Assembly, the secretary-general should decide what moves and initiatives should be taken.

Ani suspected that was the first time in the history of the United Nations that an action had not been decided by vote. And it had taken a woman to do it, of course.

That decided, Mott advised the officials that most of the UN police had been pulled from the perimeter and gathered around the Security Council chamber. He briefed them about the possibility of staging an assault by UN forces or with the NYPD's Emergency Service Unit, which had volunteered personnel.

"We can't work out any kind of military response plan until we have a better idea about what's going on in there," Mott said. "I've got two officers listening in through the double doors in the Trusteeship Council chambers. Unfortunately, the terrorists set up motion detectors in the corridors that access the media, so we can't go up there. They've also disabled the security cameras in the council chambers. Efforts are being made to look into the chambers using wire-thin fiber-optic lenses. We're going to use manual drills to punch two small holes through the floor in closets beneath the room. Unfortunately, we won't have visuals until well past the ninety-minute deadline. We've used an uplink to send copies of the surveillance camera videos of the killers to Interpol offices in London, Paris, Madrid, and Bonn, as well as to law-enforcement agencies in Japan, Moscow, and Mexico City. We're hoping that something about the attack may be similar to what agents there may have seen before.''

"The question is, will they really execute one of the hostages?'' asked Secretary-General Chatterjee.

"I believe they will,'' Mott said.

"Based on what intelligence?'' someone asked. Ani didn't recognize his voice or his accent.

"My own *intelligence*,'' Mott replied. Based on the way he said "intelligence,'' Ani could picture him pointing to his own head in frustration. "The terrorists have nothing to lose by killing again.''

"Then what are our options prior to the deadline?'' the secretary-general asked.

"Militarily?'' Mott asked. "My people are willing to go in without visuals, if they have to.''

"Is your team ready for an operation like that?'' the secretary-general asked.

Ani could have answered that question. The Military Staff strike force was not ready for action. They'd never been field-tested and they were understaffed. If one or two key people went down, there were no reserves. The problem was that along with the rest of the UN secretariat staff, the MS unit had been cut by 25 percent over the past few years. Moreover, the ablest people went into the private sector, such as corporate security and law enforcement, where pay and the opportunities for promotion were better.

"We're prepared to go in and end the standoff,'' Mott

said. "But I have to be honest, ma'am. If we enter the chambers with the intention of removing the terrorists, there is a very strong likelihood of losses not just of my team members, but among panicked delegates and children."

"We can't risk that," Secretary-General Chatterjee said.

"Our chances would certainly be better if we waited for reconnaissance," Mott admitted.

"What about using tear gas against the terrorists?" asked Deputy Secretary-General Takahara.

"The Security Council is a very large room," Mott said. "Because of that, it would take at least seventy seconds to deliver gas through the ventilation system, slightly less time by opening the doors and hurling in grenades. Either way, that would give the terrorists time to put on gas masks, if they have them, to shoot out the two windows to dilute the effectiveness of the gas, to kill the hostages when they realize what's happening, or to move to another locale with the hostages as shields. If they possess poison gas as they've said, my guess is that they probably do have masks."

"They're going to kill all the hostages anyway," said one of the undersecretaries-general. Ani believed that it might be Fernando Campos of Portugal, one of the few militants who had the secretary-general's ear. "At least if we go in now, we may be able to save some of them."

There was some loud murmuring around the table. Secretary-General Chatterjee quieted it and returned the floor to Mott.

"My recommendation, again, is that we wait until we have some images from the chamber," Mott concluded.

147

"Just so we know where the enemy and the hostages are."

"The additional time as well as your pictures will be bought with the lives of delegates," said the man Ani thought was Undersecretary-General Campos. "I say we go in and end this matter."

Chatterjee tabled the military side of the discussion and asked if Mott had any other ideas. The colonel said that thought had also been given to shutting off the air and electricity in the Security Council chambers or of turning up the air-conditioning to make the terrorists uncomfortable. But he and the Military Staff Committee had decided that those actions would be more provocative than useful. He said that as yet they hadn't come up with anything else.

There was a short silence. Ani noted that the final half-hour mark had come and gone. She had a strong feeling what Chatterjee was going to do: just what she always did.

"Although I'm sympathetic to what Colonel Mott and Undersecretary-General Campos have suggested, we cannot give the terrorists what they want," Chatterjee said at last, her husky voice lower than usual. "But a serious gesture must be made to acknowledge their status."

"Their status?" Colonel Mott asked.

"Yes," Chatterjee said.

"Such as *what*, ma'am?" Mott demanded. "They're ruthless killers—"

"Colonel, this is not the time to express our indignation," Chatterjee said. "Since we cannot give the terrorists what they want, we must offer them what we have."

"Which is?" Mott asked.

"Our humility."

"Good Christ," Mott muttered.

"This is not your former SEALs command," Chatterjee said sternly. "We shall 'seek a solution by negotiation, enquiry, mediation, conciliation, arbitration, judicial settlement—' "

"I know the charter, ma'am," Mott said. "But it wasn't written for this kind of situation."

"Then we will adapt it," she said. "The sentiment is correct. We must acknowledge that these people have the power to kill or release our delegates and children. Perhaps bowing to them will gain us time and trust."

"It certainly won't gain us their respect," Mott said.

"I disagree, Colonel Mott," Takahara said. "Submission has been known to placate terrorists. But I am curious, Madam Secretary-General. How do you intend to bow?"

Takahara always surprised Ani. Throughout history, Japanese leaders had never been comfortable with conciliation—unless they were pretending to want peace while preparing for war. Takahara was not like that. He was a genuinely pacifistic man.

"I'll go to the terrorists," Chatterjee said. "I'll express our interest in helping them and request time to arrange an opportunity for them to address their requests directly to the nations involved."

"You're inviting a *siege,*" Mott declared.

"I prefer that to a bloodbath," said Chatterjee. "Besides, we must secure one thing at a time. If we can achieve a postponement of the deadline, perhaps we will be able to find the means to defuse the situation."

"May I remind you," said Takahara, "the killers indicated that no communication would be acknowledged other than word that the money and transportation were theirs."

"It doesn't matter if they acknowledge," Chatterjee said. "Only that they listen."

"Oh, they'll acknowledge, all right," Mott said. "With gunfire. These monsters *shot* their way into the Security Council. They've got nothing to lose by shooting a few people more."

"Gentlemen," said Chatterjee, "we can't pay the ransom, and I will not permit an attack on the council chamber." It was obvious to Ani that the secretary-general was growing frustrated. "We are supposed to be the finest diplomats in the world and, at present, we *have* no options other than diplomacy. Colonel Mott, will you accompany me to the Security Council?"

"Of course," the officer said.

He sounded relieved. Chatterjee was smart going out with a soldier at her side. *Speak softly, and carry a big stick.*

Ani heard coughs and the sound of chairs being moved. She glanced at her computer clock. The secretary-general had a little over seven minutes until the deadline. That was just enough time to get to the Security Council chamber. The bug would arrive shortly thereafter. Ani removed her headphones and turned to the phone to call David Battat. The line was secure, run through an advanced TAC-SAT 5 unit inside the desk.

The phone beeped as she reached for it. She picked up the receiver. It was Battat.

"You're there," Battat said.

"I'm here," Ani said. "Canceled my hot date and came over as soon as this broke."

"Good girl," the forty-two-year-old Atlanta native said.

Ani's fingers went white around the phone. Battat wasn't as bad as some of the others, and she didn't think he meant to be demeaning. It was just something he'd gotten used to in the spy-club-for-men.

"The attack just broke on the news here," Battat said. *"God,* I wish I were there. What's happening?"

The young woman told her superior what Secretary-General Chatterjee was planning. After listening to the plan, Battat sighed.

"The terrorists are gonna waste the Swede," he said.

"Maybe not," Ani replied. "Chatterjee is pretty good at this."

"Diplomacy was invented to powder tyrants' behinds, and I've never seen it work for very long," Battat said. "Which is one of the reasons I'm calling. A former Company man named Bob Herbert phoned about twenty minutes ago. He's with the National Crisis Management Center and needs a place for his SWAT team to crash. If they get a go-ahead from above, they may make a move to get the kids out. The boys up here have no problem with them using DSA as long as they keep our noses out of it. You should expect a General Mike Rodgers, Colonel Brett August, and party in about ninety minutes."

"Yes sir," she said.

Ani hung up and waited before returning to her headphones. The news about the NCMC team was a surprise, and it took her a moment to process it. She had been monitoring Secretary-General Chatterjee's conversations for three hours. No mention had been made of military action by the United States. She couldn't believe that the

151

United States would ever become involved militarily in an action at the United Nations compound.

But if it were true, at least she would be here to watch it unfold. Maybe she could have a hand in organizing the attack plan.

Under ordinary circumstances, it was energizing to be at the center of what the CIA euphemistically called "an event," especially when there was a "counterevent" in the offing. But these were not ordinary circumstances.

Ani looked at the computer monitor. There was a detailed blueprint of the United Nations along with icons representing the presence of all the bugs. She watched the progress of the bug following Chatterjee. It would catch up to her in less than a minute.

She slipped the headphones back on. These were not ordinary circumstances because there was a group of people inside the United Nations—a group depending on her to monitor everything the secretary-general said and planned. A group that had nothing to do with the CIA. The group was led by a man she had met while she was looking for new recruits in Cambodia. A man who had been a CIA operative in Bulgaria and who, like her, had become disenchanted with the way the Company treated him. A man who had spent several years making international contacts of his own, though not to help him gather intelligence. A man who didn't care about a person's sex or nationality, only about his or her ability.

That was why Ani had come to the office at seven o'clock. She had not come after the attack began, as she'd told Battat. She'd come here because she wanted to be in place before the attack. She would make sure that if Georgiev contacted her on his secure phone, she would be able to give him any intel he needed. She was also monitoring the account in Zurich. As soon as the money was there, she'd disburse it to a dozen other accounts internationally, then erase the trail. Investigators would never find it.

Georgiev's success would be her success. And her success would be her parents' success. With her share of the two hundred and fifty million dollars, her parents would finally be able to realize the American Dream.

The irony was, Battat had actually been wrong on two counts. Ani Hampton was not a girl. But even if she were, she would not be what he had called her: a "good girl."

She was an exceptional one.

EIGHTEEN

New York, New York
Saturday, 10:29 P.M.

Mala Chatterjee stood just over five feet, two inches. She barely reached the chin of the silver-haired officer who walked slightly behind her. But the secretary-general's size was not a true measure of her stature. Her dark eyes were large and luminous, and her skin was swarthy and smooth. Her fine black hair was naturally streaked with white and reached to the middle of the shoulder of her sharply tailored black business suit. The only jewelry she wore was a watch and a pair of small pearl earrings.

There had been some very vocal dissidents back home when she was named to this post and opted not to wear a traditional sari. Even her father was upset. But as Chatterjee had just said in an interview with *Newsweek*, she was here as a representative of all people and of all faiths, not just her native land and her fellow Hindus. Fortunately, the disarmament pact with Pakistan put the sari issue to rest. It also allayed the very vocal complaints some member nations had had, that the world body had opted to appoint a mediagenic secretary-general rather than an internationally renowned diplomat.

Chatterjee hadn't doubted her ability to handle this

155

job. She had never encountered any problem that couldn't be resolved by making the first conciliatory move. So many conflicts were caused by the need to save face; remove that element, and the disputes often solved themselves.

Mala Chatterjee held tight to that belief as she and Colonel Mott rode the elevator down to the second floor. Selected reporters had been allowed into this section of the building, and she answered a few questions as she walked toward the Security Council chamber.

"We hope the matter can be resolved peaceably . . . our priority is the security and preservation of human life . . . we pray for the families of the hostages and victims to be strong. . . ."

Secretaries-general had said those exact words or words like those so many times, in so many places around the world, they had almost become a mantra. Yet they were very different here. This wasn't a situation where people had been fighting and hating and dying for years. The war was new, and the enemy was very determined. The words came from her soul, not from memory. Nor were they the only words that had come to mind. After leaving the reporters, she and the colonel walked past the sprawling *Golden Rule*, a large mosaic based on the painting by Norman Rockwell. It was a gift of the United States on the fortieth anniversary of the United Nations.

"As ye would that men should do to you, do ye also to them likewise." Chatterjee prayed that that would be possible here.

Representatives of Security Council nations were gathered to the north of the chambers of the Economic and Social Council. Between them and the adjoining

Trusteeship Council chamber were twenty-seven guards, the entire force that Colonel Mott had under his command. There was also a team of emergency medical technicians from the NYU Medical Center, which was located ten blocks south of the United Nations. The technicians were all volunteers.

Secretary-General Chatterjee and Colonel Mott neared the Security Council chamber double doors. They stepped a few yards away. The colonel removed the radio from the loop in his belt. It was preset to the correct frequency. He switched the unit on and handed it to the secretary-general. Chatterjee's hand was cold as she took it. She looked at her watch. It was ten-thirty.

She'd gone over the words in her head as she walked here, made them as concise as she could. *This is Secretary-General Chatterjee. Would it be all right if I came in?*

If the terrorists admitted her, if the deadline passed without a death, then there would be room for talk. For negotiation. Perhaps she could convince them to keep her there in exchange for the children. Chatterjee wasn't even thinking beyond that, to her own fate. For a negotiator, the goal was everything, the means secondary. Truth, deceit, risk, compassion, coldheartedness, resolve, seductiveness; everything was coin of the realm.

Chatterjee's slender fingers held the radio tightly as she raised the mouthpiece toward her lips. She had to make sure she sounded strong but nonjudgmental. She swallowed to make sure the words didn't catch. Her voice had to be clear. She moistened her lips.

"This is Secretary-General Mala Chatterjee," she said slowly. She'd decided to add her first name to deformalize the introduction. "Would it be all right if I came in?"

There was nothing but silence on the radio. The terrorists had said they'd be listening to this channel; they had to have heard. Chatterjee could swear she heard Colonel Mott's heart throbbing in his chest. She could certainly hear her own, like sandpaper up around her ears.

A moment later, there was a loud crack from behind the double doors of the Security Council chamber. It was followed by screams from deep within the chamber. An instant after that, the nearest of the two doors opened outward. The Swede fell out, except for the back of his head.

That was on the wall inside the chamber.

NINETEEN

New York, New York
Saturday, 10:30 P.M.

Paul Hood had composed himself and returned to the cafeteria. He reached it just as representatives from Department of State security police arrived. Since the parents were all U.S. citizens, the American ambassador had requested that they be moved at once to DOS offices on the other side of First Avenue. The reason given was security, but Hood suspected that sovereignty was the real issue. The United States did not want American citizens interrogated by foreign nationals about a terrorist attack on international soil. It would set a dangerous precedent to allow any government or representatives thereof to hold Americans who were not charged with breaking foreign or international law.

None of the parents liked the idea of moving from the building where their children were being held. But they went, accompanied by Deputy Chief of Security Bill Mohalley, DOS. Hood made Mohalley out to be about fifty. From the way he stood, with his big shoulders back, his manner clipped and commanding, he had probably come to DOS via the military. The dark-haired Mohalley reiterated that their own government could keep them better protected and better informed. Both statements were true, though Hood wondered how much the government would actually tell them. Armed terrorists had gotten through American security systems to reach the UN. If anything happened to the children, there would be unprecedented lawsuits.

As they were leaving the cafeteria and starting up the central staircase, the gunshot from the Security Council chamber echoed through the building.

Everything stopped. Then there were a few distant shouts among the otherwise awful silence.

Mohalley asked everyone to continue quickly up the stairs. It took a long second before anyone moved. Some of the parents insisted that they go back to the correspondents' room to be close to their children. Mohalley told them that the area had been closed off by United Nations security personnel and it wouldn't be possible to get in. Mohalley urged them to go ahead so he could get them to safety and find out what had happened. They started moving, though several of the mothers and a few of the fathers began to weep.

Hood put his arm around Sharon. Even though his own legs were weak, he helped her up the stairs. There had only been one shot, so he assumed a hostage had been killed. Hood had always felt that was the worst way to die, robbed of everything to help make someone else's point. A life used as a bloody, impersonal exclamation point, one's loves and dreams ended as though they didn't matter. There was nothing colder to contemplate than that.

When they reached the lobby, Mohalley received a call on his radio. As he stepped aside to take it, the parents filed into the spotlit park situated between the General Assembly Building and 866 United Nations Plaza. They were met there by two of Mohalley's aides.

The call was brief. When it was finished, Mohalley rejoined the group at the head. As they filed past, he asked Hood if he could talk to him for a moment.

"Of course," Hood said. He felt his mouth grow very dry. "Was that a hostage?" he asked. "The gunshot?"

"Yes, sir," Mohalley said. "One of the diplomats."

Hood felt sick and relieved at the same time. His wife had stopped a few steps away. He motioned for her to go ahead, that everything was okay. At the moment, *okay* was a very relative term.

"Mr. Hood," Mohalley said, "we did a quick background check on all the parents, and your Op-Center record came up—"

"I've resigned," Hood said.

"We know," Mohalley told him. "But your resignation doesn't become effective for another twelve days. In the meantime," he went on, "we have a potentially serious problem that you'll be able to help us with."

Hood looked at him. "What kind of problem?"

"I'm not at liberty to say," Mohalley told him.

Hood hadn't really expected Mohalley to tell him. Not here. The State Department was paranoid about security outside its own offices, though here they had a right to be. Every diplomat, every consulate was here to help their country. That included being "on the line," using everything from eavesdropping to electronics to listen in on conversations.

"I understand," Hood said. "But it's related to this?" he pressed.

"Yes, sir. Will you follow me?" Mohalley said. It was less a question than a statement.

Hood glanced toward the courtyard. "What about my wife—"

"We'll tell her we needed your help," Mohalley informed him. "She'll understand. Please, sir, this is important."

Hood looked into the man's steel-gray eyes. Part of Hood—the part that felt guilty about Sharon—wanted to tell Mohalley to go to hell. Lowell Coffey had once said, "*The needs of a state come before the needs of estate.*" Hood had gotten out of government for that reason. A delegate had just been shot, and their daughter was being held by his killers—killers who had vowed to murder another person every hour. Hood should be with his wife.

Yet there was also a part of him that didn't want to sit around and wait for others to act. If there was something Hood could do to help Harleigh, or if he could collect intel for Rodgers and Striker, he wanted to be in there doing it. He hoped Sharon *would* understand.

"All right," Hood said to the security head.

The men turned and walked briskly toward the courtyard. They headed toward First Avenue, which was blocked by police cars from Forty-second to Forty-seventh Streets. Beyond them was a wall of glare, the lights from TV cameras. Parked along the avenue were three NYPD Emergency Service Unit Radio Emergency Patrol trucks with FAT squads—Fugitive Apprehension Teams—just in case the terrorists were Americans. The bomb squad from the Seventeenth Precinct was also there, complete with their own van. Overhead was a pair of NYPD Aviation Unit blue and white Bell-412 helicopters, their powerful spotlights shining on the compound. Cleaning personnel and diplomatic aides were still being evacuated from the UN and from the towers across the avenue.

In the glow of the white lights, Hood could see his ghostly white wife being led across the street with the other parents. She was looking back, trying to catch a glimpse of him. He waved, but they were immediately blocked by the REP trucks on the UN side of the street and the wall of police on the other.

Hood followed Mohalley south toward Forty-second Street, where a black State Department sedan was waiting. Mohalley and Hood slipped into the backseat. Five minutes later, they were headed through the renovated Queens-Midtown Tunnel, out of Manhattan.

Hood listened as Mohalley spoke. And what he heard made him feel as though he'd been sucker punched, pushed into taking a big step in the wrong direction.

TWENTY

New York, New York
Saturday, 10:31 P.M.

When the gun sounded inside the Security Council chamber, Colonel Mott immediately moved in front of the secretary-general. If there had been additional gunfire, he would have pushed her back to where his security personnel were standing. The officers had grabbed blast shields, which were stacked off to the side, and were standing behind them.

But there was no more shooting. There was only the acrid smell of cordite, the cottony deafness caused by the gunshot, and the unthinkable coldness of the execution.

Secretary-General Chatterjee stared ahead. The mantra had failed. A man had died, and so had hope.

She had seen death re-created in her father's films. She had seen the aftermath of genocide in videos produced by human rights organizations. Neither of those came close to capturing the dehumanizing reality of murder. She looked at the body lying chest-down on the tile floor. The eyes and mouth were both open wide, and the dead face was like clay, flat on its cheek and turned toward her. Beneath it, blood was spreading evenly in all directions. The man's arms were twisted under his body, and his feet were turned in opposite directions.

165

Where was the shadow of the *Atman* her faith talked about, the eternal soul of Hinduism? Where was the dignity we supposedly carried with us into the cycle of eternity?

"Get him out of here," Colonel Mott said after what was probably just a second or two but seemed infinitely longer. "Are you all right?" he asked the secretary-general.

She nodded.

The emergency medical technicians came forward with a stretcher. They rolled the delegate's body on top of it. One of the medics placed a thick swatch of gauze against the gaping head wound. This was more for propriety than to help the delegate, who was beyond help.

Behind the guards, the representatives were still and silent. Chatterjee looked at them and they looked at her. Everyone was ashen. Diplomats dealt with horror every day, but they rarely got to experience it.

It was a long moment before Chatterjee remembered the radio in her hand. She quickly composed herself and spoke into the mouthpiece. "Why was that necessary?"

After a short silence, someone answered. "This is Sergio Contini."

Contini was the Italian delegate. His normally powerful voice was weak and breathy.

Colonel Mott turned toward Chatterjee. His jaw was tight, and there was anger in his dark eyes. He obviously knew what was coming.

"Go ahead, *Signore* Contini," Chatterjee said. Unlike Mott, she was holding on to hope.

"I have been asked to tell you that I will be the next victim," he said. The words came slowly, unsteadily. "I will be shot exactly one—" he stopped and cleared his throat ''—exactly one hour from now. There will be no further communication.''

''Please tell your captors that I wish to come inside,'' Chatterjee said. ''Tell them I want to—''

''They've stopped listening,'' Mott informed her.

''Excuse me?'' Chatterjee said.

The colonel pointed to the small red indicator light on top of the oblong unit. It was off.

Chatterjee lowered her arm slowly. The colonel was wrong. The terrorists never started listening. ''How long until we have pictures from inside the chamber?'' she asked.

''I'll send someone downstairs to find out,'' Mott said. ''We're maintaining radio silence in case they're listening.''

''I understand,'' Chatterjee said. She returned his radio to him.

Colonel Mott sent one of his security officers downstairs, then ordered two others to clean up the delegate's blood. If they had to move in, he didn't want anyone slipping on it.

As Mott spoke with his troops, several of the representatives tried to come forward. Mott ordered his guards to keep them back. He said that he didn't want anyone blocking the path to the Security Council chambers. If any of the hostages managed to get out, he wanted to be able to protect them.

While Mott kept the crowd orderly, Chatterjee turned her back on the group. She walked toward the picture window that overlooked the front courtyard. It was usually so active out there, even at night, with the fountain and the traffic, people jogging or walking their dogs, lights in the windows of the buildings across the street.

167

Even helicopter traffic was being routed away from mid-town—not just in case there was an explosion on the ground but in the event that the terrorists had accomplices. She imagined that barge and pleasure boat traffic was also being stopped along the East River.

The entire enclave was paralyzed. So was she.

Chatterjee took a tremulous breath. She told herself there was nothing they could have done to prevent the delegate's murder. They couldn't have put together the ransom, even if the nations had agreed to try. They couldn't have attacked the Security Council chamber without causing more death. They couldn't negotiate, though they tried.

And then suddenly it struck her: what she'd done wrong. One thing—one small but significant thing.

Walking over to the representatives, Chatterjee informed them that she was returning to the conference room to notify the delegate's family of the assassination. Then, she said, she was coming back.

"To do what?" demanded the delegate from the Republic of Fiji.

"To do what I should have done the first time," she replied, and then headed toward the elevator.

TWENTY-ONE

New York, New York
Saturday, 10:39 P.M.

Reynold Downer went over to Georgiev after killing the Swedish delegate. Except for a few of the children who were crying and the Italian delegate who was praying, everyone in the room was silent and still. The other masked members of the group remained where they were.

Downer stood close enough so that Georgiev could feel the warmth of his breath through the mask. There were tiny spots of blood on the fibers.

"We need to talk," Downer said.

"About what?" Georgiev whispered angrily.

"About throwing more logs on the fire," Downer snarled.

"Go back to your post," Georgiev insisted.

"Listen to me. When I opened the door, I saw about twenty or twenty-five armed and shielded security guards in the corridor."

"Eunuchs," Georgiev said. "They won't risk an assault. We've *talked* about this. It will cost them everything."

"I know." Downer's eyes shifted to a secure phone sitting in a duffel bag on the floor. "But your intelligence source said that only France agreed to pay. We don't have the damned secretary-general as a hostage, the way we planned.''

"That was unfortunate," Georgiev said, "but not catastrophic. We'll manage without an advocate."

"I don't see how," Downer said.

"By outwaiting them," Georgiev said. "When the United States starts to worry that the children are at risk, they will pay whatever the other nations do not. They'll charge it to their UN debt, find some face-saving way to give it to us. Now, go back and do what you're supposed to do."

"I don't agree with this," Downer insisted. "I think we need to turn up the heat."

"There's no need," Georgiev said. "We have time, food, and water—"

"That isn't what I *mean!*" Downer interrupted.

Georgiev fired him a look. The Australian was getting loud. This was exactly what he expected from Downer. A ritualistic, confrontational nay-saying, as predictable and extreme as a Japanese Kabuki. But it was going on a little too long and getting a little too loud. He was prepared to shoot Downer, to shoot any of his people if he had to. He hoped Downer could see that in his eyes.

Downer took a breath. He was calmer when he spoke. The message had been received.

"What I'm saying," Downer went on, "is these bastards don't seem to be getting the message that we want the money, that we're not going to talk. Chatterjaw tried to negotiate."

"We expected that, too," Georgiev said. "And we closed her down."

"For now," Downer grumbled. "She'll try again. Talk is all these bloody idiots *ever* do."

170

"And it never succeeds," Georgiev said. "We have contingencies for everything," the Bulgarian reminded him quietly. "They *will* comply."

The Australian was still holding the gun he'd used to kill the Swedish delegate. He shook it as he spoke. "I still think we ought to find out what they're planning and *push* the bastards," Downer said. "I say that after we put down the Italian delegate, we start serving up the kiddies. Maybe torture them first, let a few screams drift through the corridors. Like those Khmer Rouge guerrillas in Cambodia who caught the family dog and cut it up slowly to draw out the family. Put pressure on them to hurry things along."

"We knew that it would take several bullets to get their attention," Georgiev whispered back. "We knew that even if there is a willingness to sacrifice delegates, the United States won't allow the children to die. Not through an attack and not through inactivity. Now, for the last time, return to your post. We will follow our plan."

Downer left with a huff and an oath, and Georgiev turned his attention back to the hostages. The Bulgarian had also expected this. Reynold Downer was not a patient man. But resolve could be tested and teamwork strengthened by conflict and tension.

Except in the United Nations, Georgiev thought ironically. And the reason for that was simple. The United Nations promoted peace instead of gain. Peace instead of testing oneself. Peace instead of life.

Georgiev would fight it until he succumbed to the peace there was no avoiding, the peace that eventually came to every man.

TWENTY-TWO

New York, New York
Saturday, 11:08 P.M.

The large C-130 was parked and idling on the airstrip outside the Marine Air Terminal at La Guardia Airport. Originally called the Overseas Terminal when it opened in 1939, the Marine Air Terminal was the airport's main terminal building at the time. Constructed adjacent to blustery Jamaica Bay, the terminal was designed to accomodate passengers of "flying boats," the preferred mode of international air travel in the 1930s and 1940s.

Today, the Art Deco Marine Air Terminal is dwarfed by the Central Terminal Building and the buildings operated by individual airlines. In its heyday, however, the Marine Air Terminal had witnessed history. Though black, the so-called "silver tarmac" had welcomed politicians and world leaders, movie stars and celebrated artists, renowned inventors and world-famous explorers. Typically, the flashing bulbs of the press had been on hand to welcome them to New York. Limousines had been waiting to take them to the city.

Tonight, the Marine Air Terminal witnessed history of a different sort. Eleven Strikers and General Mike Rodgers stood on the dark landing strip surrounded by a dozen military police. Paul Hood was taut with rage when he saw them, literally digging his fingers into the seat cushion.

En route, Deputy Chief Mohalley had told Hood that the MPs had choppered in from Fort Monmouth, New Jersey, where they were attached to the Air Mobility Command.

"According to the information I was given," Mohalley had explained, "the Congressional Intelligence Oversight Committee refused to give your Strikers permission to become involved in the crisis. Apparently, the CIOC chairman was concerned about Striker's reputation for rule-bending, so he contacted the White House and spoke directly with the president."

Obviously, Hood thought bitterly, *no one had bothered to consider Striker's reputation for success.*

"When the president tried to phone Mike Rodgers," Mohalley went on, "he was furious to learn that Striker was already airborne. The president's next call was to Colonel Kenneth Morningside, Fort Monmouth post commander. I'm not surprised they're taking such a hard line," Mohalley added. "About fifteen minutes after the terrorists went into the United Nations, the State Department issued a general order that no units of the security police were to set foot in the United Nations complex. I understand the NYPD got a similar order. Any incursion had to be requested by the secretary-general in writing, and the parameters approved by the unit's commanding officer."

Hearing this, Hood was more afraid for Harleigh and the other children than he was before. If Striker wasn't allowed to save them, who could? But Hood's feelings of despair shaded to rage when he saw Mike Rodgers, Brett August, and the rest of the Strikers being detained.

These men and women, these combat heroes, didn't deserve to be treated like thugs.

Hood got out of the car and jogged toward the group. Mohalley hurried after him. A stiff, salty wind blew in from the bay and Mohalley had to hold his cap to keep it from blowing off. Hood didn't feel it. The anger roiled inside, burning more intensely than his fear and frustration. His muscles were cable-taut and his mind was on fire. Yet his fury was not just directed at this outrage and at the continuing ineffectiveness of the UN. Like oil feeding deep-smoldering fires, his anger spilled everywhere. He actually found himself mad at Op-Center for having intruded so much on his life, at Sharon for not being more supportive, and at himself for having managed it all so badly.

Lieutenant Solo, the military police brigade commander, walked forward to meet them. The lieutenant was a short, beefy, balding man in his late thirties. He had unyielding eyes and a no-nonsense face.

Mohalley caught up to Hood and introduced himself to the colonel. Then he went to introduce Hood. But Hood had already walked past the officers toward the ring of MPs. Frowning, the colonel turned and strode after him. Mohalley followed the colonel.

Hood stopped just short of shouldering his way through the MPs—but it was a very short stop. Enough common sense remained to remind Hood that if he fought these people, he was going to lose.

The lieutenant eased in front of Hood. "Excuse me, sir—" he said.

Hood ignored him. "Mike, are you all right?"

"Been in worse spots," he said.

That was true, Hood had to admit. Perspective joined common sense and Hood relaxed slightly.

"Mr. Hood," the lieutenant said insistently.

Hood looked at him. "Lieutenant Solo, these servicemen report to me. What are your orders?"

"We've been instructed to make certain that all Striker personnel are put back on board the C-130 and to remain at our post until the aircraft returns to Andrews," Solo informed him.

"Fine," Hood said with open disgust. "Let Washington bench the only hope the UN's got—"

"This was not my decision, sir," Solo said.

"I know, Lieutenant," Hood said, "and I'm not angry at you." He wasn't. He was angry at everyone. "But I do have a situation that requires the presence of my second-in-command, General Rodgers. The general is not a member of the Striker unit."

Lieutenant Solo looked from Hood to Rodgers, then back to Hood. "If that's true, then my instructions do not pertain to the general."

Rodgers stepped away from the Strikers and moved through the tight circle of MPs.

Mohalley scowled. "Hold on," he said. "The general order I was given *does* pertain to all security and military personnel, including General Rodgers. Mr. Hood, I'd like to know what the situation is that requires the general's presence."

"It's personal," Hood replied.

"If it pertains to the situation at the United Nations—"

"It does," Hood said. "My daughter is being held hostage there. Mike Rodgers is her godfather."

Mohalley regarded Rodgers. "Her godfather."

"That's right," Rodgers said.

Hood said nothing. It didn't matter whether the DOS security officer believed him. All that mattered was that Rodgers be allowed to go with him.

Mohalley looked at Hood. "Only immediate family are allowed to go into the waiting room with you."

"Then I will not *go* to the waiting room," Hood said through his teeth. He'd had enough of this. He had never hit a man, but if this functionary didn't step aside, Hood was going to push him aside.

Rodgers was standing directly beside the shorter State Department officer. The general was watching Hood. For a long moment, the only sound was the wind. It seemed much louder now in the silence.

"All right, Mr. Hood," Mohalley said. "I'm not going to hold your feet to the fire on this one."

Hood exhaled.

Mohalley looked at Rodgers. "Would you like a ride, sir?"

"I would, thank you," Rodgers said.

Rodgers was still looking at Hood. And Hood suddenly felt like he did when they used to sit in his office at Op-Center. He felt reconnected, tapped into a network of devoted friends and coworkers.

God help him. In the midst of everything, he felt whole again.

Before leaving, Rodgers turned to the Strikers. They came to attention. Colonel August saluted him. Rodgers saluted back. Then, on August's command, the Strikers returned to the C-130. The circle of MPs parted to let them through. The police remained on the landing strip as Hood, Rodgers, and Mohalley returned to the car.

Paul Hood didn't have a plan. He didn't imagine that

177

Mike Rodgers had one, either. Whatever Rodgers might have been thinking of doing would have involved Striker. But as the State Department sedan turned from the Marine Air Terminal and the towering C-130, Hood was slightly less anguished than he had been before. It wasn't entirely Rodgers's presence that comforted him. It was also a reminder of something he'd learned from running Op-Center: that plans made in moments of calm rarely worked in a crisis anyway.

There were only two of them, but they were backed by the strongest team in the world, and they'd think of something.

They had to.

TWENTY-THREE

New York, New York
Saturday, 11:11 P.M.

"I absolutely can't allow you to do this!" Colonel
Mott was practically shouting at Secretary-General Chatterjee. "It's insanity. No, it's worse than insanity. It's
suicide!"

The two were standing by the head of the table in the
conference room. Deputy Secretary-General Takahara
and Undersecretary-General Javier Olivo were standing
several feet away beside the closed door. Chatterjee had
just hung up with Gertrud Johanson, the wife of the
Swedish delegate, who was at home in Stockholm. Her
husband had attended the party with his young executive
assistant, Liv, who was still in the Security Council
chamber. Mrs. Johanson would be flying over as soon
as possible.

It was both sad and ironic, Chatterjee thought, that so
many political wives ended up with their husbands only
after the men were dead. She wondered if she would be
doing this if she were married.

Probably, she decided.

"Ma'am?" the Colonel said. "Please tell me you'll
reconsider."

She couldn't. She believed that she was right. And
believing that, she could do nothing else. That was her

dharma, the sacred duty that came with the life she had chosen.

"I appreciate your fears," Secretary-General Chatterjee said, "but I believe that this is our best option."

"It is not," Mott said. "We should have video images of the Security Council in a few minutes. Give me a half hour to have a look at them, and then I'll take my team in."

"In the meantime," the secretary-general pointed out, "Ambassador Contini will die."

"The ambassador will die anyway," Mott said.

"I don't accept that," Chatterjee said.

"That's because you're a diplomat and not a soldier," Mott said. "The ambassador is what we call an operative loss. That's a soldier or unit you can't get to in time unless you risk the security of the rest of the company. So you don't try. You *can't.*"

"A company is not at risk, Colonel Mott," Chatterjee said. "Only me. I'm going to the Security Council and going inside."

Mott shook his head angrily. "I think you're doing this to punish yourself, Madam Secretary-General, and you have no reason to. You did the right thing trying to radio the terrorists."

"No," Chatterjee said. "I did the shortsighted thing. I didn't think to the next step."

"That's easy to say now," Deputy Secretary-General Takahara suggested. "No one here had a better idea. And if we had thought of this option, I would have argued against it."

Chatterjee looked at her watch. They only had nineteen minutes before the next deadline. "Gentlemen, I'm going ahead with this," she said.

"They'll cut you down," Mott warned. "They've probably got someone stationed at the door to shoot anyone who tries to come in."

"If they do, then perhaps my death will count as their murder of the hour," Chatterjee said. "Maybe they'll spare Ambassador Contini. Then you, Mr. Takahara, will have to decide what to do next."

"What to do next," Mott muttered. "What else *is* there to do but move in on these monsters? And there's something else you haven't considered. The terrorists told us that any attempt to liberate the hostages would result in the release of poison gas. We're dealing with a hair-trigger situation. There's a good chance they may interpret your attempt to enter the room as an attack by my security forces or perhaps as a diversion for an attack."

"I'll talk to them through the door," Chatterjee said. "I'll make it clear that I'm coming in unarmed."

"Which is exactly what we'd say if we wanted to deceive them," Mott told her.

"Colonel, in this instance I agree with the secretary-general," Deputy Secretary-General Takahara said. "Remember, it's not just Ambassador Contini's life that's in danger. If you enter the Security Council with an armed security force, there will absolutely be extensive casualties among the hostages and possibly your own personnel, not to mention the risk of the poison gas."

Chatterjee looked at her watch again. "Unfortunately, we don't have time to discuss this further."

"Ma'am," Mott said, "will you at least put on a bulletproof vest?"

"No," Chatterjee replied. "I must go into that room with hope and also with trust."

The secretary-general opened the door. She walked into the corridor followed closely by Colonel Mott.

Despite the hopes she'd expressed in the conference room, Chatterjee knew she might be walking to her death. The awareness that she might have just a few minutes left to live made her senses hyperalert and changed the otherwise familiar complexion of the corridor. The sights and smells, even the sound of the tile under her shoes, were vivid. And for the first time in her brief career here, she wasn't distracted by talk or debate, by pressing issues of war, peace, sanctions, and resolutions. That made the experience even more surreal.

She and Mott entered the elevator. There were five minutes left before the deadline.

Only now did it occur to her how wickedly final that word sounded.

TWENTY-FOUR

New York, New York
Saturday, 11:28 P.M.

Georgiev was standing near the opening of the circular table in the Security Council chamber. He had been keeping an eye on the delegates and also on his watch. The other men were still guarding the doors, except for Barone. The Uruguayan was kneeling in the center of the room, just before the gallery, looking down. When two minutes remained until the next deadline, the Bulgarian turned and nodded at Downer.

The Australian had been pacing slowly by the northern door of the upper gallery. He had been watching Georgiev. When he got the signal, he started down the stairs.

Several of the men and women sitting on the floor inside the table began to whimper. Georgiev hated weakness. So he raised his automatic and pointed it at one of the women. He used to do that with his girls in Cambodia. Whenever one or more of them came and threatened to expose him because she was being treated poorly or was being paid less than he'd promised, Georgiev wouldn't say a word. He'd simply point a gun at her head. It never failed: Every opening in her face—her eyes, nose, and mouth—would gape and freeze there. Then Georgiev would speak: *"If you complain to me again, I will kill you,"* he'd say. *"If you try to leave, I will kill you and your family."* They never complained after that. Out of the more than one hundred girls who had worked for him during the year his ring operated, he'd only had to shoot two of them.

Everyone on the floor stopped sobbing. Georgiev lowered the gun. There were still tears but no more sounds.

Downer was nearly at the bottom of the stairs when Georgiev saw the light on the TAC-SAT flash. He was surprised. He had spoken to Annabelle Hampton an hour ago, when she let him know that the secretary-general intended to try to negotiate. For a moment, Georgiev wondered if Downer's fears were going to be realized and security forces would try to move in. But that wasn't possible. The UN wouldn't risk it. He walked to the phone.

Annabelle Hampton had been Georgiev's riskiest but most important acquisition. From the time they had first met in Cambodia, Annabelle had impressed him as a determined and independent woman. She was in Phnom Penh recruiting HUMINT and personnel for the CIA. Georgiev provided her with intelligence his girls obtained from their customers. He also gave her intel he picked up from his own Khmer Rouge contacts. Though he was paying the rebels and getting paid to spy on them, he actually made a small personal profit on the arrangement.

When the UNTAC operation ended in 1993, Georgiev sought Annabelle out in order to sell her the names of the girls he'd been using. Learning she'd been transferred to Seoul, he contacted her there. Annabelle seemed more angry than ambitious by then. When he mentioned that he was leaving the army to go into business, she half-joked that he should keep her in mind if he heard of any interesting opportunities.

He did.

Up until this afternoon, when Annabelle gave Georgiev the detailed timetable for tonight's United Nations event, he wondered if she was going to back out. He was confident she wouldn't betray him because he knew where her parents lived; he'd made a point of sending them flowers while Annabelle was visiting there for Christmas. Still, the final hours before any mission are what the great nineteenth-century Bulgarian General Grigor Halachev used to call "the times of gravest doubt." That's when the external plans are finally set, and soldiers had a chance to examine their internal condition.

Annabelle had not backed down. She had as much steel in her as any soldier in this room.

He picked up the phone. "Speak," he said. That was the only word Annabelle had been told to respond to.

"The secretary-general is on her way again," Ani informed him. "Only this time, she's planning to come into the Security Council chamber. She hopes you'll take her in."

Georgiev smiled.

"Either that," Ani said, "or she hopes you'll target her instead of the Italian delegate."

"Pacifists always hope you'll target them until you really do," Georgiev said. "Then they cry and beg. What are her advisers saying?"

"Colonel Mott and one of the undersecretary-generals are encouraging a strike as soon as they get video images of the chamber," Ani said. "The other officials have been noncommittal."

185

Georgiev glanced at Barone. The security unit wouldn't be getting any images. When Annabelle had informed them of the plan, Georgiev had sent Barone to the spot where they were said to be drilling. As soon as the tiny camera came through, he would cover it.

"Was there any further discussion about paying the ransom?" Georgiev asked her.

"None," Ani said.

"No matter," Georgiev said. "No video images, more dead—they'll turn to our needs soon."

"There is one thing more," Ani said. "I've just been informed by my superior that a SWAT team from the National Crisis Management Center is coming up from Washington."

"The NCMC?" Georgiev said. "Sanctioned by whom?"

"No one," Ani told him. "They're going to use my office as their headquarters. If the UN gives them the go-ahead, they may come in."

That was unexpected. Georgiev had heard that the NCMC staged a very creditable action in Russia during the coup attempt over a year before. Though he had poison gas and battle plans for the Security Council chamber, he didn't want to have to use either. On the other hand, the UN would have to give the SWAT team permission to come in. And if he could get Chatterjee in here, she would give Georgiev the means of forestalling that.

Georgiev thanked Annabelle and hung up.

The secretary-general would be a welcome addition to the hostages. He had always counted on having her as an advocate for the children. Telling the nations of the world to cooperate for their release. Now she would also help him to keep the military out. And when it was time to go, she and the children would make ideal hostages.

Downer arrived. The only question was what to do about the Italian delegate. If they shot him, it would undermine the secretary-general's credibility as a peacemaker. If they spared him, they'd seem weak.

Deciding that the secretary-general's credibility was not his concern, Georgiev nodded to Downer. Then he watched as the Australian half-pushed, half-pulled the weeping delegate up the stairs.

TWENTY-FIVE

New York, New York
Saturday, 11:29 P.M.

"They're going to do it again."

Brown-haired Laura Sabia was sitting on Harleigh Hood's left. She was staring ahead blankly and shaking worse than before. It was as if she were on a bad sugar high. Harleigh placed her fingertips back on the girl's hand to try and calm her.

"They're going to kill him," Laura said.

"Shhhh," Harleigh said.

Barbara Mathis, who was sitting on Harleigh's right, was watching the terrorists. The raven-haired violinist was sitting up straight and seemed very intense. Harleigh knew the look. Barbara was the kind of musician who got irrationally angry if someone made a noise that caused her to break concentration. Barbara looked like she was getting to that point now. Harleigh hoped not.

The girls watched as the masked men led the delegate up the stairs. The victim fell to his hands and knees on one of the steps and was crying, saying something fast and high in Italian. The masked man, the Australian, grabbed him by the back of his collar and yanked at him hard. The Italian's arms crumpled and he fell forward. The masked man swore, crouched, and put his gun between the man's legs. He said something to the Italian,

189

who grabbed onto a chair and quickly struggled back to his feet. The men continued to the top of the stairs.

Near the young violinists, in the center of the circular table, a delegate's wife was comforting another woman. She was holding her close and pressing her hand over her mouth. Harleigh guessed that this was the wife of the man who was about to die.

Laura was literally fluttering now, as though there were an electric current running through her. Harleigh had never seen anything like it. She closed her fingers around Laura's hands and squeezed.

"You've got to calm down," Harleigh said under her breath.

"I can't," Laura said. "I can't breathe. I need to get out of here."

"Soon," Harleigh said. "They'll get us out. Just sit back and shut your eyes. Try and relax."

Harleigh's father had once told her and her brother that if they were ever in a situation like this, the important thing was to stay centered. Invisible. Count the seconds, he'd said, not the minutes or the hours. The longer a hostage crisis went on, the better the chance for a negotiated settlement. The better the chance for survival. If there were an opportunity to escape, she had to use common sense. The question she had to ask herself was not, *Is there a chance I'll make it?* The question was, *Is there a chance I won't make it?* If the answer was yes, it was better to stay where you were. He'd also told her to avoid eye contact wherever possible. That would humanize her to her captors. It would remind them that she was one of the people they hated. She should also say nothing, in case it was the wrong thing. Above all, she was supposed to relax. Think happy thoughts, just like they did in two of her favorite musicals, *Peter Pan* and *The Sound of Music*.

"Laura?" Harleigh said.

Laura didn't seem to have heard.

"Laura, you have to listen to me."

She wasn't hearing anything. The young woman had slipped into some kind of weird state. Her eyes were staring and her lips were pressed tight.

The two men had reached the top of the stairs.

On Harleigh's other side, Barbara Mathis was the opposite of Laura, taut as a violin string. She was sneering in a way that Harleigh knew well. Harleigh felt like the statue at the Justice Department. Only instead of the scales of justice she was between emotional extremes.

Suddenly, Laura shot from her seat. Harleigh was still holding the girl's hand.

"Why are you *doing* this to us?" Laura shrieked as she stood there. "I want you to *stop* it *now!*"

Harleigh tugged gently on her hand. "Laura, don't do this—"

The leader of the gang was standing halfway up the steps. He turned and glared at the girls.

Ms. Dorn was sitting three seats away. She rose slowly but remained behind her seat. "Laura, sit *down,*" she said firmly.

"No!" Laura pulled away from Harleigh. "I can't stay here!" she screamed, and ran around the table. She was headed toward the door on the other side of the chamber, the door the leader had been guarding.

The leader started down the stairs as Laura ran across the carpeted floor. Ms. Dorn ran after Laura, shouting for her to come back. The man who'd been standing on the other side of the room, guarding the other door, left his post and ran after the teacher. The Australian man at the top of the stairs had stopped and was looking down at them.

Everyone was watching Laura as the leader, Ms. Dorn, and the other man all reached the door. The other man grabbed Ms. Dorn around the waist, pulled her back, swung her around, and literally flung her on the floor. The leader reached the door as Laura was pulling it open. He threw his shoulder into it, closing it, and pushed Laura back. The girl stumbled, fell, got up, and rushed toward the stairs. She was still shrieking.

The door isn't locked.

The thought hit Harleigh like a bright light. Of course it wasn't locked. The men had opened the doors and they didn't have the keys to lock them.

They'd opened the door Laura had run toward, and they'd opened the door behind Harleigh. Harleigh had watched them do it. They'd spent some time putting equipment into the hallway down here.

The door that was about twenty feet behind where Harleigh and Barbara were sitting. The door the man had just run from in order to catch Laura.

The door no one was guarding.

The leader was running after Laura. Ms. Dorn had had the wind knocked from her but was fighting with the man who'd thrown her down. The pressure must have gotten to her; the music teacher wasn't thinking. But Harleigh was, clearly and confidently. She was thinking not only of getting out and saving herself, but of bringing what "Uncle" Bob Herbert called "intel" to the outside.

The teenager turned slowly and stole a sideways look at the door. She could run a dash like that easily. She'd blue-ribboned the fifty-yard dash in high school two out of four years. She could certainly get to the double doors before any of the men could stop her. And once she was out of here, there had to be a way to get into the Economic and Social Council chamber. She'd seen the double doors on that side during the tour they'd been given.

Harleigh used the toe of her right high-heeled shoe to slip off her left shoe. Then she slowly did the same with the right. Her fellow students were watching the struggle.

Harleigh eased the chair back. Slowly, without rising, she pivoted the chair on one leg so she could turn her body around slightly. Have a clear, straight run at the exit.

"Don't do it," Barbara said from the side of her mouth.

"What?" Harleigh said.

"I know what you're thinking," Barbara said, "because I'm thinking the same thing. Don't go for it. I am."

"No—"

"I'm faster than you," Barbara murmured. "I beat you two years in a row."

"I'm two steps closer," Harleigh pointed out.

Barbara shook her head slowly. Her eyes were angry and her mind was made up. Harleigh didn't know what to do. She didn't want to race Barbara for the door. They'd only trip each other up.

The girls looked over as the leader caught Laura midway up the stairs. He lifted her off the floor and threw her backward, down the stairs. Laura bounced and rolled and came to a stop at the bottom. She was moving her arms and head slowly, painfully. The leader hurried down to her.

Barbara took a few slow, shallow breaths. She put her hands on the edge of the wooden table. She waited until she was sure that no one was looking her way. Then she pushed off from the table, rose, and ran.

Her legs were hindered by the tight gown she was wearing. Harleigh heard a rip along the side, but Barbara kept running. Her arms churned, she kept her eyes on the doorknob, and she ignored whichever of the terrorists or delegates or whoever was shouting at her to stop.

Harleigh watched as she reached the door.

Go! Harleigh thought.

Barbara stopped to pull it open. She heard the latch click, the door came open, and then she heard a whip-loud crack. It stayed inside her ears, filling them, like the first blast of music when her Walkman was turned too high.

The next thing Harleigh knew, Barbara was no longer standing. She was still holding the doorknob, but she was on her knees. Her hand slipped from the knob, and her arm flopped to her side.

Barbara's body remained upright, but only for a moment. Then she fell to the side.

She was no longer angry.

TWENTY-SIX

New York, New York
Saturday, 11:30 P.M.

Secretary-General Chatterjee stopped when she heard the muffled gunshot. It was followed by shrill cries, and then a few moments later there was a second gunshot, closer to the corridor than the first. Almost immediately after that, the door of the Security Council chamber opened. Ambassador Contini was thrown out, and the door was quickly shut.

Colonel Mott ran over to the body at once, his footsteps breaking the utter stillness of the corridor. He was followed by the emergency medical crew. The delegate's well-dressed body was lying on its side, Contini's dark face toward them. His expression was relaxed, his eyes shut, his lips slightly parted. The man didn't look dead, not the way Ambassador Johanson had. Then the blood started to pool beneath his soft cheek.

Mott squatted beside the body. He looked behind the head. There was a single wound, just like before.

As the medical team placed the body on a stretcher, Chatterjee walked toward the doors of the Security Council chamber. She looked away from the body as she passed. Mott rose and intercepted her.

"Ma'am, there's nothing you can gain by going in

there now," he said. "At least wait until we have the video."

"Wait!" Chatterjee said. "I've already waited too long!"

Just then, one of the security force personnel came from the Economic and Social Council chamber. Lieutenant David Mailman was assigned to a makeshift, two-person reconnaissance team. He and his partner had pulled a fifteen-year-old Remote Infinity Eavesdropping Device out of storage. Designed to work over a telephone line, they rigged it to pick up voices through the headphones of the translating units at each seat in the Security Council chamber. Since the range was only twenty-five feet, they had to work from the adjoining room. They were situated in the small corridor that led to the second-floor media center and was common to both the Trusteeship Council and Security Council chambers.

"Sir," Lieutenant Mailman said to the colonel, "we think someone just tried to get out of the Security Council. We saw the doorknob twist and heard that latch jiggle right before the first shot."

"Was it a warning shot?" Mott asked.

"We don't believe so," Mailman replied. "Whoever was back there moaned after the report." The lieutenant looked down. "It—it didn't sound like a man, sir. It was a very soft voice."

"One of the children," Chatterjee said with horror.

"We don't know that," Mott said. "Is there anything else, lieutenant?"

"No, sir," Mailman said.

The officer left. The colonel balled his fists, then looked at his watch. He was waiting for word about the video surveillance. Secure phones had been requested from the U.S. State Department Diplomatic Security forces; until they arrived, all communications had to be done person-to-person. Chatterjee had never seen a man look so helpless.

The secretary-general was still facing the door. Ambassador Contini's death hadn't hit her like the first one did, and that disturbed her. Or maybe her reaction had been blunted by the news Lieutenant Mailman brought.

A child may have been shot—

Chatterjee started toward the door.

Mott gently grabbed her arm. "Please don't do this. Not yet."

The secretary-general stopped.

"I know that there's nothing I can do from the outside," she said. "If it becomes necessary to take action, you won't need me here. But inside, I may be able to make a difference."

The colonel looked at the secretary-general for a long moment, then released her arm.

"You see?" she said with a soft smile. "Diplomacy. I didn't have to pull my arm away."

Mott seemed unconvinced as he watched her go.

TWENTY-SEVEN

New York, New York
Saturday, 11:31 P.M.

Paul Hood and Mike Rodgers sat in the backseat of the sedan while Mohalley sat up front with his driver. Manhattan seemed like a very different place as Hood returned to it.

The Secretariat Building stood out more than it had when he and his family first arrived—was it only a day before? The building was lit by spotlights that had been placed on the rooftops of adjoining skyscrapers. But the offices themselves were dark, making the structure seem cadaverous. The UN no longer reminded him of the proud and hale "bat symbol." It wasn't the living chest of the city but seemed like a thing already dead.

When they left the airport shortly after eleven P.M., Deputy Chief Mohalley called his office to find out if there were any new developments. His assistant informed him that as far as they knew, nothing had happened since the first execution. Meanwhile, Hood had brought Rodgers up to date. Characteristically, Rodgers listened and said nothing. The general didn't like to reveal what he was thinking in public. To Rodgers, being with people who weren't part of his trusted circle was "in public."

Both men were silent as they crossed through the tun-

199

nel back into Manhattan. When they were through, Mohalley turned to them for the first time.

"Where will I be dropping you off, Mr. Hood, General Rodgers?" Mohalley asked.

"We'll get out where you do," Hood said.

"I'm getting off at the State Department."

"That'll be fine," Hood said. He said nothing more. He still intended to go to the CIA shell at the United Nations Plaza, though he didn't want Mohalley to know that.

Once again, Mohalley didn't seem happy with that answer, but he didn't press it.

The car emerged from the tunnel on Thirty-seventh Street. As the driver made his way up First Avenue, Mohalley looked at Mike Rodgers.

"I want you to know I hate what happened back there," the State Department officer said.

Rodgers nodded once.

"I've heard about Striker," Mohalley said. "They've got quite a rep. As far as I'm concerned, we couldn't do much better than to send your people in and get this thing over with."

"It's sick," Hood said. "Everyone probably feels that way, but no one will authorize it."

"This whole thing is a mess," Mohalley said as his car phone beeped. "Hundreds of heads and no brain. It's almost breathtaking, in a tragic sort of way."

Mohalley answered the phone as the car stopped at the Forty-second Street barricade. A pair of police officers in riot gear walked over. While the driver showed them his State Department ID, Mohalley listened in silence.

Hood watched the man's face under the glow of a

streetlight. Curiosity gnawed at him. He looked over at the United Nations complex. From this angle, looking up, the Secretariat Building seemed large and imposing against the black sky. His baby seemed so small and vulnerable as he thought about her inside that blue white monstrosity.

Mohalley hung up. He looked back.

"What is it?" Hood asked.

"Another delegate was shot," Mohalley told him. "And possibly," he said, *"possibly* one of the children."

Hood stared at him. It took an instant for *"one of the children"* to translate as *possibly Harleigh*. When it did, life seemed to lose all forward momentum. Hood knew that he would never forget Mohalley's somber expression at that moment, the brilliant white glare on the windshield, and the looming Secretariat behind it. It was now and forever the picture of lost hope.

"There was a gunshot prior to the one that killed the delegate," Mohalley went on. "One of the UN security people in the adjoining chamber heard someone trying to get out the side door there. There was a cry or a groan after that."

"Is there any more information?" Rodgers asked as the police let the car through.

"There's been no communication from the Security Council," Mohalley said, "but the secretary-general is going to try to get inside."

The sedan pulled up to the curb. "Mike," Hood said. "I've got to go to Sharon."

"I know," Rodgers said. He cracked the door and stepped out.

"General, would you like to come with me?" Mohalley asked.

Rodgers stepped aside as Hood climbed out. "No," he said, "but thanks."

Mohalley handed Hood his business card. "Let me know if you need anything."

"Thanks," Hood said. "I will."

Mohalley once again looked like he wanted to ask something but didn't. Rodgers shut the door. The car pulled from the curb and Rodgers stood facing Hood.

Hood heard the distant sounds of traffic and the hum of the helicopters hovering over the river and the UN. He heard the shouts of police and the clump of sandbags being dropped behind wooden barricades along Forty-second and Forty-seventh Streets. Yet he didn't feel like he was there. He was still in the car, still staring at Mohalley.

Still hearing him say, *"And possibly one of the children."*

"Paul," Rodgers said.

Hood was staring at the buildings as they shrank into the darkness of upper First Avenue. He had to force himself to breathe.

"Don't go away on me," Rodgers said. "I'm going to need you later, and Sharon needs you now."

Hood nodded. Rodgers was right. But he couldn't seem to get out of that damn car, away from Mohalley's sad face and the horror of that moment.

"I'm going across the street," Rodgers went on. "Brett is going to meet me at the shell."

That got Hood's attention. His eyes shifted to Rodgers. "Brett?"

"We saw the MPs when we were taxiing to the terminal," Rodgers said. "We had a pretty good idea why they were there. Brett told me he'd get out somehow and meet me here." The general found a little smile. "You know Brett. No one tells him to run."

Hood came back a little. Whoever the possible victim was, there were still lives at risk. He looked over at the State Department tower. "I've got to go."

"I know," Rodgers said. "Take care of her."

"You have my cell phone number—"

"I do," Rodgers said. "When we find something out or have any ideas, I'll call."

Hood thanked him and started toward the redbrick building.

TWENTY-EIGHT

New York, New York
Saturday, 11:32 P.M.

Georgiev was carrying the panicked girl back to her seat when Barbara Mathis went down. Downer, who had fired the shot, was running from the top of the gallery. Barone was also running over. It was he who had shouted for Barbara to stop.

Heedless of her own safety, one of the Asian delegates' wives had gotten up from the table and was walking over to Barbara. She was smart. She didn't run. She also stopped with her back to the door; she didn't intend to run. The Bulgarian didn't order the woman back. She set her purse down, knelt beside the girl, and carefully plucked the blood-soaked gown from around the wound. The bullet had struck the teenage girl in the left side. Blood was oozing from the small opening. The girl wasn't moving. The flesh of her slender arms was pale.

Georgiev continued toward the circular table. He wondered if that whole thing had been planned: One girl runs screaming to get everyone's attention while another girl runs in the opposite direction and tries to get out. If so, it was a clever, dangerous maneuver. Georgiev admired courage. But just like some of the girls who used to work for him in Cambodia—some of whom were no older than this girl—she had acted disobediently. And she had been punished.

Unfortunately, the lesson was probably lost on the other hostages. They were already getting surprisingly bold. Some were pushed by fear, others by outrage over what had happened to the girl and the delegates. A mob mentality, even among hostages, had a way of shutting down reason. If they turned on him, he'd have to shoot them. Shooting them would rob him of his leverage, and the sound of gunfire and cries would embolden security forces to move in.

Of course, he would shoot them if he had to. All he really needed to get out of this were the children. Even one child would do, if it came to that.

Suddenly, two other delegates stood up. That was the problem with giving one person some extra leash. Everyone assumed they had it, too. Georgiev dropped the stunned Laura into her seat, where she sat sobbing. He ordered the other delegates to sit down. He didn't want too many people on their feet or someone else might be tempted to run.

"But that girl is hurt!" one of the delegates said. "She needs help."

Georgiev raised his gun. "I haven't selected the next one to die. Don't make my choice easy."

The men sat down. The one who'd spoken looked like he wanted to say something else; his wife urged him to be silent. The other one looked sadly toward Barbara.

To their right, Contini's wife was sobbing hysterically. One of the other wives was hugging her tight to keep her from wailing.

Vandal brought the music teacher back and ordered her to sit as well. Ms. Dorn said that she was responsible for Barbara and insisted that she be allowed to take care of her. Vandal pushed her back down. She started to get back up. Angrily, Georgiev swung toward the woman. He pointed his gun at her head and walked forward. Vandal backed away.

"One more word from you or anyone else and they will die," he said through his teeth. "One more word."

Georgiev watched as the woman's nose flared and eyes widened, just like the whores in Cambodia. But she was silent. Reluctantly, she sat down and turned her attention to the girl who'd tried to run.

Vandal lingered a moment longer and then returned to his post. Downer reached Georgiev's side at the same time as Barone. Barone got very close to the Australian.

"Are you insane?" Barone snarled.

"I had to do it!" he snapped.

"Had to?" he said, careful to keep his voice low. "We were going to try not to hurt the children."

"The mission would have been in jeopardy if she'd gotten away," Downer said.

"You heard me yelling, saw me running toward her," Barone said. "I would have gotten to her before she reached the outer door."

"Maybe yes, maybe no," Georgiev said. "The important thing is, she didn't get away. Now, go back to your posts, both of you. We'll care for her here as best we can," Georgiev said.

Barone glared at him. "She's a young girl."

Georgiev glared back. "No one told her to run!"

Barone was furiously silent.

"Now we have a door unprotected, and you should be watching for the fiber-optic cable," Georgiev said, quietly. "Or would you rather see our planning and effort lost because of that!'' He pointed toward Barbara.

Downer grunted and returned to the top of the gallery. Barone huffed, shook his head in frustration, then went back to the front of the gallery.

Georgiev watched them go. Whether he liked it or not, this had changed things. Crime is a mood-intensifying effort. Close quarters heightens emotions, and an unexpected drama makes things even worse.

"You have to let me send her out of here."

Georgiev turned. The Asian woman was standing beside him. He hadn't even heard her approach.

"No," he said. He *was* distracted. He had to refocus, get his men back. Push the United Nations harder. And he thought he knew how.

"But she's going to bleed to death," the woman said.

Georgiev walked toward one of the duffel bags. He didn't want the girl to die because it might incite a rebellion. He pulled a small blue case from inside and came back. He handed her the box.

"Use this," Georgiev said.

"A first aid kit?" the woman said. "That isn't going to help."

"That's all I can give you."

"But there may be internal bleeding, organ damage—" the woman said.

Downer waved and caught Georgiev's eye. The Australian was pointing toward the door.

"You'll have to make do," the Bulgarian said to the woman and motioned Vandal over. When the Frenchman arrived, Georgiev told him to make sure the Asian woman didn't try to get out. Then Georgiev walked toward the stairs.

He stepped up to Downer. "What is it?"

"She's here," the Australian whispered thickly. "The secretary-general. She knocked on the bloody door and asked to come in."

"Is that all she said?" Georgiev asked.

"That's all," Downer told him.

Georgiev looked past the Australian. *Focus,* he told himself. Things had changed. He had to think this through. If he let Chatterjee in, her efforts would become focused on getting the girl medical attention, not on getting them the money. And if he did let the girl out, the press would find out that a child had been hurt, possibly killed. There would be increased pressure for military action, despite the risks for the hostages. There was also the chance that the girl might became conscious in the hospital. If she did, she could describe the distribution of the men and hostages to security personnel.

Of course, Georgiev could let the secretary-general in and refuse to let the girl out. What would Chatterjee do, risk the lives of the other children by refusing to cooperate?

She might, Georgiev thought. And just having her challenge his authority in here might embolden the captives or else weaken his influence among his own people.

Georgiev looked back at the hostages. He had told the UN how to contact him and what to say when they did. His instincts told him to go downstairs, get another one, and have him make the same speech the last delegate had made. Why should he change his plan, let them think he lacked resolve?

Because situations like these are fluid, he told himself.

209

Then it came to him, suddenly, like his best ideas always did. A way to give Chatterjee what she wanted without compromising his demands. He would see her. Only not in the way she expected.

TWENTY-NINE

Washington, D.C.
Saturday, 11:33 P.M.

Most of the time, Bob Herbert was an easygoing man.

Over a decade and a half before, his injuries and the loss of his wife had tossed him into a depression that lasted for nearly a year. But physical therapy helped him to overcome self-pity, and getting back to work at the CIA bolstered the sense of self-worth that had been destroyed in the Beirut embassy explosion. Since helping to organize and launch Op-Center nearly three years before, Herbert had enjoyed some of the greatest challenges and rewards of his career. His wife would have found it very amusing that the chronic grouch she had married, the man whose spirits she'd always tried to raise, was known around the National Crisis Mangement Center as Mr. Upbeat.

Sitting alone in his dark office, which was lit only by the glow of the computer monitor, Herbert was neither easygoing nor upbeat. He wasn't only troubled by the fact that Paul Hood's daughter was one of the United Nations hostages. It wasn't only the knowledge that situations like this invariably ended in bloodshed. Sometimes it happened quickly, if the host nation or entity ousted the intruders before they could become entrenched. Sometimes it happened slowly, evolving from a standoff to a siege, which turned into an assault as soon as a plan could be formulated. On those rare occasions when a negotiated settlement could be reached, it was usually because the terrorists had only taken hostages to get attention for a cause. When they wanted money or the release of prisoners—which was most of the time—that was when things got messy.

What bothered him most were two things. First, the United Nations was the target. It had never been attacked in this way, and it did not have a record of taking a hard line with hostile agencies under any circumstances. Second, he was concerned about the E-mail he'd just received from Darrell McCaskey about the United Nations party roster. What the *hell* kind of an organization were those international innocents running?

McCaskey was at the Interpol office in Madrid. The former FBI agent had recently helped his friend Luis Garcia de la Vega break up the coup attempt and had stayed on to spend some time with his injured associate Maria Corneja. Security camera images of the United Nations assault had been sent to Interpol to see if any attacks in their files matched the modus operandi of this team. Interpol had also been sent a list of delegates and guests who attended the Security Council reception. A half hour before, McCaskey had forwarded that information to Herbert in Washington. All of the attendees were legitimate representatives of their nations though that did not, of course, make them diplomats. For over fifty years, innumerable spies, smugglers, assassins, and drug runners had been slipped in and out of the United States under the guise of being diplomats.

However, the United Nations had set a new personal worst for not running checks on two of the party guests.

When they came to the UN just two days ago, they had listed biographical data that could not be corroborated in the files of any of the schools or businesses they cited. Either there hadn't been time for their government to hack those files and insert the data, or the two didn't expect to be in New York long enough to be found out. The question Herbert needed to answer was, who *were* they?

McCaskey had obtained their ID photos from the deputy secretary-general of Administration and Head of Personnel at the United Nations. When they were E-mailed over, the Op-Center intelligence chief ran the photographs through a database comprised of images of more than twenty thousand international terrorists, foreign agents, and smugglers.

The two attendees were in that file.

Herbert read what little personal history was available on the pair—their real history, not the fake ones they'd given the United Nations. He didn't know anything about the people who had taken over the Security Council chamber, but he did know this: However bad those five terrorists were, these two could very well be worse.

Herbert had been informed by Striker that they were returning to Washington without General Rodgers or Colonel August. He didn't know where August could have gone, but he knew that Rodgers was with Hood. With no time to waste, Herbert called Hood on his cell phone.

THIRTY

New York, New York
Saturday, 11:34 P.M.

Not once in its long history has Cambodia known peace.

Prior to the fifteenth century, Cambodia was an expansive military power. Under the martial rule of the mighty Khmer emperors, the nation had conquered the entire Mekong River Valley, governing the lands that comprise modern-day Laos, the Malay Peninsula, and part of Siam. However, armies arose in unconquered sections of Siam and in the state of Annam in central Vietnam. Over the centuries that followed, these forces slowly pushed the Khmer armies back until the monarchy itself was threatened. In 1863, the desperate king of Cambodia agreed to the formation of a French protectorate over the country. A slow and steady arms buildup reclaimed lost lands, though the gains were forefeited when the Japanese occupied Indochina during World War II. Self-government was restored after the war, with Prince Norodom Sihanouk leading the country. Sihanouk was ousted in 1970 in a U.S.-backed military coup led by General Lon Nol. Sihanouk formed an exile government in Beijing while the Communist Khmer Rouge fought a civil war that overthrew Lon Nol in 1975. Sihanouk was restored to power as part of a shaky coalition government in what was now known as Democratic Kampuchea. Sihanouk's prime minister was the rabidly anti-Communist Son Sann. Sann was a cold bastard. But Sihanouk and his government were soon replaced by the more moderate and ineffective Khieu Samphan, who had as his prime minster the ruthless and ambitious Pol Pot. Pol Pot was a Maoist who believed that education was a curse and that returning to the land could transform Cambodia into a utopia. Instead, under his cruel hand, Cambodia became synonymous with "the killing fields" as torture, genocide, forced labor, and famine took the lives of over two million people—one of every five Cambodians. Pol Pot's rule lasted until 1979, when Vietnam invaded the nation. The Vietnamese seized control of Phnom Penh and established a Communist government led by Heng Samrin. But Pol Pot and the Khmer Rouge still controlled vast areas of what was now called the People's Republic of Kampuchea, and war continued to ravage the land. The Vietnamese withdrew in 1989 after sustained guerrilla warfare took a heavy toll on the occupation forces. Their withdrawal left new Prime Minister Hun Sen to struggle with groups that included the leftist Khmer Rouge, the rightist Khmer Bleu, the Sihanouk National Army loyal to the deposed prince, Lon Nol's Khmer National Armed Forces, the Khmer Loeu, which was comprised of ethnic hill tribes, and Khmer Viet Minh, who were supported by Hanoi, and nearly a dozen others.

In 1991, with the nation's economy and agriculture a shambles, the warring groups finally signed an accord that agreed to a cease-fire, widescale disarmament, and the presence of UN peacekeeping forces as well as UN-supervised elections. A new coalition with Hun Sen's party was formed, which reestablished the monarchy and placed Sihanouk on the throne as king. Feeling that they were being forced to give up too much power, the Khmer Rouge resumed fighting. The battle lost some of its momentum in 1998 with the death of Pol Pot. However, other senior Khmer Rouge officers and cadres remained in the field and vowed to continue the war.

As a result of so many political and military entities vying for power, secret government police and rebel agents vied ferociously for intelligence and weapons. Their needs gave rise to an unprecedented underground network of spies, killers, and smugglers. Some of these worked for what they believed was the good of their homeland. Others worked only for themselves.

For nearly ten years, thirty-two-year-old Ty Sokha Sary and her thirty-nine-year-old husband Hang Sary had been counterterrorist operatives for the Khmer People's National Liberation Armed Forces, the military component of the Khmer People's National Liberation Front. The KPNLF had been formed in March 1979 by former prime minister Son Sann. Initially, their goal was to oust the Vietnamese from Cambodia. When that had been accomplished, the KPNLF turned to cleansing all foreign influence from the nation. Even though Son Sann was named to the Supreme National Council, which governed the nation under Sihanouk, the leader privately opposed the involvement of the United Nations. Sann was especially opposed to the involvement of Chinese, Japanese, and French soldiers. He did not believe there could be such a thing as a benevolent occupying army. Even if the soldiers were engaged in peacekeeping, their very presence corrupted the nation's character and strength.

Ty and Hang agreed with Son Sann. And in coming to Cambodia, one foreign officer had done more than pollute their culture. He destroyed something very personal to Hang.

Ty Sokha knelt over the body of the wounded American girl. She couldn't be older than fourteen or fifteen. The Cambodian woman had seen so many girls like her, wounded or dying. And the dead. She had once helped Amnesty International locate a mass grave outside of Kampong Cham where over two hundred decomposed bodies were buried, most of them old women and very young children. Some of them had antigovernment slogans painted or sometimes carved on their bodies. Ty had also caused at least three dozen deaths by leading Hang to enemy officers or undercover operatives so that he could strangle them or slip a stiletto into their hearts while they slept. Sometimes Ty didn't bother to lead Hang there. Sometimes she did the work herself.

Like most military operatives who worked alone or in pairs, Ty had been trained in field medicine and was experienced in wound debridement. Unfortunately, the first aid kit she'd been given was inadequate for the task. There was no exit wound, which meant the bullet was still inside. If the girl moved, she could cause further damage. Ty used the antiseptic to clean the small, round hole as best she could. Then she covered it with gauze and strips of tape. She worked carefully, efficiently, but less dispassionately than usual. Though Ty had long ago become desensitized to terrorism and murder, this girl and the circumstances of the attack were too painfully familiar.

It was about Phum, of course, Hang's dear young sister.

As she worked, Ty thought back to the event that had brought them to such an unlikely place. A place so far from where they'd started.

Ty had grown up in a tiny farming hamlet midway between Phnom Penh and Kampot on the Gulf of Thailand. Her parents died in a flood when she was six years old, and she went to live with second cousin Hang Sary and his family. Ty and Hang adored one another, and it was always a given that they would marry. Eventually, they did, right before leaving on a mission together in 1990. They were alone save for a priest and his son, in a thunderstorm that had blown away the priest's hut. It was the happiest time of Ty's life.

Hang's father had been a very vocal supporter of Prince Sihanouk, contributing articles to the local newspaper about how the prince's free market policies had helped farmers. On a dark, muggy summer night in 1982, while Ty and Hang were in the city, soldiers of Pol Pot's National Army of Democratic Kampuchea came and carried Hang's father, mother, and young sister off. Hang found his parents two days later. His father was lying in a gully beside a dirt road. His arms had been tied behind his back, dislocating his shoulders. His feet and knees had been broken so he couldn't walk or crawl. Then his mouth had been packed with dirt and his throat had been punctured so that he would slowly bleed to death. His mother had been strangled before his helpless father. Hang did not find his younger sister.

Ty and Hang's world changed. Hang contacted Son Sann's KPNLF, which supported the prince. Hang told them he wanted to continue writing the kinds of articles his father wrote, but not just to promote Sihanouk. He wanted to draw the NADK killers out and repay them for what they did to his family. Before allowing Hang and Ty to use themselves as bait, the KPNLF's chief intelligence officer trained them in the use of weapons. Two months later, the small band of Khmer Rouge terrorists came to their hut. Hang and Ty had planned well and cut them down even before the KPNLF guard could summon help.

After that, the two were taught surveillance techniques. Along the way, they also learned the art of assassination. A CIA manual that had been found in Laos taught them how to use hat pins, rock-filled stockings, even stolen charge cards to stab eyes, break necks, and slice throats. They learned these skills to serve their country and also in the hope that one day they would find the monster who had ordered Phum's death.

The monster who had eluded them because he was under the protection of the Khmer Rouge.

The monster who they had lost track of when he left Cambodia, and who they had found again only recently.

The monster who was somewhere in this room.

A monster named Ivan Georgiev.

THIRTY-ONE

New York, New York
Saturday, 11:35 P.M.

Hood felt lonely and scared as he rode the elevator to
the seventh-floor lounge of the State Department. That
was where the other parents were waiting. There was no
one else in the elevator; just his own sorry reflection,
distorted and tinted by the highly polished gold-colored
walls.

If he weren't certain that security cameras were
watching him and that he'd end up getting hauled away
as a menace, Hood would have screamed and thrown
uppercuts at the air. He was deeply worried about the
rumors of a shooting, and he was miserable being on
the sidelines.

The elevator door opened, and as Hood stepped toward the security desk, his cell phone beeped. He
stopped walking and turned his back on the guard before
answering.

"Yes?" he said.

"Paul, it's Bob. Is Mike with you?"

Hood knew Herbert's voice very well. The intelligence chief was talking fast, which meant that he was
worried about something. "Mike went to see that local
office manager you told him about. Why?"

Hood knew that Herbert would have to speak

obliquely, since this was a potentially open line.

"Because there are two people in the target zone that he needs to know about," Herbert said.

"What kind of people?" Hood pressed.

"Heavy-duty rappers," Herbert replied.

People with rap sheets, a long history of no good. This was maddening. He had to know more.

"Their presence and the timing could be a coincidence," Herbert said, "but I don't want to risk it. I'll call Mike at the other office."

Hood walked back to the elevator and pushed the button. "I'll be there when you do," he said. "What's the name?"

"Doyle Shipping."

"Thanks," Hood said as the elevator arrived. He folded up the phone and stepped inside.

Sharon would never forgive him for this. Never. And he wouldn't blame her. She was not only alone among strangers, but he was certain the State Department wasn't telling the parents anything. But if the terrorists had associates on the inside that no one else knew about, he wanted to be on hand to help Rodgers and August think things through.

On the way down, Hood pulled his Op-Center ID from his wallet. He hurried through the lobby back to First Avenue and ran across the street and up four blocks. He flashed the ID to an NYPD guard who had been posted outside the United Nations Plaza towers. Though the towers were not part of the UN complex per se, a lot of delegates maintained offices here. He went inside.

Hood was breathless as he signed the security register and went to the first bank of elevators that led to the lower floors. He still wanted to scream and punch the air. But at least he was going to get involved in what was going on. At least he would have something to focus on other than fear. Not hope, but something almost as good.

An offensive.

THIRTY-TWO

New York, New York
Saturday, 11:36 P.M.

It was him.

The flat voice, the cruel eyes, the arrogant carriage—it was him, damn his soul. Ty Sokha couldn't believe that after nearly ten years they had found Ivan Georgiev. Now that she'd heard his voice beneath the mask, been close enough to smell his sweat, she knew which of these monsters it was.

Several months before, an arms dealer named Ustinoviks, who provided the Khmer Rouge with weapons, had been asked to talk to Georgiev about a buy. An informant with the Khmer Rouge knew that Ty and Sary Hang were looking for him. The informant sold them the name of the arms dealer. Though they had missed the Bulgarian when he came to New York to talk to Ustinoviks the first time, they managed to get to Ustinoviks after Georgiev had gone. The offer they made the Russian was simple: Let them know when he was coming to pick up his weapons or they would turn Ustinoviks over to the American FBI.

The Russian had let them know when Georgiev was scheduled to pick up his purchase with the provision that they didn't take him at that time. They agreed. As it happened, they didn't want him then. They wanted him

225

doing whatever it was he'd come here for, when the rest of the world could see, when they could draw attention to their own people, put an end to the countless murders in which they'd taken part as they tried to stop the Khmer Rouge and undermine the pathetically weak government of Norodom Sihanouk.

They'd watched Georgiev's team make their buy from the roof of the club next door to the shop owned by Ustinoviks. Ty couldn't really see him clearly then. Not as clearly as she had when she'd been at the UN camp, working as a cook, watching for Khmer Rouge infiltrators and seeing the degrading things for which Georgiev was responsible. But the government couldn't do anything without proof of what was going on, and anyone who tried to get that proof—or who tried to get away, like poor Phum had—died.

After Georgiev and his people made their arms purchase, Ty and Hang followed them back to their hotel. The adjoining rooms had been booked, so they took the room beneath theirs. They ran a wire through the ceiling fixture to the floor of his room, attached a sound amplifier, and listened as Georgiev and his allies reviewed their plans.

Then they'd gone to the Permanent Mission of the Kingdom of Cambodia across the street and waited.

Ty Sokha turned her large, dark eyes from the stricken young girl lying beside her. The one who was barely older than Phum had been when she'd been murdered by one of Georgiev's thugs. Ty looked over at Sary Hang, who was sitting on the floor, inside the circular table. The Cambodian operative had shifted his position slightly so that he could see Ty without seeming to watch her.

She nodded. He nodded back.

When Georgiev came back down the stairs, it would be time.

THIRTY-THREE

New York, New York
Saturday, 11:37 P.M.

Georgiev stopped when he reached the double doors
at the back of the Security Council chamber. He was
holding his automatic, though he didn't think he would
need it. Reynold Downer was standing to the right of
the doors. He had a weapon in either hand.

"Are you going to let her in?" Downer whispered.

"No," Georgiev said. "I'm going out there."

Georgiev could see that Downer was surprised, even
through his mask. "In God's name *why?*"

"They need a lesson in futility," Georgiev explained.

"Futility? They'll take *you* hostage!" Downer said.

The secretary-general spoke again. She asked to be
admitted.

"They wouldn't take the chance," Georgiev told
Downer. "This will convince them they have no choice
but to cooperate, and quickly."

"You're sounding like a bloody diplomat now. What
about them recognizing your accent?"

"I'll speak softly and deeply," Georgiev said.
"They'll probably assume I'm Russian." Now that he
thought of it, he would enjoy it if this entire takeover
were blamed on Moscow or the Russian Mafia.

"I don't agree with this," Downer said. "I bloody don't."

You wouldn't, Georgiev thought. Downer only knew how to bully, not how to finesse.

"I'll be all right," Georgiev said. Slowly, he reached for the knob on the left-side door. He turned and pushed the door open a crack.

Mala Chatterjee was standing there, her arms straight at her sides, her shoulders and head back. Behind her several paces was her head of security. Beyond him, Georgiev could see a few of the security guards with their blast shields.

Chatterjee's face was calm but resolute; the officer looked as though he wanted to snort fire. Georgiev liked that in an adversary. It kept one from becoming complacent.

"I'd like to speak with you," Chatterjee said.

"Tell everyone to step back, past the council chambers," Georgiev said. He didn't feel it was necessary to add that if anything happened to him, the hostages would suffer.

Chatterjee turned and nodded to Colonel Mott. Mott motioned for the rest of the security team to step away. They did. Mott remained where he was.

"Everyone," Georgiev said.

"It's all right, Colonel," Chatterjee said without turning.

"Madam Secretary—"

"Go, please," she said firmly.

Mott exhaled through his nose, then turned and joined his security team. He stood nearly thirty feet away, glaring at Georgiev.

That was good, Georgiev thought. She had just emasculated her chief of security. The colonel now looked like he wanted to draw his gun and put a bullet in Georgiev.

Chatterjee continued to stare at the Bulgarian.

"Now, you step back," Georgiev said.

She seemed surprised. "You want me to step back?"

He nodded. She took three steps back, then stopped. Georgiev opened the door farther. Shields rose slightly as arms tensed behind them. He could see a ripple of anxiety roll across the security team. He hoped the secretary-general could see, could *feel* how impossible her position was. Talkers and poor, untested schoolboys were all she had in her corner.

Georgiev holstered his weapon and stepped through the open door. Facing the security team, he shut the door behind him. Slowly, fearlessly. He was tempted to scratch his head or his side and watch them jump. But he didn't. Just knowing they would was enough. And more importantly, they knew it, too. They knew who had more courage and who was more at ease. Coming out here was the right thing to do. He looked at Chatterjee.

"What do you want?" he asked her.

"I want to resolve this situation without further bloodshed," she told him.

"You can," he replied. "Give us what we asked."

"I'm trying," she said. "But the nations have refused to pay."

He had expected that. "Then someone else must pay," he told her. "Let the United States rescue the world again."

"I can talk to them," she said, "but it will take time."

"You can have it," he said. "The price is one life every hour."

"No, please," Chatterjee said. "I would like to suggest something. A moratorium. I'll have a better chance of getting what you ask if I can tell them you're cooperating."

"Cooperating?" he said. "You're the one who's wasting time."

"But it will take hours, maybe days," she said.

Georgiev shrugged a shoulder. "Then the blood is on your hands, not on mine."

The secretary-general continued to look at him, though she was less composed than before. Her breathing was faster, her eyes more restless. That was good. He wanted compliance, not a negotiation. Behind her, Georgiev noticed the security chief shifting uneasily. He must not have come from the UN command ranks. He had the bearing of a tethered bull.

Chatterjee looked down. She shook her head slowly. She'd never had to deal with anything like this before. He almost felt sorry for her. What does a diplomat do when you keep saying no?

"I give you my word," she said. "Stop the killing. I will get you everything you want."

"You will get it for me anyway," he said.

Chatterjee looked at him. She seemed to be searching for something else to say, but it had all been said.

Georgiev turned toward the door.

"Don't do this," Chatterjee said.

He continued walking. He reached for the doorknob.

Chatterjee moved after him. "Don't you understand? No one will benefit from this," she said. She grabbed his arm in desperation.

Georgiev stopped and wrenched his arm toward him. The woman held on.

"Listen to me!" she implored.

So the peacemaker had claws. The big man threw his arm back. Chatterjee fell against the wall that stood out beyond the door. Georgiev turned back toward the door.

There were footsteps behind him. Georgiev reached for his automatic and turned just as an elbow came swinging across his line of vision.

His vision swirled red, the bridge of his nose and his forehead were numb, and he was light-headed. He was fighting to stay alert when a second blow turned everything black.

THIRTY-FOUR

New York, New York
Saturday, 11:42 P.M.

"Something just happened," Mike Rodgers said to Paul Hood.

Rodgers was sitting at the computer with Ani Hampton. Hood had arrived moments before, still breathing hard from the run. Ani had checked him on the video surveillance camera at the door and then buzzed him in. Rodgers wanted to know what had brought Hood here, but what was happening with Mala Chatterjee was what the military called "breaking news." Ani had put the bug's audio on the computer speakers. Even though the sound was being recorded, he didn't want to miss a word of the very faint conversation between the secretary-general and the terrorist.

"Paul Hood, Annabelle Hampton," Rodgers said, introducing them now that he found it difficult to hear anything at all.

Ani acknowledged Hood with a quick look and a nod. She seemed extremely intent on what was happening.

"We think something just happened outside the Security Council," Rodgers told Hood. "One of the terrorists came out to talk with the secretary-general. From the sound of things, she shouted and then someone—probably Colonel Mott of the UN security team, who we believe was closest to her—apparently attacked the terrorist. It sounds like they have him, but we can't be certain. Everyone is being very quiet."

They listened silently for a moment more. Then Hood spoke.

"This may not have anything to do with what's going on," he said, "but I just got a call from Bob. There are two people inside the Security Council who've spent at least eight years with the Cambodian Khmer People's National Liberation Armed Forces. They started as counterterrorists fighting the Khmer Rouge and then became assassins working for Son Sann."

Ani fired him a look.

"They came into the country two days ago with the permission of someone in their government, though their backgrounds were intentionally obscured," Hood continued. "The question is, are they there by chance, are they working with the terrorists, or is something else going on that we don't know about?"

Rodgers shook his head as there was another buzz at the door. Ani put the surveillance image on the computer; it was Brett August. Rodgers okayed him and Ani reached under the table to buzz him in. Rodgers excused himself to greet the Striker leader.

As Rodgers hurried to the office reception area, he reflected on the fact that this was the kind of situation that hostage negotiators in every country encountered every day. Some of the crises were large-scale political events that made the news; others were small and involved no more than one or two people in an apartment or convenience store. But all of them, wherever they were and whoever was involved, had one thing in common: volatility. In his experience, battles could change quickly, but they tended to change en masse. They'd pick up inertia and continue in one direction as the participating armies surged and flowed.

Hostage situations were different. They were subject to hair-trigger fluidity. They lurched, stalled, jerked, turned, and then ran in unpredictable ways. And the more people that were involved, the more likely that things would change dramatically at any given moment. Especially if those people were a mixture of frightened kids, fanatical terrorists, single-minded assassins, and diplomats whose only weapon was talk.

Colonel August was sweaty and grease-stained when he arrived. He saluted Rodgers, then explained that he'd done a pencil roll from the C-130's hydraulically operated cargo ramp while it was being raised. Since it was dark, no one saw him as he rolled tight and low down the ramp. There was a four-foot drop from the lip to the tarmac, and apart from a few bruises, the colonel was okay. He was wearing a Kevlar bulletproof vest under his sweatshirt and that had taken some of the impact. Because August was a fully equipped tourist, he'd had his wallet with him and enough cash for the cab ride to Manhattan.

Rodgers brought him up to date as they walked to Ani's office. As they neared, August stopped suddenly.

"Hold on," August said quietly.

"What's wrong?"

"You've got a pair of Cambodian assassins in the Security Council?" August asked.

"That's right."

August thought for a moment, then nodded toward the offices in back. "Did you know that your lady here worked for the CIA in Cambodia?"

"No," Rodgers said. He was openly surprised. "Tell me about it."

"I downloaded her file on the flight over," August said. "She recruited operatives in Cambodia for nearly a year."

Rodgers let his mind run through possible scenarios, looking for possible connections. "She signed in downstairs about fifteen minutes before the attack began. She said she'd come here to catch up on some work."

"That could very well be true," August said.

"It could," Rodgers agreed. "But she got here early *and* she has the ability to eavesdrop on the secretary-general. She also has a TAC-SAT in the office."

"Not standard CIA office issue," August said.

"No," Rodgers agreed. "Sounds like a nice setup if you want to pass intel to people who are involved in this takeover."

"But which side of the takeover?" August asked.

"I don't know," Rodgers said.

"Is the TAC-SAT turned on?" August asked.

"Can't tell. It's in a sack."

August snickered. "You spend too much time behind a desk. Roll up your sleeves."

"What do you mean?" Rodgers asked.

"Get the back of your arm near the unit," August said.

"I still don't follow."

"The hair. Static electricity," August told him.

"Shit," Rodgers said. "You're right."

An insulated piece of equipment, when active, would generate an electric discharge—static electricity. That would cause the hairs on his arm to stand up when he got close.

Rodgers nodded, and they continued toward the office.

Neither man was an alarmist. But from the start of their careers, with anywhere from one life to thousands of lives hanging on any decision they made, neither man had ever been complacent. And as Rodgers turned into the office, he reminded himself of something that the CIA had learned the hard way. That volatility didn't always come from the outside.

THIRTY-FIVE

New York, New York
Saturday, 11:43 P.M.

For a moment, the silence in the corridor outside the
Security Council was absolute. Then Secretary-General
Chatterjee pushed herself off the wall where she'd been
flung. She looked from the prone terrorist to Colonel
Mott.

"You had no right to do that!" she whispered harshly.

"You were attacked," he whispered back. "It's my
job to protect you."

"I grabbed *him*—"

"It doesn't matter," Mott said. He pointed to two of
the men on the security line and motioned them forward.
Then he turned back to Chatterjee. "We're in this now."

"*Against my wishes!*" she shot back.

"Ma'am, we can discuss this later," Mott said. "We
don't have much time."

"For what?" she demanded.

The two men arrived. "Strip him," Mott said quietly,
pointing to the terrorist. "Fast."

They got to work.

"What are you doing?" Chatterjee said.

The colonel began unbuttoning his own shirt. "Going
in there," he said. "As him."

Chatterjee seemed stunned. "No. Absolutely not."

241

"I can pull this off," he said. "We're about the same size."

"Not without my authority," she said.

"I don't need your authority," he replied as he removed his shirt and took off his shoes. "Section 13C, subsection 4, of the security regulations. In the event of a direct threat against the secretary-general, all appropriate precautions must be taken. He struck you. I saw it. Now the fiber-optic camera is not getting through for some reason. We're coming up on another hour, and a child may be hurt in there. Help me end this situation, ma'am. Did he have an accent?"

"They're going to find you out."

"Not soon enough," Mott said. He was aware of every second passing, wondering how long the terrorists inside were going to wait for their man to return. Fearing what they might do to get him back. "Now please," Mott pressed. "Did he have an accent?"

"Eastern European, I believe," Chatterjee said. She seemed dazed.

Mott looked down as one of his men removed Georgiev's mask. "Do you recognize him?"

Chatterjee looked at the beefy, unshaven face. There was blood on the thick bridge of the nose. "No," she said softly. "Do you?"

Mott looked from the fallen man to the Security Council door. "No." Whether it was his own anxiety or the instincts of an old undercover cop, he felt tension from inside the chamber. He had to defuse it before it exploded. The colonel motioned for his man to give him the mask. He pulled it over his head, then stooped and wiped some of the blood from Georgiev's nose onto the

242

mouth of the mask. "Now I don't have to do any accent," he said.

Chatterjee watched as he quickly finished pulling on the man's sweater, trousers, and shoes.

"Get everyone into the Trusteeship Council chambers," the colonel said to his second-in-command, Lieutenant Mailman. "I want you at the adjoining doors, fast but stealthy. Form two groups: a defensive perimeter and a team to get the hostages out. Go in when you hear gunfire." Mott picked up Georgiev's automatic and checked the clip. It was nearly full. "I won't fire until I'm in position to take out one or more of the terrorists. I'll try and stay on the north side to draw their fire away from you. You know how they're dressed; take them out. Just make sure you don't shoot the guy who's shooting at them."

"Yes, sir," the officer replied.

"Ma'am, I'd get Interpol in here to find out who this *individual* is." Mott practically spit out the word. "If something goes wrong, the information may help you stop them."

"Colonel, I'm against this," Chatterjee said. The secretary-general had collected herself and was growing angry. "You're risking the lives of everyone in the room."

"Everyone in there is going to die unless we get them out," he replied. "Isn't that what this person told you?" He indicated Georgiev with his foot. "Isn't that why you tried to stop him from going back?"

"I wanted to stop the killing—"

"And he didn't give a damn what you wanted," Colonel Mott said in a raspy whisper.

243

"No, he didn't," she agreed. "But I can still go in there, try to talk to the others."

"Not after this," Mott said. "They'll want to know where their man is. What will you tell them?"

"The truth," she said. "It might persuade them to cooperate. Perhaps we can even give him back in exchange for hostages."

"We can't," Mott said. "We may need him for information. And whatever else happens, this bastard's got to stand trial." Mott had always admired Chatterjee's persistence. Right now, though, it seemed more naive than visionary.

While the lieutenant formed his two teams, the colonel signaled over the emergency medical team. They placed the fallen terrorist on a stretcher and used handcuffs from one of the security officers to keep him there.

"Take him over to the infirmary, and keep him handcuffed to the cot," Mott told the head emergency medical technician.

The lieutenant signaled Mott that he was ready to go. Colonel Mott signaled back thirty with his fingers. He looked at his watch as Lieutenant Mailman's two teams headed into the Trusteeship Council chamber. Then he started marking off thirty seconds.

"Colonel, please," Chatterjee said. "I can't go in if you do."

"I know," he said. Twenty-five seconds to go.

"But this is a mistake!" she said, raising her voice for the first time.

There was a creak at the Security Council door, as though someone had leaned against it. Chatterjee immediately fell silent. Mott looked from the door to Chatterjee to his watch. Twenty seconds remained.

"It's only a mistake if it fails," Colonel Mott said quietly. "Now, please, Madam Secretary-General. There's no time to debate this. Just step back so you won't be hurt."

"Colonel—" she started, then stopped. "God be with you," she said. "God be with you all."

"Thank you," Mott replied. There were fifteen seconds to go.

Reluctantly, Chatterjee backed away.

Colonel Mott turned his attention to what he was about to do. He could taste the terrorist's blood through the mask. There was something appropriately barbaric, Viking about it. He stuck the terrorist's gun in his belt, where it had been when he came out. Then he flexed and unflexed his gloved fingers, anxious to get in there and do his job.

Ten seconds.

Twenty-odd years ago, when he was an NYPD cadet at the academy on Twentieth Street and Second Avenue, a strategy and tactics instructor told him that the job really came down to dice. Every police officer, every soldier, had a die with six pips. The pips were resolve, skill, ruthlessness, ingenuity, courage, and strength. Most of the time, you practice-rolled. You trained, you walked a beat, you patrolled the street, trying to get the wrist action right, the finesse, the feel. Because when it came time to roll for real, you had to come up with more of those qualities than the other guy, sometimes in an instant. Mott remembered that during his twenty years in Midtown South. He remembered it each time he went to an apartment with no idea what was on the other side of the door, or stopped a car without knowing what was hidden under the newspaper lying next to the driver. He remembered it now. He brought up every reflex that was stored in his memory, in his bones, in his soul. And for good measure, he threw in the words of one of the original Mercury astronauts, he forgot which one, who said, as he waited to be launched into space: *"Dear God. Please don't let me screw this up."*

Five seconds.

Alert and ready, Mott walked toward the door of the Security Council. He moaned, as though he'd been hit and was hurting.

He yanked open the door and stepped inside.

THIRTY-SIX

New York, New York
Saturday, 11:48 P.M.

Telephones were put at the disposal of the parents
when they arrived at the State Department lounge. Se-
lecting an armchair in the corner of the brightly lighted
lounge, Sharon's first call had been to Alexander back
at the hotel. She wanted to make sure he was all right.
He was fine, though she suspected he'd stopped playing
video games and had accessed the room's SpectraVision
channel. Alexander always sounded edgy when he was
playing video games, as though the fate of the galaxy
rested on his shoulders. When she called around eleven
o'clock he sounded awestruck and humbled. Like Charlton Heston when he saw the burning bush in *The Ten
Commandments.*

Sharon let him be. She didn't even tell him what was
going on. She had a feeling that Alexander would be
sleeping very well tonight. Hopefully, it would all be
over in the morning before he woke. Then she called
her home answering machine. She wasn't going to call
her parents unless they'd seen the news report and left
a message. They were not in the best of health, and they
were worriers. She didn't want to burden them.

But her mother had phoned. She had seen the news
flash, so Sharon called her back. She told her mother

247

what she'd been told, that officials were trying to negotiate a solution and that there was no other news.

"What does Paul think?" her mother asked.

"I don't know, Mom," Sharon replied.

"What do you mean?"

"He went off with one of the military people from the UN and hasn't come back yet," Sharon said.

"He's probably trying to help," her mother said.

Sharon wanted to say, *He's always trying to help—them.* Instead, she said, "I'm sure that's what he's doing."

Her mother asked how she was doing. Sharon said that she and the other parents were holding tight to hope, and that was all they could do. She promised to call if anything else happened.

Thinking of Paul and his devotion to *them* upset her. She wanted her daughter back and was willing to make any sacrifice to save her. But she knew that Paul would be doing this even if Harleigh weren't inside. Sharon hadn't cried very much since this began, but that pushed her over the rim.

She turned from the other parents and wiped tears away as they formed. She tried to convince herself that Paul was doing this for Harleigh. And even if he weren't, whatever he did would help her.

But she felt so alone now. And not knowing what was happening, how her baby was, made her angry again. The least Paul could do was call her. Tell her what was happening.

Then she thought of something. Taking a tissue from her purse, Sharon blew her nose and picked up the phone. Paul still had his cell phone with him. She punched in his number, finding strength in anger that had not come in reflection.

THIRTY-SEVEN

New York, New York
Saturday, 11:49 P.M.

Ty Sokha continued to squat beside the girl on the floor. There was nothing more she could do for her, but then she hadn't come here to save lives. Taking care of the girl had done one thing and one thing only: It had enabled her to establish which of these men was Ivan Georgiev. Which of them owned the voice she had heard in the UN camp as it ushered customers in and out of tents. Which of them had ordered his aide to pursue and shoot Phum when she tried to escape. In case Ty and Hang could not get all the terrorists, they wanted to make sure they got him.

Ty had a compact 9mm Browning High Power handgun in her purse. Hang had one in a holster hooked to the back of his belt. The weapons had been smuggled past UN security in diplomatic pouches. Between the two of them, they'd get the bastard in a cross fire and then take down the rest of the terrorists. Not only would they have their revenge, not only would they be seen as heroes for rescuing the hostages, but their cause—a strong, right-wing Cambodia under Son Sann—would acquire worldwide attention. Injustice would end. The Khmer Rouge would finally be hunted down and destroyed. Cambodia would be free to become an Asian political and financial power.

But all of that depended on what happened next. Ty was sorry she'd let Georgiev go, but she hadn't expected him to leave. And she didn't want to fire on her own without identifying him to Hang, in case the other terrorists managed to bring her down.

Ty opened her purse and removed a silk handkerchief. She left her purse open on the floor as she dabbed the forehead of the wounded girl. The butt of the Browning was pointing toward her. When she replaced the handkerchief, she took the opportunity to unlock the safety. She was getting anxious. She hoped the miserable creature didn't negotiate a deal with Secretary-General Chatterjee. Ty grew quietly furious with herself for not having taken him out when she had the chance. He had been standing right next to her. She might have died, but she would have died knowing how proud Hang and the spirits of his family were of her.

Suddenly, one of the double doors flew open at the top of the stairs on the opposite side of the chamber. The terrorist who had been standing behind it jumped to the side as Georgiev stormed back in. The Bulgarian was holding the lower part of his mask. He slammed the door shut, drew his pistol, and shook it angrily at the door. Then he turned and stalked past his associate. When the other man tried to follow, Georgiev motioned for him to remain where he was. Then he half-walked, half-stumbled down the stairs. He seemed a little groggy, as though he'd been struck. He did not look happy.

That was good. According to the doctrine of the elders in the Theravada Buddhist faith, a man who died un-

250

happy remained so in the next life. Ty felt that Georgiev deserved no less.

The Bulgarian was holding his gun. He stopped midway down the stairs and rubbed his chin. He seemed to waver.

The man at the top of the steps came toward him. So did one of the men at the bottom of the steps.

Damn, Ty thought. It had to be now. Soon there would be three of them in one place; she might not have a clear shot.

She looked at Hang. He was obviously thinking the same thing. She reached into her purse as Hang rose. He drew his weapon from the holster and turned toward his target. Ty slipped her own handgun free and followed his lead. Hang fired first, putting three shots into Georgiev before the others arrived. One bullet missed, but two red blotches popped from his forehead, and the Bulgarian was flung back-first against the wall. He slid straight to the ground, dragging three long red smears down the green and gold wallpaper.

The couple began running foward, seeking cover on the stairwell. The two other men on the stairs stopped, ducked behind the chairs, and swung their guns toward the shootists. The two terrorists on the other side of the chamber also ducked and aimed at the attackers. As they did, the door that led to the Trusteeship Council chamber opened. Four members of the United Nations security force rushed in. There was a heart-stopping moment when the only sounds were the sobbing of children. The two Cambodians turned to see who was behind them, and the terrorists paused to aim at the nearest targets.

The distraction enabled the terrorists beside Georgiev along the south wall to fire at Ty and Hang. The Cambodians were crouched near the wall at the foot of the gallery and went down. Hang took a bullet in the shoulder, Ty in the thigh. Ty twisted and fell silently onto her back; Hang went to his hands and knees and screamed, though his cry was cut short by a head shot. The bullet came in at an angle from the front and dropped him flat on the floor.

Ty had lost her handgun when she fell and was reaching for it when a second shot caught her in the upper arm and a third struck her in the belly. She reached for her abdomen, stopping suddenly when a fourth shot cracked through the top of her skull.

It took slightly more than a second for the Cambodians to fall and die. But their presence had confused the UN police, who weren't sure whether to fire at them or not. The delay enabled the terrorists on the north side of the chamber to turn, aim, and fire straight down the stairs, at the door. One security officer went down, shot through the leg, and had to be pulled out. The other three who had entered squatted and returned fire to cover the withdrawal. Noticing the wounded girl, one of the men grabbed her under the arms and dragged her back.

One of the terrorists on the southern side of the chamber went down. He rolled down several steps before his head struck one of the chairs. One of the UN officers was shot in the face and simply fell over. The room was an echo chamber of thundercrack shots and screams as the terrorists battled the UN police and the hostages cried out. Many of those who were screaming were trying to duck and at the same time attempting to keep other panicked hostages from running madly into the line of fire.

The firefight ended when the UN forces withdrew and

the door to the Trusteeship Council chamber crashed shut. The gunshots stopped but not the screaming. Nor the sense of madness that, for a few deadly seconds, seemed to infect everyone in the chamber.

THIRTY-EIGHT

New York, New York
Saturday, 11:50 P.M.

Reynold Downer lay Georgiev's bloody body down while Etienne Vandal knelt over him.

"You better go back to the door," Vandal said. "They may try to come in again."

"I will," Downer said. He pulled his bloodred gloves from under Georgiev and looked across the room. The smaller of the two terrorists was running down the stairs. That meant Sazanka had taken the hit. Downer watched as Barone bent over him. The Uruguyan stood and dragged a finger across his throat. Their pilot was dead.

Downer swore. So did Vandal. Downer looked down.

Vandal had removed Georgiev's mask. Only it wasn't Georgiev who was lying on the landing.

"Then they've got him," Downer said. "I thought I heard noise out there. The bastards have got him." He spit on the American-looking face that lay lifeless on the carpet.

Vandal pulled back the man's glove and felt for a pulse. He dropped the man's wrist. "He's dead." Vandal looked down at the bodies lying near the gallery. "Those were UN security police who came in, and I'll bet this man was with them. But who were those other two?"

"Probably undercover police," Downer said. "Working security for the party."

"Then why didn't they move sooner?" Vandal wondered aloud. "Try and save the delegates?"

"Maybe they sent some kind of silent signal for reinforcements," Downer said. "They were just waiting."

"I don't think so," Vandal said. "They almost seemed surprised when they saw the United Nations team come in."

Downer went back up the stairs, and Vandal turned and hurried down the steps. He was worried about the doors, though he didn't really think there would be another attack now. The UN forces had gotten hurt. They took away the wounded girl, but he didn't think that was their objective. They came in looking like they wanted to establish a beachhead. Four in with reinforcements waiting to move through the center. Why didn't the reinforcements pull the girl out?

The firefight had put the hostages low on the floor or sent them ducking under the table. Vandal would leave them where they were for now. There was a lot of sobbing and whimpering, but everyone had been rattled by the attack. No one was going anywhere.

Vandal reached the two people who had been killed at the foot of the gallery. They were Asian. He squatted and checked the pockets of the man's jacket. He had a Cambodian passport. There was a connection, at least. Georgiev was into a number of unsavory businesses during the UNTAC operation, from spying to prostitution. Maybe this was supposed to be some kind of payback. But how did they know he was here?

Barone had come over. Vandal dropped the passport and rose.

"Is he dead?" Barone asked, nodding toward Georgiev.

"It isn't him," Vandal said.

"What?"

"They got him when he went out," Vandal said. "Made a switch."

"Who would have thought they had the *cajones?*" Barone said. "That could be why the security team came in. They were following their man's lead."

"Very possibly," Vandal said.

Barone shook his head. "If he gives them information about the bank accounts, then even if we get out of here with the money, they'll take it right back."

"Agreed," Vandal said.

"So what do we do?" Barone asked.

"We still have what they want," Vandal said, thinking aloud. "And we still have the means to kill the hostages if the security forces come in again. So I suggest we stick to our plan with two differences."

"What?" Barone asked.

Vandal turned toward the conference table. "We tell them we want cash," he said as he walked forward, "and we speed up the clock."

His eyes moved from the empty seat where the girl who ran had been sitting. They settled on Harleigh Hood. There was something about her, something defiant, that hit him wrong.

He told Barone to get her.

THIRTY-NINE

New York, New York
Saturday, 11:51 P.M.

The audio bug in the corridor picked up the shots from the Security Council chamber. The reports were muffled, as were the shouts in the corridor, but it was clear to Paul Hood and the others that one side or the other had made a move. The shouts continued after the gunfire had stopped.

Hood was standing behind Ani. Except for swinging over to a laptop on another desk—to try and boost the audio quality, she said—the young agent had stayed at her post. She was calm and very focused.

August was standing to Hood's left. Rodgers had removed his jacket, rolled up his sleeves, and had pulled a chair from the other desk. He had asked for, and was given, a book of blueprints of the United Nations. Hood had a look at the book over Rodgers's shoulder. The FBI had obviously assembled the blueprints in order to plant primitive eavesdropping devices in structural materials back in the 1940s. Updated notations on the pages suggested that the CIA also used the blueprints to program routes for their mobile bugs.

On the floor near where Rodgers had pulled his chair was an upright canvas case. The zippered bag was open on top, and Hood could see a TAC-SAT phone inside.

As Hood stood there listening, he heard his cell phone beep. He assumed it was Bob Herbert or Ann Farris with information. Hood slipped the phone from his pocket. Mike Rodgers rose and came over.

"Hello?" Hood said.

"Paul, it's me."

"Sharon," Hood said. *Christ, not now,* he thought.

Rodgers stopped. Hood turned his back to the room.

"I'm sorry, hon," Hood said quietly. "I was on my way up to see you when something happened. Something that had to do with Mike."

"He's here?"

"Yes," Hood said. He wasn't really listening to the phone. He was trying to hear what was happening in the Secretariat Building. "Are you holding up okay?" he asked.

"You've got to be kidding," she said. "Paul, I need you."

"I know," he said. "Look, we're in the middle of something here. We're trying to get Harleigh and the others out. Can I call you back?"

"Sure, Paul. Just like always." Sharon hung up.

Hood felt like he'd been slapped. How could two people be so close one night, then be totally unconnected the next day? But he didn't feel guilty. He felt angry. He was doing this to try and save Harleigh. Sharon wasn't happy being alone, but that wasn't what the hang-up was about. It was about the fact that Op-Center had separated them again.

Hood folded his phone and put it away. Mike placed a hand on Hood's shoulder.

Suddenly, they heard Chatterjee's voice clearly.

"Lieutenant Mailman, what happened?" the secretary-general asked.

"Someone shot Colonel Mott before the rest of the team went in," he said breathlessly. "He may be dead."

"No," Chatterjee said while he was still speaking. "God, no."

"They killed one of my people and then we got one of the terrorists before withdrawing," the lieutenant went on. "We also pulled a girl out. She'd been shot. There was no way we could get in without taking a lot of casualties."

Hood felt his knees weaken.

"I'll find out who it is," Rodgers said. "Don't call Sharon. You may worry her for nothing."

"Thanks," Hood said.

Rodgers went to the office phone and called Bob Herbert. In order to keep track of known terrorists and underworld figures—many of whom were regularly hurt in explosions, car accidents, or gunfights—Op-Center had a program that was connected with all the big-city hospitals and interfaced with the Social Security Administration. Whenever a social security number was entered on a hospital computer, it was checked against Op-Center's database to make sure that the person wasn't someone the FBI or police were looking for. In this case, Herbert would have Matt Stoll check on everyone who was admitted to a UN-area New York hospital in the last half hour.

The conversation continued in the Secretariat.

"You did the right thing pulling out," Chatterjee said.

"There's something else," the lieutenant said. "Two of the delegates were armed and firing."

"Which two?" Chatterjee said.

"I don't know," the lieutenant replied. "One of the team members who got a good look said it was an Asian man and woman."

"It could be Japan, South Korea, or Cambodia," Chatterjee said.

"Both of the delegates were killed by the terrorists."

"Who were the delegates shooting at?" Chatterjee asked.

"Believe it or not, they were firing at Colonel Mott," he replied.

"At the colonel?" she said. "They must have mistaken him for—"

"The terrorist he replaced," the lieutenant said.

A radio beeped as the lieutenant was speaking. Chatterjee answered it. "This is Secretary-General Chatterjee."

"That was stupid and reckless," said the voice on the other end. The man's voice was scratchy and faint and spoken with an accent, but Hood was able to make out most of what was being said. Concentrating on that was a welcome distraction from thinking about the wounded girl.

"I'm sorry for what happened," Chatterjee said. "We tried to reason with your partner—"

"Don't try and make this *our* fault!" the caller snapped.

"No, it was all mine—"

"You knew the rules, and you ignored them," he said. "Now we have new instructions for you."

"First tell me," Chatterjee said. "What is the condition of our officer?"

"He's dead."

"Are you sure?" Chatterjee implored.

There was a shot. "Now I am," the caller replied. "Do you have any other questions?" he asked.

"No," Chatterjee said.

"You can come and get him when we're gone," said the terrorist. "How soon that happens is up to you."

There was a short, painful silence. "Go ahead," Chatterjee said. "I'm listening."

"We want the helicopter with six million American dollars," he said. "We want cash, not transfers. You have our man; he may tell you our names. I don't want our accounts frozen. Let us know when the helicopter is here. We will resume the killing in eight minutes and again every half hour. Only this time we won't be killing delegates. We'll continue on the young ladies."

Hood realized he had never known hate until that instant.

"Oh please, no!" Chatterjee cried.

"You made this happen," the caller said.

"Listen to me," Chatterjee said. "We'll *get* what you want but there must be no more killing. There has been too much already."

"You have eight minutes."

"No! Give us a few hours!" Chatterjee implored. "We'll cooperate with you. Hello? *Hello!*"

All was quiet. Hood could imagine the depth of the secretary-general's frustration.

August shook his head. "The troops ought to go back in now, hit them fast when they don't expect it."

"We ought to go in," Hood said.

"They said they'll release poison gas," Ani told them.

"But they didn't during the first assault," August said. "Hostage-takers want to live. That's why they've

263

got hostages. They won't give up that advantage."

Rodgers turned from the phone. "It wasn't Harleigh who was shot," he said. "The girl's name is Barbara Mathis."

Everything was relative. Harleigh was still a prisoner, and one of her ensemble mates was injured. Yet relief washed over Hood from the inside out.

Despite the fact that Harleigh was still in there, Hood had to agree with August. The men in the Security Council chambers were not suicide bombers or political terrorists. They were pirates, here for plunder. They wanted to get out alive.

After a moment, Chatterjee informed the lieutenant that she was going to the infirmary. She wanted to talk to the captured terrorist. There was no further audio after the secretary-general left.

"She's out of range of the bug," Ani said.

Rodgers looked at his watch. "We've got less than seven minutes," he said sharply. "What can we do to stop them?"

"There isn't enough time to go to the Security Council and get inside," August said.

"You've been listening to this for nearly five hours," Rodgers said to Ani. "What do you think?"

"I don't know," she said.

"Guess," Rodgers pressed.

"They're leaderless," she said. "There's no telling what they might do now."

"How do you know that?" Hood asked.

She looked at him.

"That they're leaderless?" he said.

"Who else would have gone out to talk for them?" she asked.

The phone rang, and Ani picked up. It was Darrell McCaskey for Rodgers. Ani passed him the phone. Something else passed between Rodgers and the woman as well. A disapproving look. Or was it doubt?

The conversation was short. Rodgers stood there saying very little as Darrell McCaskey briefed him. When he was finished, he handed the receiver back to Ani. She turned and lay it in the cradle.

"UN Security fingerprinted the captured terrorist," Rodgers said. "Darrell just got the intel." Rodgers looked back at Ani. He leaned over her chair, his hands on the armrests. "Talk to me, Ms. Hampton."

"What?" she said.

"Mike, what is it?" Hood asked.

"The terrorist's name is Colonel Ivan Georgiev," Rodgers said. He was still looking down at Ani. "He served with UNTAC in Cambodia. He also worked with the CIA in Bulgaria. Did you ever hear of him?"

"Me?" Ani asked.

"You."

"No," she said.

"But you know something about this that we don't," Rodgers said.

"No—"

"You're lying," Rodgers said.

"Mike, what's going on?" Hood asked.

"She came to the office before the attack," Rodgers said. He moved closer to Ani. "To work, you said."

"That's right."

"You're not dressed for work," Rodgers said.

"I was stood up," she said. "That's why I came here. I had reservations at Chez Eugenie, you can check. Hey, I don't know why I have to defend myself to—"

"Because you're lying," Rodgers said. "Did you know this was going to happen?"

"Of course not!" she said.

"But you knew *something* was going to happen," Rodgers said. "You served in Cambodia. Colonel Mott was killed by a pair of Cambodians posing as delegates to the United Nations. Did they think they were shooting Ivan Georgiev?"

"How the hell should I know?" Ani cried.

Rodgers shoved the chair back. It rolled across the tile floor and slammed into a filing cabinet. Ani started to rise, and Rodgers pushed her back down.

"Mike!" Hood shouted.

"We don't have time for this bullshit, Paul," Rodgers said. "Your daughter could be the next one they kill!" He glared down at Ani. "Your TAC-SAT is on. Who were you calling?"

"My superior in Moscow—"

"Call him now," Rodgers said.

She hesitated.

"Call him now!" Rodgers yelled.

Ani didn't move.

"Who's on the other end of that line?" Rodgers demanded. "Was it the Cambodians, or is it the terrorists?"

Ani said nothing. Her hands were on the armrests. Rodgers slapped one of his hands on top of hers. She couldn't move it. He pushed a thumb under her index finger and bent it back. She screamed and reached over with her other hand to try and pry him off. He used his free hand to shove her hand back to the armrest and kept up his pressure on the other.

"Who's on the other end of the goddamn *phone?*" Rodgers yelled.

"I told you!"

Rodgers bent the finger back until the nail was nearly touching the wrist. Ani screamed.

"Who's on the other end?" Rodgers pressed.

"The terrorists!" Ani cried. "It's the terrorists!"

Hood felt sick.

"Are there any other outside units besides you?" Rodgers demanded.

"No!"

"What are you supposed to do next?" Rodgers asked.

"Tell them if the money's really being delivered," she said.

Rodgers released her hand. He rose.

Hood was staring at the young woman. "How could you help them? *How?*"

"We don't have time for that now," Rodgers said. "They're going to kill someone else in three minutes. The question is how do we stop them?"

"By paying them," August said.

Rodgers looked at him. "Explain."

"We get Chatterjee's number from Op-Center," August said. "We ask her to get on the radio to tell the terrorists she has the money. Then our lady here corroborates that. We contact the NYPD, get a chopper over there like they asked for, and have a SWAT unit take them when they come out."

"They'll come out, but with hostages," Hood said.

"We're going to have to risk the hostages at some point," August said. "At least this way we'll save more than we could in the Security Council—and one of them for sure."

"Do it," Hood said, glancing at his watch. "Fast."

FORTY

New York, New York
Saturday, 11:55 P.M.

Secretary-General Chatterjee raced down the escalator
to the infirmary, which was located on the first floor not
far from the visitor's lobby. An aide had joined her at
the foot of the escalator and was walking with her. Enzo
Donati was a young graduate student from Rome who
was earning credits for his degree in international relations. He had her cell phone and he was in touch with
the New York office of Interpol. They had learned that
the prisoner's name was Ivan Georgiev, a former officer
in the Bulgarian army. The Bulgarian ambassador had
not been at the soiree and had been notified.

Chatterjee passed through the Delegates Only doorway near the Hiroshima exhibit and made her way along
the brightly lighted corridors. She tried not to think of
the loss of Colonel Mott or the other security personnel,
or of the deaths of the delegates. She focused on the
approach of midnight, on the impending death of one of
the young violinists, and how to avoid it. Chatterjee had
it in mind to offer Georgiev a deal. If he would urge his
accomplice to postpone the shooting, and help to defuse
the situation, she would do what she could to get him
clemency.

Chatterjee assumed, of course, that Georgiev was even

269

awake. She hadn't spoken to the emergency medical people since they'd brought him down here. If not, she didn't know what she was going to do. They had less than five minutes. Mott's military approach had been repulsed, and her own diplomatic efforts had failed. Co-operation was an option, but the six million dollars they asked for would take time to put together. She had called Deputy Secretary-General Takahara and asked him to sit down with the other members of the emergency team to figure out how to do that. She knew that even if they paid, there would still be further bloodshed. The NYPD or the FBI would move in as soon as the terrorists tried to leave. But at least there was a chance that they could still get some of the delegates and young violinists away safely.

Why did international crises seem so much more man-ageable than this? Because the ramifications were so se-vere? Because there were two or more sides where no one really wanted to pull the trigger? If that were true, then she really wasn't a peacemaker. She was simply a medium, like a telephone or even one of her father's movies. She may have come from the land of Gandhi but was nothing like him. Nothing.

They turned a corner and approached the door to the infirmary. Enzo slipped ahead of the secretary-general and opened it for her. Chatterjee walked in. She stopped abruptly.

Two EMTs were lying on the floor in the reception area. The attending nurse was also lying on the floor, in the doctor's office. So were a pair of security guards.

Enzo ran to the nearest bodies. There were spots of blood on the tile. The technicians were alive but unconscious, evidently from blows to the head. The nurse was also unconscious.

There were no tears in their clothes, no indication that there had been a struggle.

There was no trace of the handcuffs and no sign of Georgiev.

As Chatterjee took a moment to process what had happened, there was only one conclusion to be drawn: that someone had been here waiting.

FORTY-ONE

New York, New York
Saturday, 11:57 P.M.

Hood called Bob Herbert and told him to get them
Chatterjee's mobile phone number. While Hood held the
line, Rodgers bound Ani Hampton to her chair. He used
black electrical tape he'd found in the supply closet to
tie her left wrist to the armrest. There had been pack-
aging twine on the shelf, but using tape was a habit from
field interrogations: it didn't leave marks or tear the skin,
and it was tougher to work lose. Rodgers had also found
several handguns and other CIA field gear in the closet.
The guns were locked in a metal gun rack. After binding
Ani, Rodgers took the key case from her blazer, which
was hanging in the closet. CIA regulations required that
whoever was in charge of a shell have access to the
"self-defense matériel." Rodgers found the key that unlocked the rack and took a pair of Berettas for himself
and another pair for August. Each handgun held a clip
with a fifteen-shell capacity. He also grabbed a pair of
point-to-point radios along with a brick of C-4 and det-
onators. He put the explosives in a foam-lined backpack
and slung it over one shoulder. It wasn't the usual
Striker kit—night vision glasses and Uzis would be
ideal—but it would have to do. He hoped he didn't need
any of these, but he wanted to be prepared for the worst.

273

Upon returning to the office, Rodgers looked down at Ani. "If you cooperate, I'll help you when we get out of here."

She didn't respond.

"Do you understand?" Rodgers pressed.

"I understand," she said without looking up.

After handing August his guns, Rodgers took the colonel's arm. He led him to where Hood was standing, still holding the phone.

"What's wrong?" August asked.

"I don't have a good feeling about our prisoner," Rodgers said quietly.

"Why?" Hood asked.

"In a few minutes, she's going to have us by the short hairs," Rodgers said. "Suppose Chatterjee calls the terrorists for us. Then this woman refuses to back up the lie. Where are we then?"

"I'd say pretty much where we are now," August told him.

"Not exactly," Rodgers said. "The terrorists will have been attacked and then lied to. They're going to want to hit back. Shoot a hostage as scheduled and add another as payback."

"Are you saying we shouldn't do this?" Hood asked.

"No, I don't think we have a choice," Rodgers said. "Because, if nothing else, we can buy ourselves a few extra minutes."

"For what?" Hood asked.

"To take control of this situation," Rodgers said. "To launch a bottleneck operation."

August seemed pleased.

Hood shook his head. "With what kind of force?" he asked. "The pair of you?"

274

"It can work," Rodgers told him.

"I repeat—with just two soldiers?" Hood asked.

"In theory, yes," Rodgers said.

Hood didn't seem happy with that answer.

"We've run simulations," Rodgers went on. "Brett has drilled for this."

"Mike," Hood said, "even if you can get in there, the hostages are going to be extremely vulnerable."

"Like I said, what do you think is going to happen if our lady friend here turns on us?" Rodgers asked. "We've got human gunpowder in a keg, and we're applying a match. The terrorists are going to blow."

Hood had to admit that Rodgers had a point. He looked at his watch. "Bob?" he said into the phone.

"I'm here," said Herbert.

"What's happening with the phone number?"

"The State Department still only has the number for Secretary-General Manni, if you can believe it. I've got Darrell working on getting the number through Interpol and Matt trying to hack it," Herbert said. "I'm betting on Matt getting it first at this point. Another minute or two."

"Bob, we're measuring time in seconds," Hood said.

"Understood," Herbert replied.

Hood looked at Rodgers. "How do you both get inside?"

"Only Colonel August has to go in," Rodgers continued. "I'll take the base position, which will be outside the Security Council." He looked at August. "The entrance to the UN garage is located on the northeast side of the compound, down a flight of stairs that are on a direct line from the front door of this building. That's where you get in."

"How do you know the garage will be open?" Hood asked.

"It was open when I came here," Rodgers said, "and they're obviously keeping it that way in case they want to move personnel or equipment in. The terrorists might hear the sound of a big door like that shutting and then opening. It could tip them off, if something were up."

That was a good point, Hood thought.

"There probably won't be any security personnel in the rose garden leading to the garage," Rodgers said to August. "They'll keep the perimeter itself guarded to maximize manpower. If there are choppers, you'll have sufficient cover under the bushes or statues. Once you get through the park and into the garage, your only problem will be the corridor between the elevator and the Security Council. According to the blueprints, the elevator shaft lets off about fifty feet down the main corridor from the Security Council."

"Isn't that a big problem?" Hood asked.

"Not really," August said. "I can cover fifty feet pretty quick. I'll bowl people down if I have to. Surprise works against your own people, too."

"What if the security personnel fire at you?" Hood asked.

"I heard foreign accents on our little bug," August said. "I'm sure there are UN personnel I can use as a shield. Once I get inside the Security Council, it doesn't matter what they do."

"It's still an extra impediment," Hood said.

"Maybe we can convince Chatterjee to help us, if it comes to that," August suggested.

"If the lie about the ransom doesn't work, I doubt she'll go with a second lie," Hood said. "Diplomats

276

who were never soldiers don't understand the quicksilver nature of warfare."

"She may not have a choice by that time," Rodgers said. "Colonel August will be inside."

"Who do you think will be watching the garage door?" August asked Rodgers.

"They're probably letting the NYPD take charge of that," Rodgers said. "Most of the UN police are probably upstairs."

Bob Herbert came back on then. Op-Center's computer genius Matt Stoll had managed to pull it from the restricted on-line United Nations directory before Darrell McCaskey was able to get the number from his Interpol people. Hood wrote it down. The phone line wouldn't be secure, but Hood would have to risk it. There wasn't much time left.

He would have to risk a number of things, he decided. He okayed Rodgers's plan and August left at once.

Hood punched in the number.

A man with an Italian accent answered. "This is the secretary-general's line."

"This is Paul Hood, the Director of Op-Center in Washington," Hood said. "I need to speak with the secretary-general."

"Mr. Hood, we have a situ—"

"I know!" Hood snapped. "And we can save the next victim if we act quickly! Put her on."

"Just a moment," the man told him.

Hood glanced at his watch. Assuming the terrorists didn't rush the deadline, there was just over a minute left.

A woman came on the line. "This is Mala Chatterjee."

"Madam Secretary-General, this is Paul Hood," he said. "I'm the director of a crisis management team in Washington. One of the hostages is my daughter." Hood's voice was quaking. He realized that what he said now could save or doom Harleigh.

"Yes, Mr. Hood?"

"I need your help," Hood went on. "I need you to radio the terrorists and tell them that you have the money and the helicopter they've asked for. If you do that, we can make sure they believe you."

"But we don't have those things," Chatterjee told him. "Nor are we likely to."

"By the time the terrorists figure that out, they'll be outside the building," Hood said. "I'll have the NYPD ready to get them there."

"We've already tried one very costly attack," Chatterjee said. "I won't authorize another."

Hood didn't want her to know that he knew that. "This will be different," Hood said. "If the terrorists are outside, they can't control all the hostages. We can get some of them away. And if they use poison gas, we'll be in a better position to help the victims. But you've got to call the terrorists *now*. You've also got to tell them that the offer is only good if they don't kill any more hostages."

Chatterjee hesitated. Hood couldn't understand what she was hesitating *about*. After the hit the security forces had just taken, there was only one answer: I'll do it. I'll help save a life and smoke the bastards out. Or did she still think she could open a dialogue, talk the terrorists into surrendering? If he had the time to finesse the situation, he would point out that Colonel Georgiev had apparently helped to turn the UNTAC operation into a sham. He would ask how she could still believe her own propaganda, that peacekeeping and negotiation were somehow the high road and force was the low road.

"Madam Secretary-General, please," Hood said. "We have less than a minute."

She continued to hesitate. Hood had never been as disgusted with despots as he was right now with this so-called humanitarian. What was there to fret over? Lying to terrorists? Having to explain to the Gabonese Republic why the United Nations charter was being side-stepped, why the surviving members of the General Assembly weren't consulted before the United States was permitted to terminate a hostage situation?

But this wasn't the time for a debate. Hopefully, Chatterjee would see that, too. And quickly.

"All right," the secretary-general replied. "I will place the call to save a life."

"Thank you," Hood replied. "I'll be in touch."

FORTY-TWO

New York, New York
Sunday, 12:00 A.M.

Harleigh Hood was on her knees, facing the closed doors of the Security Council chamber.

The Australian man was standing behind her, holding her hair tightly, painfully. The other man, the Spanish-sounding man, was behind him, looking at his watch. Harleigh's face was badly swollen above the right cheek where she'd been pistol-whipped when she'd tried to bite him. There was blood on her mouth where she'd been backfisted, hard. Her gown was torn at both shoulders, her neck rug-burned from being dragged up here, all the while kicking at the floor, walls, and chairs. And her left side hurt with every breath because she'd been jackbooted there just a few seconds before.

Harleigh had not gone willingly to her execution.

Now that the young woman was here, she was staring ahead blankly. She hurt everywhere, but nothing was as painful as the utter loss of her humanity, something she couldn't even touch. She realized, in a surprisingly lucid instant, that this was probably what it was like to be raped. Choice taken away. Dignity taken away. Future fear of any stimulus reminiscent of the experience, whether it was something pulling at your hair or the feeling of a rug under your knees. Perhaps worst of all,

281

this wasn't about anything she had done or said or been. She was just a convenient target for some animal's hostility. Is that what death was supposed to be like? No angels and trumpets. She was just meat.

No.

Harleigh screamed a cry of rage that came from deep inside. She screamed again, and then her bruised muscles exploded and she tried to get to her feet. Death was that if you let it *be* that. The Australian tugged hard on her hair, twisting her around. Harleigh fell to the ground, onto her back. She fought to get up, wriggling from side to side. Her captor dropped his knee on her chest, hard, and remained there. He put the barrel of his gun in her mouth.

"Scream into this," he said.

Harleigh did, defiantly, and he pushed the barrel down her throat until she gagged.

"Go on, one more time, angel," he said. "Scream again and it will scream back."

Metallic-tasting saliva quickly pooled in the bottom of Harleigh's throat. Blood mixed with the saliva, and she stopped screaming; she had to as she tried to swallow around the gun. But she couldn't swallow, cough, or breathe. She was going to drown in her own saliva before he could shoot her. She reached up and tried to push his hand back, but he used his free hand to grab her wrists. He easily forced Harleigh's slender arms to the side.

"It's time," Barone said.

Downer glared down as Harleigh made a guttural sound around the gun barrel.

Just then the radio beeped.

"Hold it," Barone said quickly. He answered the radio. "Yes?"

"This is Secretary-General Chatterjee," said the caller. "We have your money, and a helicopter is on the way."

Downer and Barone exchanged looks. Barone hit the mute button. His eyes narrowed suspiciously.

"She's lying," Downer said. "She couldn't have gotten it this fast."

Barone disengaged the mute. "How did you get it?" he asked.

"The United States government has guaranteed a loan from the Federal Reserve Bank in New York," she said. "They're putting together the currency and bringing it over."

"Wait until you hear from me," the Uruguayan said. He turned and started running down the stairs.

"You won't execute the hostage?" Chatterjee said.

"I'll execute two hostages if you're lying," he replied. He punched the radio off and hurried to the TAC-SAT phone at the front of the Security Council chamber.

FORTY-THREE

New York, New York
Sunday, 12:01 A.M.

While they waited for the TAC-SAT to ring, Rodgers
called Bob Herbert and briefed him. Herbert said he
would get in touch with New York Police Commissioner
Kane. The men had worked together when Russian spies
in Brighton Beach were helping to orchestrate a coup in
Moscow. Herbert had a good rapport with the commissioner and felt that Gordon would welcome the chance
to save the hostages—and the UN.

When Rodgers was finished, he made another call—
to check messages, he said. That wasn't true, but he
didn't want the young woman to know it. He asked to
borrow Hood's cell phone to make the call. While Hood
looked on, Rodgers stood between the woman and the
desk so she couldn't see what he was doing. It was a
trick he had learned from Bob Herbert, who used his
wheelchair phone to spy on people after he left a meeting. Rodgers turned off the ringer on the office phone
and then called the number, using Hood's cell phone.
He answered the office phone, switched it to speaker,
and left both lines open. Then he put the cell phone in
his pants pocket, making sure he didn't disconnect.

Rodgers went back and sat on the desk, across from
Annabelle Hampton. Hood paced between them. As the

minutes inched by, Rodgers became more convinced that this wasn't going to go the way he wanted.

The young woman was staring ahead fixedly the entire time. Rodgers did not doubt what she was looking at. The future. Ani Hampton didn't strike Rodgers as the PGA type—a postgame analyst. Many intelligence and military people worked like chess masters or ballroom dancers. They followed carefully tested patterns and deviated as little as possible from often-complex moves and strategies. When deviations did occur, they were later studied and either incorporated into the playbook or discarded.

But there were also many CIA field personnel who took a more ephemeral approach to tactics. These were the so-called "sharks." Typically, sharks were loners whose modus operandi was to continually move and look ahead. It didn't matter if the bridge burned behind them; they probably weren't going back, anyway. These were the kinds of people who managed to infiltrate foreign villages, terrorist cells, and enemy bases.

Rodgers was betting that Ani Hampton was a shark. She wasn't sitting here regretting anything. She was figuring out what to do next. Rodgers had a damn good idea exactly what that was, which was why he'd asked Colonel August to leave. Just in case.

Looking at the young woman, Rodgers felt cold— inside, not out. What she'd done here reminded him of something he'd learned during his first tour of duty in Vietnam: that while treason was the exception rather than the rule, it was everywhere. In every nation, every city, every town. And there were no reliable profiles, no rules, to sort out the practitioners. Traitors came in all ages, sexes, and nationalities. They worked in public places and private places and held jobs where they came into contact with information or people. And what they did could be personal or it could be motivated entirely by profit.

There was something else about traitors, something unique to them. They were most dangerous when they were caught. Faced with execution for their crimes, they had nothing to lose. If they had a final gambit, however futile or destructive it was, they'd try it.

In 1969, the CIA had received intelligence that North Vietnam was using a South Vietnamese military hospital in Saigon to distribute drugs to American servicemen. Rodgers went there, ostensibly to visit a wounded comrade. He watched as South Vietnamese nurses accepted American dollars from "wounded" South Vietnamese soldiers—actually, fifteen- to eighteen-year-old Viet Cong infiltrators—as payment for moving heroin and marijuana from the basement to field-bound medical kits. When arrested, two of the three nurses pulled pins from hand grenades that killed them and seven wounded soldiers in the ward.

Caregivers and teenagers becoming killers. Vietnam was unique that way. It was the reason so many veterans had snapped when they came home. In quiet villages, young girls frequently greeted American soldiers. Some asked for candy or money. Often, that was all they wanted. Other times, girls carried dolls that were rigged to explode. Sometimes the girls blew up with them. Old women occasionally offered bowls of cyanide-laced rice to the Americans, rice which they ate first to put the soldiers at ease. These were shapes of destruction more frightening than an M16 or a land mine. More than any other war, Vietnam had robbed American soldiers of the notion that anything anywhere could be trusted. And returning from that war, many soldiers found that they could no longer open up to wives, relatives, even children. That was one of the reasons Mike Rodgers had never married. Getting close to anyone other than a fellow soldier was impossible. And all the therapy, all the reasoning in the world couldn't change that. Once killed, innocence could not be revived.

Rodgers was not happy to revisit those feelings of mistrust again through Annabelle Hampton. The young woman had sold innocent lives for profit and dishonored the government she worked for. He wondered how anyone could be content with blood money.

The building was quiet, and there were no ambient sounds coming from outside. First Avenue had been shut down just beyond this building and the FDR Drive had been closed because it passed right behind the United Nations. Obviously, the New York Police Department wanted to have clear access if they needed it. The dead-end street in front of this building was also closed.

When the TAC-SAT beeped, it startled them all.

Hood stopped pacing and stood beside Rodgers. Annabelle's gaze shifted to the general. Her mouth was set, and there wasn't a hint of compliance in her pale blue eyes.

Rodgers wasn't surprised. Annabelle Hampton was a shark, after all.

"Answer the phone," Rodgers said.

She stared at him. Her eyes were cold. "If I don't, are you going to torture me again?"

"I'd rather not," Rodgers said.

"I know that," Annabelle said. She grinned. "Things have changed, haven't they?"

There was definitely something different in the young woman's voice. Aggressiveness. Confidence. They'd given her too much time to think. The dance had begun, and Annabelle Hampton was leading. Rodgers was glad he'd taken the precautions he had.

"You could force me to answer by bending my finger back again," she said. "Or you could hurt me in other ways. Open a paper clip or find a push pin and press the point through the soft skin under one of my eyes. Standard CIA method of persuasion. But then the pain would show in my voice. They'd know I was being coerced."

"You said you'd cooperate," Hood pointed out.

"And if I don't cooperate, what will you do?" she asked. "If you shoot me, the hostage dies for sure." She made a point of looking at Hood. "Possibly your daughter."

Hood's body stiffened.

She was better than he'd expected, Rodgers thought. The dance had become a quick, dirty game of chicken. Rodgers already knew which way this was going. What he needed now was to buy August time.

"What do you want?" Rodgers asked.

"I want you to cut me loose and leave the room," she said. "I'll make the call you want, then I go free."

"I won't do it," Rodgers said.

"Why not?" Ani asked. "Don't want to dirty your hands cutting a deal with me?"

"I've cut deals with worse than you," Rodgers said. "I won't cut a deal because I don't trust you. You need this operation to succeed. Terrorists don't pay in advance. That's how they ensure loyalty. The situation you're in now, you need your cut of the ransom."

The TAC-SAT beeped a second time.

289

"Whether you trust me or not," Annabelle said, "if I don't answer the phone, they're going to assume that something has happened to me. They'll execute the girl."

"In that case," Rodgers replied evenly, "you'll either be executed or spend your life in jail as an accomplice."

"I end up with ten to twenty years if I cooperate with you," Ani said. "I get life or death if I don't. What's the difference?"

"About thirty years," Rodgers said. "It might not matter now, but it will when you're sixty."

"Spare me the recon from the front," she replied.

"Ms. Hampton, please," Hood said. "It's not too late to help yourself and dozens of innocent people."

"Tell your partner, not me," she said.

The TAC-SAT beeped a third time.

"There will be a total of five rings," Ani said. "Then a girl in the Security Council Chamber will have her head blown open. Is that what you want? Either of you?"

Rodgers took a half-step forward. He shouldered between Hood and the woman. He didn't know if Hood would take the bait and order him to comply with her, but he didn't want to risk it. Hood was still the director of Op-Center, and Rodgers didn't want them fighting each other. Especially since Hood didn't know what else was going on right now.

"Let me go, and I'll tell them what you want," she said.

"Why don't you say what we want and then we'll let you go?" Rodgers countered.

"Because as much as you don't trust me, I don't trust

you," she said. "And right now, you need me more than I need you."

The TAC-SAT beeped a fourth time.

"Mike—" Hood said.

Though Hood had been there for the planning of the bottleneck, he was obviously hoping the original idea could be adhered to: drawing the terrorists outside. But Rodgers waited. A few seconds more could make the difference between success and failure.

"I'm against this," Rodgers said to Annabelle.

"And you hate the fact that that doesn't matter," she replied.

"No," Rodgers told the young woman. "I've eaten shit before, too. We're all grown-ups here. What I hate is having to trust someone who has already broken one promise."

The general tucked a gun into his belt, reached into his pants pocket, and pulled out a switchblade. He snapped it open with a flick of his hand and began cutting her free.

The TAC-SAT beeped a fifth time.

Annabelle reached for the knife. "I'll finish that," she said.

Rodgers released the knife. He stood back, in case she decided to use it on him.

"I want you out of here," the young woman said. "I want to see you on my security camera, in the hallway. And leave me my keys."

Rodgers took the key case from his pants pocket and tossed it on the floor in front of her. Then he grabbed his jacket from the back of a chair and followed Hood out.

The young woman finished cutting herself loose, then

switched the computer monitor to a security view. As Rodgers crossed the office lobby toward the corridor, Ani leaned over and picked up the TAC-SAT.

"Speak," she said.

Rodgers was just going out of earshot as she said that. Fortunately, he wasn't out of earshot for long. He hurried into the hallway and passed under the security camera.

Like Annabelle Hampton, Rodgers was a shark. But for all her bold threats and lies, for all the bluster she'd just thrown at them, he had something the young woman lacked.

Thirty years in the water.

FORTY-FOUR

New York, New York
Sunday, 12:04 A.M.

As soon as Rodgers and Hood passed beyond the fish-eye lens of the security camera, Rodgers took Hood's cell phone from his pocket. The general stopped in the corridor and listened in silence for a moment, then disconnected. He handed Hood the cell phone along with one of his two guns.

"She told him the truth?" Hood asked.

"She screwed us good," Rodgers said.

Rodgers pulled the point-to-point radio from his jacket pocket. He pushed the transmit button on top.

"Brett?" he said.

"Here, General."

"The bottleneck is a go," Rodgers said. "Will you make it?"

"I'll make it," August replied.

"Good," Rodgers said. "When do you want the feedback?"

"In two minutes," August said.

Rodgers looked at his watch. "You've got it. I'll get in position, north side of the building. I'll be ready in seven minutes."

"Understood," August said and signed off. "Good luck."

"Godspeed," Rodgers said. He put the radio back in his pocket.

Hood shook his head. "You called this one right."

"Unfortunately," Rodgers admitted. He looked at his watch. "Listen. I've got to get going. Call the NYPD and have them close off this floor and take our lady into custody. She'll probably be armed, so if she comes out before they get here, you may have to take her down."

"I can do that," Hood said.

All of Op-Center's executive officers had taken extensive weapons training, since they were likely targets of terrorism. Right now, Hood didn't think he would have any trouble firing at Annabelle Hampton. And it wasn't only because she had betrayed them. It was because Rodgers was so completely prepared, so much in charge, that there was no questioning his orders. Which was what military leadership was all about.

"I'll also need you to try what you suggested before."

"Chatterjee?"

Rodgers nodded. "I know it's a long shot, but explain what's going to happen. If she doesn't want to cooperate, tell her there's nothing she can do to stop what we've set in—"

"I know the drill," Hood said.

"Right," Rodgers said. "Sorry. Tell her there's only one thing I want from her and her people."

"What's that?" Hood asked.

Rodgers looked for the exit sign and then hurried toward the stairs. "To stay out of our way."

FORTY-FIVE

New York, New York
Sunday, 12:05 A.M.

Colonel Brett August moved like a leopard through the silent park. There were no helicopters positioned over this sector; their lights were all on the UN and its immediate approaches. Save for the spillover from the spotlights around the UN complex, the grounds were dark.

August's stride was long and sure, his body bent low, his balance perfect. The high stakes energized rather than daunted him. Despite the odds against him, he was eager to engage, eager to test himself. And despite the fact that nothing was ever guaranteed in combat, he was confident. Confident of his training, his abilities, and the necessity of what he was doing.

He was also confident of the plan. What General Rodgers had said about the chaotic, quicksilver nature of combat was absolutely true. And the bottleneck gave a unit the ability to contain it somewhat.

The bottleneck operation is a classic maneuver that was first used, as far as anyone could determine, by a small, ragtag army of Russian peasants serving under Prince Alexander Nevsky. The Russians were battling heavily armed and armored Teutonic invaders in the twelfth century. The only way they could conceivably defeat the larger, better-equipped force was by squeezing them onto a frozen lake, where the ice cracked beneath the weight of their armor. Virtually all of the enemy soldiers drowned. The strategy had been adapted by Striker's former commander, Lieutenant Colonel Charles Squires, for low-personnel offensives.

The idea was to select an area where there was sufficient cover on two sides of an enemy force—such as a gorge, a forest, or a lakeshore. Finding such a spot, the unit, however small, would split into two sections. One group would flank the opposing force, leaving the enemy between them. One part of the divided force would then advance in a tight formation, moving down the neck of a bottle, so to speak. The enemy couldn't afford to flee, since a hidden army dogging their progress would be able to snipe at them. And if the enemy tried to counterattack, the force in the bottleneck would be able to attack to the front, left, or right. As the attack forced the enemy back, they'd find themselves surprised by the force that had moved behind them. Both sections of the divided unit would then hammer them. Done well, under cover of night or geography, the bottleneck made it possible for a small force to overcome a much larger one.

Colonel August would not have the darkness to cover his move into the chamber. Even if he could kill the lights for a second or two, that would give the terrorists a heads-up. He preferred surprise. Unfortunately, with the lights on, the enemy would know that he was just one man. They would see him come into the chamber, just as they'd seen the United Nations security team enter. If they acted quickly, the bottleneck could be broken.

If that happened, August would still have several advantages. He had been trained as a soldier, not as a security guard. The seats in the Security Council would offer him cover. Thanks to the long, open staircases, the terrorists would find it difficult to sneak up on him, especially if he kept moving low through the upper tiers. And if the terrorists tried to use hostages as a shield, the Striker leader had two other advantages. One was his eye. Brett August was one of the deadliest shots in the combined special forces, and he had the medals to prove it. Only Mike Rodgers had won more. The other advantage was that August wouldn't be afraid to fire. If he had to risk killing a hostage to take out a terrorist, he was prepared to do that. As Mike Rodgers had said earlier, if they didn't act decisively and soon, the hostages were going to die anyway.

The garden stretched southward for several blocks. It was actually a small, tree-filled park anchored by a towering sculpture of Saint George slaying the dragon. The statue, a gift of the former Soviet Union, was made from pieces of Soviet SS-20 and American Pershing nuclear missiles that had been destroyed under the terms of the Intermediate-Range Nuclear Forces Treaty of 1987. Like the UN itself, the statue was a public relations gesture: a loud, bold lie saluting peace. The Soviets knew damn well that peace didn't work unless you had the SS-20s and Pershing missiles to back it up.

Or a good tactic like the bottleneck, he thought. That was a Russian monument he could respect.

Large, gray rats were moving furtively among the rosebushes. Rats were good scouts that way. If they were out, it meant there probably wasn't anyone up ahead. The animals scattered as August moved by.

The Colonel crouched lower as he neared the end of

the park. Beyond the greenery was an open courtyard roughly seventy feet across that led to the main lobby of the General Assembly Building. There were still too many bushes and trees for him to see it clearly.

August was carrying one of the two Berettas that Rodgers had given him. The other handgun was in his right pants pocket. The colonel had posed as a tourist on his recent mission to Spain, a disguise that had taught him to wear pants with pockets deep enough to carry a concealed weapon. He was also still carrying the radio, just in case he needed it to help him get inside. Otherwise, August would have shut it off and left it behind. A communication or a burst of static at the wrong time could give his position away. Ironically, that was the very thing he might need to get inside the building.

Pausing when he was about two hundred and fifty feet from the General Assembly Building, August looked past the other, smaller sculptures toward the United Nations compound itself. In addition to three helicopters hovering over the area, the spotlights were on in the wide courtyard and a half-dozen NYPD officers were stationed at the main lobby entrance. Rodgers was right. The police had been allowed to move from their command booths on the street to the grounds when the UN guards were called away. August couldn't risk taking the steps and being spotted. The NYPD wasn't like the UN police. They were more like Striker. They knew how to take people down and keep them down. When he was a NATO adviser, August had spent time with a former NYPD Emergency Service chief of department who had briefed NATO strategists on hostage situations. New York Police Department policy was to establish and secure an inner perimeter, as tight as possible, then bring in specialized weapons, heavy vests, and be ready to tackle the hostage-takers in case negotiations broke down. This situation would have ended hours ago if Chatterjee hadn't been so obliging. It was all part of the post–Desert Storm world mind-set. Someone breaks the law. Then, in the cause of world peace, everyone else talks and negotiates while the lawbreaker grows stronger and more entrenched. When you finally decide to do something about it, you need a coalition.

That was crap. All you needed was the guy who started it in your gunsight. He'd back down fast enough.

August rarely paid attention to clocks. He always moved as fast as he could, as efficiently as he could, and assumed that he had less time than he did. To date, he'd never missed a deadline. But even without checking his watch, he knew he didn't have time to explain who he was or what he was doing here. Instead, he decided to leave the garden and go down to the FDR Drive. The highway ran under the wide esplanade that bordered the garden on the east. Though he'd have to drop down instead of using the stairs behind the UN, it was the only way he'd get to the garage unseen.

Turning toward the river, August made his way alongside the gravel path that led to the concrete walkway. Crossing the esplanade, he came to a low metal fence and swung over it. Lying on his belly, facing east, he looked over the edge of the walkway. It was a drop of about twelve feet to the highway, but there was nothing to hold onto. Removing the radio from his pocket, he replaced it with the gun. Then he took off his belt, slid the flap-end through the radio case, and pulled until the case rested against the buckle. Then he looped the belt around one of the thin stanchions that supported the rail.

Holding the two ends of the strap, he lowered himself over the side. Still holding the buckle end of the belt and the radio, he let go of the other end and dropped the five feet to the asphalt.

August landed with his knees slightly bent. He stood quickly. The United Nations garage was to the south, directly ahead. August couldn't see the site clearly yet, since it was blocked by the corner of a building on the northeastern side of the street.

August put his belt back on as he crept through the eerie silence under the highway. As he neared the garage entrance, he saw two policemen standing to the east of the open door. The inside of the garage was lighted, but the outside was dark. If he could draw the officers away, then getting to the door unseen wouldn't be a problem.

August looked at his watch. In twenty seconds, Rodgers would turn his own radio to maximum volume. With his own radio turned up, the overload would generate a static feedback. When that happened, the police would do one of three things. Both officers would go to investigate; one officer would investigate while the other remained at his post; or they would call for backup.

August expected that both officers would go. They couldn't afford to leave a possible threat unchecked, and he imagined that the NYPD followed the field policy of most big-city police departments. That officers were not allowed to enter a potentially dangerous situation alone.

If that didn't happen, August was going to have to take down one or both officers. He didn't relish attacking men who were on the same team, but he was prepared to do it. He shifted to a confrontational mind-set, with his focus on the goal and not the means.

The colonel moved quickly through the shadows under the highway, then put his radio down beside the curb. He made sure the volume was turned all the way up. Then, with just seconds remaining, he ducked into a darkened doorway across from the garage. He was approximately thirty feet from the corner and roughly the same distance from the garage.

August slipped off his shoes.

Less than five seconds later, a piercing screech ripped through the night. August watched as the officers looked over. One drew his gun and flashlight and started toward the street while the other radioed in the 10-59, which identified it as a non–crime-related noise.

"Sounds like a radio," said the officer who was reporting the incident. "We have anyone else on the block?"

"Negative," said the dispatcher.

"I copy that," said the officer. "I'm going over with Orlando."

The first police officer approached cautiously with his flashlight turned toward the side of the building on the northeast corner. The second officer stayed slightly to the side, his gun drawn and his radio on. He was betting that these men would shoot him on sight if they saw him. He had to make certain that they did not.

While the radio continued to crackle loudly, August watched the officers. When they reached the corner, he ducked low and ran across the street in his stocking feet. He made no sound, did not feel anything he stepped on. The goal was all that mattered. And as he entered the garage and saw the elevator ahead, he had only one goal.

To win.

FORTY-SIX

New York, New York
Sunday, 12:06 A.M.

The secretary-general was still standing in the corridor outside the Security Council. Little had changed since the siege began. A few of the delegates had left, and others had come up. Security personnel were more agitated than before, especially those who had taken part in the aborted assault. Young Lieutenant Mailman, a British officer who had come here after helping to plan Desert Fox, was the most restless of all. After Chatterjee had phoned the terrorists to relay Hood's message, the officer walked over.

"Ma'am?" he said.

The silence was oppressive. Though he was whispering, his voice sounded very loud.

"Yes, Lieutenant?"

"Ma'am, Colonel Mott's plan was a good one," he insisted. "We couldn't have anticipated the variable, the other gunmen."

"What are you asking?" she said.

"There are only three terrorists left now," he told her, "and I have a plan that might work."

"No," she said adamantly. "How do you know there won't be other variables?"

"I don't," he admitted. "Soldiering isn't about predicting the future. It's about fighting wars. And you can't do that standing on the sidelines.''

There were sounds from behind the door of the Security Council. Whimpering, knocking, snarls. Something was happening.

''I've given you my answer,'' she replied.

A moment later, Paul Hood called back. Enzo Donati handed her the cell phone.

''Yes?'' Chatterjee said anxiously.

''She turned on us,'' Hood said.

''God, no,'' Chatterjee said. ''Then that's what's happening inside.''

''What's happening?'' Hood said.

''A struggle,'' she said. ''They're going to execute the hostage.''

''Not necessarily,'' Hood said. ''One of my men is on the way up. He's dressed in civilian clothes—''

''No!'' the secretary-general said.

''Madam Secretary, you've got to let us handle this,'' Hood said. ''You don't have a plan. We do—''

''You had a plan, and we tried it,'' she said. ''It failed.''

''This one won't—''

''No, Mr. Hood!'' Chatterjee said as she cut him off. She felt like screaming. The phone beeped again. She shut it off and handed it to Donati. She told her assistant to leave.

It was as though someone had spun the world like a top. She was dizzy, electrified, and exhausted at the same time. Is this what war was like? A white-water river that carried you to places where the best you could do, the best you could *hope* for, was to take advantage of someone who was slightly more dizzy and exhausted than you?

Chatterjee looked at the Security Council door. She would have to try to go in again. What else was there to do?

Just then, there was a commotion from the hallway just past the Economic and Social Council chambers. Several of the delegates turned around, and members of the security force were going over to see what was happening.

"Someone's coming!" shouted one of the security police.

"Quiet, damn you!" Mailman hissed.

The lieutenant ran over to the police line. He arrived just as the barefoot Colonel August shouldered through the crowd of delegates. August raised both hands to show the security people that he was unarmed, but he didn't stop moving.

"Let him through!" Mailman said, his voice an insistent whisper.

The line of blue shirts parted immediately, and August stepped through. As he did, he reached into his pants pockets and withdrew both Berettas. The officer's movements were fast and sure, no wasted action. He was less than ten feet from the door. All that stood between him and the Security Council chamber was Mala Chatterjee.

The secretary-general looked at August's face as he neared. His eyes reminded her of a tiger she'd once seen in the wild in India. This man had smelled his prey, and nothing was going to come between them. At the moment, those eyes seemed like the only steady thing in her universe.

This wasn't how it was supposed to be. Leon Trotsky

had once written that violence seemed to be the shortest distance between two points. The secretary-general didn't want to believe that. When she was a student at the University of Delhi, Professor Sandhya A. Panda, an acolyte of Mohandas Gandhi, had taught pacifism as though it were a religion. Chatterjee had practiced that faith devoutly. Yet in five hours, everything that could go wrong did. Her best efforts, her self-sacrifice, her calm thoughts. At least Colonel Mott's aborted attempt had managed to get a wounded girl to the hospital.

Just then, there was a soft cry from the other side of the door. It was a girl's voice, high and muffled.

"No!" the voice sobbed. *"Don't!"*

Chatterjee choked on an involuntary cry of her own. She turned reflexively to go to the girl, but August stopped her with a firm nudge as he rushed past.

Armed with a handgun, Lieutenant Mailman followed August. He stopped several paces behind the colonel.

Chatterjee started after them. Mailman turned and held her back.

"Let him go," the lieutenant said quietly.

Chatterjee didn't have the energy or will to resist. In a madhouse, only the insane are at home. They both watched as the Colonel paused at the door, but only for a moment. He turned the handle with the heel of his left hand and remained standing. Once again, his movements were clean and efficient.

A hearbeat later, he followed both guns in.

FORTY-SEVEN

New York, New York
Sunday, 12:07 A.M.

Shortly after answering the TAC-SAT call from Barone, Annabelle Hampton went to the closet, took one of
the last remaining Berettas, and walked into the hallway.
The corridor was empty. The bastards who had tried to
bully her were gone. She headed past the closed offices,
custodial closet, and rest rooms toward the stairwell.

Annabelle didn't want to take the elevator for two
reasons. First, there were security cameras built into the
ceiling. Second, the men from Op-Center might be waiting for her in the lobby. She wanted to take the stairs
to the cellar and slip out the side door. She would re-
connect with Georgiev later, as planned. She had sent
the two CIA floaters to pick him up at the UN infirmary.
Annabelle would tell her superior that she had Georgiev
removed because of what he knew about CIA operations
in Bulgaria, Cambodia, and in the rest of the Far East.
She didn't want that information falling into the hands
of the United Nations. She would also tell him that the
men from Op-Center were in league with the terrorists.
That would keep them at bay long enough for her to
collect her share of the ransom and get out of the country. If there was no ransom, she'd still use the money
Georgiev had paid her up front to go to South America.

The door opened in. It was solid metal, as required by fire laws. There was no window, so the young woman opened it cautiously in case anyone was on the other side.

No one was waiting there. Annabelle let the door shut and started across the concrete landing. There were five floors to the cellar; Hood or one of his men could still be waiting for her down there. She didn't think the police would be there. NYPD policy was to throw a tight net. They would have come up to the fourth floor to shut her in, not give her an opportunity to get away.

She started down the steps. And then the lights went off. Even the security spots went down, which could only be controlled from the utility room. The young woman thought angrily, *Right next to the men's room. Goddam whichever of those bastards thought of that.* She was angrier at herself for not having checked the room.

Annabelle considered going back, but she didn't want to waste the time or risk a showdown with whoever had cut the lights. Switching the gun to her left hand, she grabbed the handrail with her right hand and made her way down slowly. She reached the landing, turned the corner, and started down the second half of the stairs. She was pleased with the progress she was making.

Until a bright light snapped on in front of her and then a sharp, crippling pain struck her left thigh.

She fell over, unable to breathe and losing the gun as pain rocked her entire left side.

"Put 'em back on!" someone shouted.

The stairwell lights snapped back, and Annabelle looked up. She saw a beefy, black-haired man looming over her. He was dressed in a white shirt and wearing navy blue trousers. In his thick hands were a radio and a black police-style baton. He was State Department Security. The name tag on his shirt said Deputy Chief Bill Mohalley.

Mohalley picked up her gun and tucked it in his waistband. Annabelle tried to get up but couldn't. She could barely breathe. As she lay there, she heard the door open on the fourth-floor landing.

While the State Department officer radioed for the rest of his team to come to the third floor, Hood ran down the stairs. He must have been the one who turned off the lights. Hood stopped on the landing and looked down at the young woman. His expression seemed sad.

"I thought—we had a deal," she gasped.

"So did I," Hood replied. "But I know what you did. I heard."

"You're lying," she said. "I—saw you—in the camera."

Hood just shook his head. Mohalley stepped over as his team ran up the stairs.

"My team will take it from here," Mohalley said to Hood. "Thanks for your help."

"Thanks for having given me your card," Hood said. "Have you heard anything about the wounded girl?"

Mohalley nodded. "Barbara Mathis is on the operating table. She's lost a lot of blood, and the bullet's still in her. They're doing everything they can, but it doesn't look good." He looked down at Annabelle. "She's just fourteen years old."

"I didn't want—any of the children hurt," Annabelle said.

Hood stepped back. Shaking his head again, he turned and ran down the stairs.

Annabelle lay back as other State Department security personnel arrived. Her thigh was throbbing painfully, and her back hurt where it had hit the stairs. But at least she was able to breathe again.

What Annabelle had said to Mohalley was true. She felt sorry that one of the young musicians might die. That wasn't supposed to happen. If the secretary-general had cooperated, if she had done the right thing, none of the girls would have been hurt.

Without quite being able to wrap her brain around the idea, Annabelle knew that she was probably going to spend the rest of her life in prison. As disturbing as that was, however, what bothered her most was the fact that Paul Hood had outsmarted her.

That once again, a man had come between her and her goal.

FORTY-EIGHT

New York, New York
Sunday, 12:08 A.M.

The wooden door of the Security Council opened outward. Colonel August stood in the doorway, simultaneously looking for the killer and making himself the target. He was wearing his bulletproof vest and was willing to trade hits if it would save a hostage's life. The terrorist couldn't shoot a hostage if he was shooting at August.

The first person August saw was a slender, teenage girl. She was on her knees less than five yards away. She was whimpering and shaking. August wasn't sure who the girl was. The terrorist was standing very close behind her. Using peripheral vision, August noted the location of the other two terrorists. One of them was standing in the front of the Security Countil chamber, behind the semicircular desk. The other terrorist was standing right beside the door that led to the adjoining Trusteeship Council.

The terrorists were all dressed in black and wearing ski masks. The one nearest him was holding the girl's long blonde hair by the roots, close to her forehead, so that her face was staring straight up. He had a gun pointed directly ahead, at the top of her skull.

August had the middle of the man's mask in his gun

sight, but he didn't want to fire first. If he hit the terrorist, the man's finger might tighten around the trigger and take the top of the girl's head off. August knew that was wrong; if he had the shot, he should take it. The thought that this could be Paul Hood's daughter stopped him.

The terrorist hesitated and then he did something that surprised August. He dropped directly behind the kneeling girl and then threw himself to his right, into the row of seats. Still holding the girl's hair, he pulled her with him. Obviously, he did not want to trade gunfire. And now he had a shield.

You should have taken the damn shot, August reprimanded himself. Instead of having one less terrorist to deal with, everyone was at risk.

The terrorist and the girl were four rows down the sloping gallery. August pocketed the Beretta that was in his right hand, turned to his left, and jogged a few feet along the back of the gallery. Silent in his bare feet, he put his free hand on the railing that ran along the seat backs of the last row. He leaped the green-velvet seats and immediately jumped the next row. He was now two rows from the terrorist and the girl.

"Downer, he's coming for you!" one of the terrorists shouted. He had a French accent. "Behind you—"

"Get out or I'll kill her!" shouted Downer, the pinned terrorist. "I'll blow her goddam brains out!"

August was still two rows away. The man with the French accent started running toward him. He would be on the stairs in two or three seconds. The third man was covering the hostages.

"Barone, the gas!" the Frenchman said.

The third terrorist, Barone, ran toward a duffel bag

that sat open in the front of the chamber, near the north-side window. August finished hopping over the third row. He could now see Downer and the girl. They were on the floor of the next row. The terrorist was on his back with the girl faceup on top of him. But August had a problem.

The bottleneck had required preventing the girl's death, disabling the nearest of the three terrorists, and establishing a beachhead in the back of the chamber before General Rodgers got here. That hadn't happened. Unfortunately, not only was the bottleneck dead, but the colonel had to reorder his priorities. He had to deal with the gas.

Barone was on the opposite side of the semicircular table, protected by the table and by the hostages. He had already removed his ski mask and had pulled three gas masks from the duffel bag. The terrorist slipped one of the masks on as he handed the others out. The other men didn't put them on yet because the goggles impaired their peripheral vision. Then Barone returned to the bag and removed a black canister.

August turned and ran toward the north side of the chamber. The French terrorist had reached the stairs on the south side of the Security Council and was running up. August didn't want to stop and shoot it out with him. Even if the Frenchman tagged him, August would be in a better position to kill Barone if he were on the same side of the chamber.

The table and the tightly huddled hostages were still in August's way.

"No one move!" August shouted. Running, they might get between him and Barone.

No one moved at all.

August reached the stairwell and started down. He kept his right arm across his chest. Cocked at his side, the arm would be more vulnerable. The Frenchman was directly across the room. The terrorist suddenly stopped and fired several rounds. Two of the four shots hit August in the waist and ribs. The impact threw him against the wall, though the bulletproof vest stopped the slugs.

"You're down, you bastard!" the Frenchman cried triumphantly. "Downer, cover me!" he yelled as he cut through one of the middle rows of the gallery, heading toward the north side.

The Australian threw the girl aside and stood. He screamed in raw, frustrated rage.

Pulling himself off the wall, August continued crawling down the steps. He ignored the sharp pain in his side. Where he was, behind the seats, the Frenchman did not have a shot at him. And Barone was almost in view.

Just then, a loud crack broke from the back of the room. From the corner of his eye, August saw the Frenchman fall forward between the rows. Downer ducked fast as Lieutenant Mailman crouched behind his gun in the open door.

"Keep going, sir!" Mailman shouted.

Good man, August thought. Mailman had shot at the Frenchman, though August couldn't tell whether or not the terrorist had been hit.

August reached the bottom step as Barone carefully peeled a red plastic strip from the mouth of the canister. He threw the tape aside and began unscrewing the cap. August fired twice. Both bullets punched holes in the side of Barone's head, spilling him toward the front of the chamber. The canister fell to the carpet, a thin wisp of green vapor slipping around the neck of the container.

August swore. He got to his feet and ran toward the door that adjoined the Trusteeship Council. He had it in mind to get to the canister and shut it. If he couldn't do that, then maybe he could cover the hostages as they ran out through that door.

He never made it.

The Frenchman emerged on the north side of the gallery. He was unhurt and opened fire. This time he aimed at August's legs.

August felt two sharp bites, one in his left thigh and one in his right shin. He went down, the wounds burning fiercely. August ground his teeth together and crawled forward. Pain management training had taught him to set small, attainable goals. That was how soldiers stayed conscious and functioning in the field. He concentrated on where he needed to be.

Behind him, Downer fired at Mailman, driving him back outside the door. Meanwhile, the Frenchman crept down several steps.

The canister was just a few feet away. The cap was still on, but the gas was beginning to spread. August needed to screw it back on. He didn't have time to turn and fire.

Suddenly, there was a massive pop about ten feet in front of August. The great brown drapes on the northernmost window blew open and bulletproof glass flew straight across the front of the Security Council. Almost simultaneously, there was a terrific crash as the upper part of the towering window came crashing down.

A moment later, right on schedule, Mike Rodgers stepped into the room.

FORTY-NINE

New York, New York
Sunday, 12:11 A.M.

This is not a bottleneck operation, Mike Rodgers thought gravely as he looked across the Security Council chamber. This was proof of the Striker axiom that nothing was guaranteed.

Rodgers had crossed the rose garden the same way August had. By the time he'd reached the courtyard, however, the gun battle had begun, and most of the police who were outside the lobby had gone inside. He was able to reach the hedges on the east side of the courtyard unseen. Creeping ahead to the north-side window of the Security Council chamber, he immediately placed and detonated the C-4. He only used a small amount in order to keep the flying glass to a minimum. He suspected that once the bottom of the window was blown in, the rest of the pane would collapse. He was right.

Entering the chamber, Rodgers saw Colonel August roughly four yards in front of him. The colonel was on his knees and bleeding from both legs. Between them was a dead terrorist and a container leaking gas. Rodgers also saw the armed terrorist in the northside gallery stairwell. Obviously, something had gone terribly wrong.

Firing two shots to drive the terrorist gunman back

between the seats, Rodgers turned and grabbed the drape. The blast had torn it in the middle and, yanking hard, he ripped the bottom half from the window. Many kinds of poison gas were lethal if they came into contact with flesh. He would rather try to contain the gas this way than close the canister.

Rodgers pulled the heavy fabric over the container. He figured that should buy them about five minutes in here—enough time to get everyone out. He'd have them leave through the broken window; since it was behind him, it would be easier for him to cover.

As Rodgers turned to the girls who were gathered around the table, August swung onto his back and sat up. He was facing the back of the chamber and still holding one of his Berettas.

"All right!" Rodgers said, looking at their faces. "I want all of you to go out through the window, quickly!"

Led by Ms. Dorn, the girls hurried toward the outside terrace and safety. As they did, Rodgers turned back to August.

"Where's the third terrorist?" he asked.

"Fourth row from the top of the gallery," August said. "He's holding one of the girls."

Rodgers swore. He hadn't seen Harleigh Hood among the girls down here. It had to be her.

As August spoke, he had maneuvered onto his knees and crept back toward the stairwell. Raising himself up on the wooden banister, he started up the steps. Walking was obviously agony for the colonel, who put most of his weight on his left arm. He held his right arm out, Beretta pointed ahead. Rodgers didn't have to ask him what he was doing; he was using himself as bait to draw the terrorist's attention. He watched as the colonel made his way up the stairs.

Rodgers stood between the hostages and the gallery. Several of the delegates also rose and scrambled to get out, pushing the girls aside as they ran. If it were up to Rodgers, he would have shot them. But he didn't want to turn his back on the gallery. Not with one of the terrorists still up there.

The chamber was emptying, and the thick drapery seemed to be holding down the gas for now. Rodgers wished he could move over to the north side of the chamber to cover August, but he knew he had to look out for the safety of the hostages. He watched as August limped higher.

Rodgers turned for a moment to check on the girls. All of them had been evacuated, and the last of the delegates were heading toward the window. Then, as Rodgers turned back, he heard a shot from the gallery. He saw August's arms fly back as the colonel lost his gun and he stumbled against the wall. A moment later, August went down back-first.

Rodgers swore and ran toward the stairwell. The terrorist rose and fired at the general. Since Rodgers wasn't wearing a bulletproof vest, he had to drop to the floor in front of the gallery.

"Don't worry!" the terrorist shouted at Rodgers. "You'll get your turn!"

"Give it up!" Rodgers yelled back as he wriggled toward the stairwell on his belly.

The terrorist didn't answer. Not with words. The next thing Rodgers heard were two shots and then a cry.

Rodgers swore. *I'll kill him,* he thought bitterly as he

rose quickly, hoping to nail the terrorist before he could turn and aim.

But Rodgers was too late. He watched as the terrorist dropped his gun, twisted, and then slumped over the back of one of the seats. There were two large red exit wounds in his back. Stepping toward the stairway, Rodgers saw August still lying on his back. There was a bullet hole in his left pocket.

"Son of a bitch should have paid closer attention," August said as he removed the second gun from his pocket. The barrel of the gleaming Beretta was still smoking.

Rodgers was relieved, though he was far from happy as he turned toward the steep gallery. There was still a third terrorist, the one who apparently was holding Harleigh Hood hostage. He had been ominously silent throughout the exchange. A UN security officer was crouched in the doorway. Save for the muted hissing of the gas canister under the drapery, the chamber was quiet. And then they heard a voice from the aisle of the upper gallery.

"You have not won," said Reynold Downer. "All you have done is gotten more of the ransom for me."

FIFTY

New York, New York
Sunday, 12:15 A.M.

"They're out!" a young man yelled into the waiting room. "The kids are out, and they're safe!"

The parents responded with laughter and tears, all of them rising and hugging one another before making their way to the door. Official word came as they were filing into the hallway. A uniformed State Department security official met them. A middle-aged woman with short brown hair, big brown eyes, and a name tag that said Baroni told them that the children appeared to be well but were being taken to the NYU Medical Center as a precaution, and that a bus would be along to bring the parents downtown. The parents were all grateful and thanked the woman as though she had personally been responsible for the rescue.

The DOS official made her way inside as she directed the parents toward an elevator at the end of the hall. She appeared to be looking for someone. When she saw Sharon Hood, she touched her forearm.

"Mrs. Hood, my name is Lisa Baroni," she said. "Can I have a few words with you?"

The request brought an instant welling of nausea.

"What's wrong?" Sharon asked.

Lisa gently maneuvered Sharon away from the last of

the parents. The two women stood just inside the door, beside one of the couches.

"What is it?" Sharon demanded.

"Mrs. Hood," she said, "I'm afraid your daughter is still inside."

The words sounded ridiculous. A moment ago, everyone was safe. She was happy. "What do you mean?" Sharon asked.

"Your daughter is still inside the Security Council."

"No, they're out!" Sharon said, growing angry. "That man just said they're out!"

"Most of the children were evacuated through a broken window," the woman said. "But your daughter was not with the group."

"Why not?"

"Mrs. Hood, why don't you sit down?" Lisa said. She urged her back toward the seat. "I'm going to stay with you."

"Why wasn't my daughter with them?" Sharon demanded. "What's happening in there? Is my husband with them?"

"We don't know everything about the situation," Lisa said softly. "What we *do* know is that there are now three SWAT officers inside the Security Council chamber. Apparently, they were able to get all but one of the terrorists—"

"*And he has Harleigh!*" Sharon screamed. She clawed at her temples. "*Oh my God, he has my baby!*"

The woman grabbed Sharon's wrists and held them gently but firmly. She moved her fingers into Sharon's tightly curled fingers and squeezed them.

"Where's my husband!" Sharon cried.

"Mrs. Hood, you've got to listen to me," Lisa said.

322

"You know they're going to do everything they can to protect your daughter, but it may take a little time. You're going to have to be strong."

"I want my husband!" Sharon sobbed.

"Where did he go?" the woman asked.

"I don't know," Sharon said. "He—he said he had to do something about this. He has a cell phone. I have to call him!"

"Why don't you give me the number; I'll do it," the woman said.

Sharon gave the woman Paul's cell phone number.

"Okay," Lisa said. She released Sharon's hands and pointed to one of the tables. "I'm just going over there to make the call. You sit here, and I'll be right back."

Sharon nodded. Then she started to cry again.

She sat there sobbing as Lisa Baroni walked over to the table with the telephones. She tried the number. Hood had shut off his phone.

Sharon couldn't remember a time when she'd felt such anger and despair. She didn't need a State Department official holding her hand right now. She needed her husband. She needed to talk to him, not to feel so utterly alone. Whatever he was doing, wherever he was, at least he could have given her that. Just that.

However this ended, Sharon knew one thing for certain.

She could never forgive Paul for this.

Never.

FIFTY-ONE

New York, New York
Sunday, 12:16 A.M.

Paul Hood was running through the park when he heard the explosion and saw the flash behind the UN. Since he didn't see or hear shards of glass, he assumed that it was Mike Rodgers blowing the window in. Hood ran ahead hard, watching as the police who had been guarding the lobby entrance hurried around back. By the time Hood arrived, children and delegates were already running out through the shattered window.

They did it, Hood thought proudly. He hoped that Rodgers and August were all right.

Hood was out of breath by the time he reached the courtyard. One of the police officers had run ahead toward First Avenue. He had obviously radioed EMT personnel and wanted to show them where to set their stations up—in the parking lot, away from the building. Meanwhile, the other officers were ushering the young women and delegates through the courtyard toward the lot. Everyone was walking under their own power. They appeared relatively unhurt.

Hood stopped and watched as they approached. He didn't see Harleigh among them, but he recognized one of her friends, Laura Sabia. He went over to her.

"Laura!" he cried.

One of the police officers moved to intercept him. "Excuse me, sir, but you'll have to wait for your daughter—"

"She isn't my daughter, officer. I'm Paul Hood of Op-Center in Washington. We organized this rescue."

"Congratulations," said the officer, "but I still need you to get out of the area and let us—"

"Mr. Hood!" Laura said, stepping out of the line.

Hood slid around the police officer. He ran over and took the young girl's hand. "Laura, thank God. Are you all right?"

"I'm okay," she said.

"What about Harleigh?" he asked. "I don't see her."

"She's—she's still inside."

Hood felt like he'd been punched hard in the gut. "In there?" he asked. "In the Security Council?"

Laura nodded.

Hood looked into the girl's bloodshot eyes. He didn't like what he saw. "Is she hurt?"

"No," Laura said as she shook her head and started to cry. "But he has her."

"Who does?"

"The man who shot Barbara."

"One of the terrorists?" Hood asked.

Laura nodded.

Hood didn't wait to hear any more. Releasing Laura's hand and ignoring the officer's shout to stop, he ran toward the terrace.

FIFTY-TWO

New York, New York
Sunday, 12:18 A.M.

Harleigh's head rose above the back of the seats and
stopped. Downer was below the seats, still holding her
hair tightly. The girl's face was pale and upturned, her
eyes straining from the sides. The tip of the gun barrel
was pressed to the back of her head.

Mike Rodgers was at the foot of the gallery, in the
center. Because of the steep slope of the rows and the
intervening seats, the only target he had was the hostage-
taker's left hand. That was too close to Harleigh's neck,
and it still left his right hand free, holding the gun. He
kept his gun trained on the hand, though he knew that
they weren't going to be able to let this go on for very
long. The drape would only contain the poison gas for
another few minutes. Even if he could get to a gas mask,
that wouldn't help Harleigh.

August was crawling up the stairs on the north side
of the chamber, to Rodgers's right. Though hobbled by
the gunshot wounds to his legs and clearly in pain, the
colonel had no intention of sitting this out. Behind the
terrorist, the UN security agent entered the room cautiously from the back door. That had to be Lieutenant
Mailman, the one who briefed Chatterjee after the failed
attack on the Security Council.

Suddenly, Rodgers heard a sound behind him. He turned as Hood appeared in the frame of the shattered window. Rodgers motioned him back.

Hood hesitated, but only for a moment. He stepped away, into the darkness of the terrace.

Rodgers faced the gallery and turned his gun back to the terrorist.

"Hey, hero!" the terrorist cried. "You see that I have her?"

His voice was loud, challenging, uncompromising. They weren't going to be able to bully this man. But Rodgers had another idea.

"You *see?*" the terrorist asked again.

"I see," Rodgers said.

"And I'll kill the bloody girl if I have to!" Downer yelled. "I'll put a hole in the back of her goddamned head!"

"I saw you kill my partner," Rodgers said. "I believe you."

August stopped and looked at Rodgers. Rodgers motioned for him to stay still. August did. He was supposed to be dead.

"What do you want us to do?" Rodgers asked.

"First, I want whoever's creeping up behind me to get the hell out of here," the terrorist said. "I can see his feet from here. I can also see the window, so if anyone tries to sneak in, I'll know it."

"No tricks," Rodgers said. "I hear you."

"I hope so," Downer said. "When he's gone, I want you to put your gun down and raise your hands straight up. When you're both out of here, I want you to send that bitch secretary-general in with her hands on her head."

"You don't have a lot of time," Rodgers pointed out. "The gas will come through the—"

"I know about the gas," Downer cried. "I won't *need* a lot of time if you shut up and move!"

"All right," Rodgers said. He looked up at the door. "Lieutenant—please make sure the secretary-general is outside and then stay out of the room. I'm coming up to join you."

Mailman hesitated.

Rodgers moved the gun from the terrorist's hand to Mailman's forehead. "Lieutenant, I said I want you out of here."

Mailman scowled and backed from the Security Council.

Rodgers squatted, put his gun on the floor, and lifted his hands high. Then he walked toward the staircase on the south side of the chamber. He quickly made his way up the stairs. He didn't think the terrorist would bother firing at him. Until Secretary-General Chatterjee came in, Rodgers was his only means of communicating with the outside.

Rodgers continued up the stairwell. He was nearly level with the fourth row from the top, where the terrorist was hiding. He was looking at Harleigh, whose back was toward him. The slender girl was locked in place, with her hair pulled tight. She wasn't crying, but that didn't surprise him. From talking to POWs, Rodgers knew that pain provided focus. It was often a mercy, a distraction from danger or a seemingly hopeless situation.

He wanted to say something encouraging to Harleigh. At the same time, he didn't want to do anything that might annoy the terrorist. Not when there was a gun barrel pressed against the girl's skull.

Rodgers backed out the door. That gave him one last chance to glance toward the north side of the chamber. He couldn't see Brett August from where he was standing. Either the colonel had snuggled up close to the seats or else he'd lost so much blood from his wounds that he'd passed out.

Rodgers hoped that wasn't the case. This was going to be difficult enough as it was.

Rodgers stepped into the hallway. Chatterjee was there. She looked at him for a moment, then put her hands on her head and started toward the door to the Security Council.

Rodgers put his arm in front of her, barring her way.

"You know about the poison gas?" he asked.

"The lieutenant told me," she replied.

Rodgers stepped closer. "Did he also tell you that one of my men is still in there?" he whispered.

She seemed surprised.

"The terrorist thinks my man is dead," Rodgers said. "If Colonel August can get a shot, he's going to take it. I didn't want you to be surprised and give him away."

Chatterjee's expression darkened.

Rodgers lowered his arm, and the secretary-general walked past him. As she entered the Security Council and shut the door behind her, Rodgers felt like running in after her and dragging her out. He had a sick feeling deep in his belly, the feeling that despite everything that had happened, Chatterjee still believed in an unwritten United Nations policy. A policy that the world organization had upheld repeatedly against the weight of common sense and fundamental morality.

The idea that terrorists had rights.

FIFTY-THREE

New York, New York
Sunday, 12:21 A.M.

Mala Chatterjee's mind and soul were tortured as she entered the Security Council chamber.

The terrorist was lying on the floor. Chatterjee saw the head of his prisoner, and she saw the gun being held against it. She ached for the child and was revulsed by the act of terrorism. Chatterjee would do anything to save the girl.

But the secretary-general was troubled by the idea of allowing a murder to take place when there might be another way. If she became like these people, if she killed without conscience, without the law, what kind of meaning would her life have? She didn't even know whether this man had actually killed anyone, whether he *could* kill anyone.

Chatterjee walked down the steps toward the row. "You asked to speak with me," she said.

"No, I asked you to come in," Downer said. "I don't want to talk. I want out of here. I also want what I came for."

"I want to help you," Chatterjee said. She stopped at the foot of the aisle. "Let the girl go."

"I said no more *talk!*" Downer screamed. Harleigh shrieked as the Australian tugged harder on her hair.

''There's poison gas leaking up front. I need you to arrange a place where the lady and I can wait while you get my money and transportation. I want the six million dollars.''

"All right," she said.

Chatterjee saw something move on the northern staircase. There were eyes peering over the armrest of the last seat. The man who had been left inside raised himself up slightly. He put his index finger to his lips.

The secretary-general was torn. Was she about to be part of a rescue effort or an accomplice to a cold-blooded killing? This American soldier and his partner had rescued most of the hostages. Perhaps it had been necessary for them to kill, but that didn't give them the right to continue killing. Chatterjee's goal had always been to find a bloodless solution to conflict. She couldn't give that up while there was still a chance. There was also the matter of trust. If she could convince the terrorist that she wanted to help him, perhaps she could convince him to surrender.

"Colonel August," she said, "there has been enough killing today."

August froze. For a moment, Chatterjee wondered if he were going to shoot her.

"Who are you talking to?" Downer demanded. "Who's *here*?"

"Another soldier," she told him.

"Then he wasn't killed, the bastard!" Downer cried.

"Please put down your weapons and leave, Colonel," Chatterjee said.

"I can't," August replied bitterly. "I've been shot."

"You'll be shot again if you don't get the hell out of here!" Downer screamed.

The Australian swung Harleigh around roughly. He pulled her up by her hair, knelt behind her, and aimed his automatic at August. He fired a burst as the Striker leader dropped back onto the stairwell. Wood from the armrests flew in every direction. The bursts echoed for a moment after he stopped firing.

Snarling, Downer looked back at Chatterjee. He kept Harleigh between himself and August. At the bottom of the chamber, the secretary-general could see the poison gas beginning to creep around the edges of the drape.

"Get him out!" Downer cried.

"I'm trying to help you!" Chatterjee shouted at Downer. "Let me handle—"

"Shut up and do what I said!" Downer screamed. He turned to face her as he did. For a moment his chest was facing the front of the chamber.

A gunshot ripped through the chamber. The bullet punched a hole in the right side of Downer's neck, away from Harleigh. He dropped the gun and released Harleigh as the impact sent his arms back.

Paul Hood rose from the bottom of the Security Council chamber. He was holding the Beretta Mike Rodgers had left behind.

"Get down, Harleigh!" he cried.

She covered her head and dropped straight down. A moment later, a second gunshot cracked from the north-side staircase. Colonel August put a shot cleanly through the terrorist's left cheek. A second bullet drilled through Downer's temple as he fell.

Blood collected on the floor even before his body landed.

Chatterjee screamed.

Paul Hood dropped the gun and ran around to the north-side staircase. Waved on by August, Hood continued up to his daughter's side.

FIFTY-FOUR

New York, New York
Sunday, 12:25 A.M.

When he first left the Security Council chamber, Mike Rodgers notifed the NYPD's hazardous materials squad to tell them about the poison gas leak. The team assembled in the north-side courtyard and was ready to move in as soon as everyone was out. The entire UN complex had been closed off; now it was quarantined, the doors and windows covered with plastic sheets, the edges of which were sealed with fast-drying foam. Because there was no one left to tell the police exactly what the poison gas was, an Emergency Service mobile laboratory had been driven to the scene for on-site analysis. New York Fire Department Emergency Medical Service Command crews were on hand, setting up tents in the Robert Moses Playground just south of the United Nations. So was the FDNY's Marine 1. The fire department presence was required by law in situations involving hazardous materials. Many terrorist groups follow a scorched-earth policy. If they can't win, they'll make sure that no one does. Since one of the terrorists had vanished from the United Nations infirmary, and the NYPD didn't know if there were additional accomplices, they had to be prepared for anything. Including a final act of spite.

Paul Hood and his daughter took a long moment to

embrace. Hood was crying openly. Harleigh was shaking violently. Her head was on his chest and she was clutching his arms. One of the medical technicians threw a blanket over her shoulders before leading them out to the EMSC tents.

"We've got to get word to your mother," Hood said through his tears.

Harleigh nodded.

Mike Rodgers was standing behind them, watching as medics carried Brett August away. Rodgers said he'd take care of bringing Sharon over. He also told Hood that he was proud of him. Hood thanked him. But the truth was that when Rodgers left the Security Council and Hood snuck in, he knew that nothing—not his own safety, not national or international law—was going to keep him from trying to save Harleigh.

Hood and his daughter headed toward the escalators along with delegates and security personnel. As they started downstairs, he couldn't imagine what was going through Harleigh's mind. She was still holding him tightly and staring ahead with glazed eyes. Harleigh wasn't in shock; she hadn't suffered any of the physical injuries that brought on hypovolemic, cardiogenic, neurogenic, septic, or anaphylactic conditions. But the young girl had spent about five hours in that room watching people being shot, including one of her best friends. She had nearly been executed herself. The posttraumatic stress would be intense.

Hood knew from experience that what had happened today was going to be with his daughter every moment of every day for the rest of her life. Former hostages were never truly free. They were haunted by a sense of hopeless isolation, the humiliation of being treated as a thing and not as a human being. Dignity could be rebuilt, but in an unintegrated, patchwork fashion. The sum of the parts would never equal the shattered whole.

What life puts us through, Hood thought.

But his daughter was safe in his arms. As they reached the bottom of the second elevator, Hood saw Sharon running across the lobby. If anyone had tried to keep her out, obviously they'd failed. A woman from the State Department was behind her, desperately trying to keep up.

"My baby!" Sharon was screaming. *"My girl!"*

Harleigh broke away from Hood and ran to her mother. They clutched each other and wept convulsively, Sharon threatening to engulf the girl with her arms. Hood stood back.

Rodgers walked in, accompanied by Bill Mohalley. Beyond them, in the courtyard, Secretary-General Chatterjee was talking to reporters. She was gesturing angrily.

"I want to shake your hand," Deputy Chief Mohalley said. He offered Hood a powerful handclasp. "You three rewrote the crisis management book today. I'm honored to have been here to see it."

"Thanks," Hood said. "How's Brett?"

"He'll be okay," Rodgers told him. "The bullets missed the femoral artery. The wounds caused more pain than damage."

Hood nodded. He was still looking at Chatterjee. There were spots of the terrorist's blood on her outfit, hands, and face.

"She doesn't seem very happy," Hood said.

Mohalley shrugged. "We're going to hear a lot of shit about what you did here," he said. "But the hostages are safe, four of the terrorists are taking a dirt nap, and one thing is certain.''

"What's that?" Rodgers asked.

"It'll be a blustery day in hell before anyone tries something like this again," Mohalley said.

FIFTY-FIVE

New York, New York
Sunday, 12:51 A.M.

Alexander was asleep when Hood walked into the hotel room.

Sharon had gone to the NYU Medical Center with Harleigh. In addition to a physical checkup, it was important that she talk to a psychologist as soon as possible. Harleigh had to understand that she did nothing to bring this on herself and shouldn't feel guilty about having survived it. Before any of the other damage could be attended to, she had to understand that.

Hood stood by the side of the king-size bed and looked down at his son. The boy's life had changed, his sister's needs would be different, and he didn't even know it. The innocence of sleep.

Hood turned and went into the bathroom. He filled the sink and washed his face. His life had changed, too. He'd killed a man. And whether the man deserved to die or not, Hood had killed him on international territory. There would probably be a trial, and it might not be in the United States. The process could take years, and it might very well compromise the security of Op-Center.

How did they know certain things? To what extent were the CIA and the State Department involved? What was the connection between the U.S. government and the missing Bulgarian Georgiev? The government agencies had no authority in any of these areas.

The irony was that the United Nations might come out of this looking like the wounded party, the victim of a United States conspiracy. From withholding dues to bugging the secretary-general, we'd broken many of the rules that States Members of the United Nations promised to uphold. Nations that sponsored terrorism, trafficked in narcotics, and crushed human rights would be able to wag their fingers indignantly at the United States.

And we would take it. We would take it because the media would be watching. Hood had always felt that television and the United Nations were made for each other. In their eyes, everyone was the same size.

Hood toweled off and looked at himself in the mirror. Sadly, he didn't think the most difficult fight would be with his enemies. That would come when he and Sharon tried to talk. Not just about his behavior tonight but about a future that suddenly looked very different from what they'd been planning.

"Enough," he said quietly.

Hood dropped the towel on the counter and took a drink of tap water. He walked slowly back to the bedroom. The night was starting to catch up with him. His legs were weak from all the running, and he'd strained his lower back when he'd run crouching into the Security Council chamber. He eased himself down beside Alexander. He kissed the boy lightly behind the ear. He hadn't done that in years and was surprised. He could still smell the remnants of little boyhood there.

The peace of the child gave comfort to the man. And as he slipped into sleep, Hood's last thought was how strange it all was. He had helped to make these two children. Yet by their needs and by their love, the reverse was also true.

These children had created a father.

FIFTY-SIX

New York, New York
Sunday, 7:00 A.M.

A call from Bill Mohalley startled Hood awake at seven A.M.

The State Department official was calling to inform Hood that his wife, daughter, and the other families were being brought to La Guardia Airport for a flight to Washington. Mohalley said that his wife had been notified at the hospital and that the NYPD would arrive at the hotel in an hour to escort him and his son to the airport.

"Why the quick evac?" Hood asked. He was sore and groggy, and the bright, white sunshine was like an acid bath in his skull.

"It's mostly for you," Mohalley said, "though we don't want it to seem like we're hustling you out."

"I don't follow," Hood said. "And why is the NYPD handling this instead of the State Department?"

"Because the police are used to protecting news makers," he said. "And like it or not, you just became one."

Hood's cell phone beeped. It was Ann Farris. Hood thanked Mohalley and got out of bed. He walked toward the door where he wouldn't wake Alexander and it was mercifully much darker.

"Good morning," Hood said.

"Good morning," Ann said. "How are you?"

"Surprisingly well," he said.

"I hope I didn't wake you—"

"No," Hood said, "the State Department did."

"Anything important?" she asked.

"Yeah," he said. "They want me up and out of here."

"I'm glad," she said. "You're pretty exposed right now."

"And obviously out of the loop," he said. "What the hell's been happening, Ann?"

"It's what we press professionals call a shitstorm," she said. "Since no one has the names of what they're calling the two 'SWAT men' who went in before you, this whole thing has become the Paul Hood Show."

"Courtesy of Mala Chatterjee," Hood said.

"She's not very happy with you," Ann said. "She says you risked your daughter's life needlessly for a speedy and criminal resolution to the crisis."

"Up hers," Hood replied.

"Can I quote you on that?" Ann quipped.

"Banner headline," Hood replied. "What's the fall-out so far?"

"Security-wise, Bob Herbert's on top of that," she said. "You're the only face on a team that helped kill terrorists from three different countries. Bob's just starting to sift through the possible links they had with other terrorist groups or the sicko nationalists who may want to avenge them."

"Yeah, well, forgive me for not having worried about that," Hood said bitterly.

"This isn't a question of blame or forgiveness," the press liaison said. "It's about special interests. It's what

344

I've been telling all of you for years. Spin control isn't a luxury anymore. The way every system in the world is interconnected, it's a necessity.''

That symbiosis was true, Hood had to admit. And it was sometimes true in unexpected ways. Fifteen years before, intelligence collected by Bob Herbert's CIA team was routinely made available to other American intelligence groups, including Naval intelligence. When Naval analyst Jonathan Pollard turned over U.S. intelligence secrets to the Israelis in the 1980s, several of those secrets were subsequently given to Moscow in exchange for the release of Jewish refugees. Hard-line Communists in Moscow used that intelligence to plot against the Russian government. Years later, when Op-Center became embroiled in thwarting the coup attempt, Herbert's own data was used against him.

"How *is* this playing in the press?" Hood asked.

"On the national op-ed pages it's playing very well,'' Ann said. "For the first time in history, the liberal and conservative press are united. They're portraying you as a 'hero-dad.' ''

"And on the international op-ed pages?" he asked.

"You could run for Prime Minister in Great Britain and Israel and probably win,'' she said. "Other than that, the news isn't good. The secretary-general described you as 'just another impatient American with a gun.' She's demanding an investigation and house arrest. The rest of the world press I've seen so far has picked up that mantra.''

"Bottom line?" Hood asked.

"Just what you said,'' she told him. "You're being evacuated. No one in the State Department or the White House has decided how to play any of this yet. I guess they want you here to help figure it out. Though I will tell you that Bob has taken the precaution of contacting the Chevy Chase police and ordering up some security for your home. They're there now. Just in case.''

Hood thanked her, then woke Alexander to get him ready. Hood had always been very open with his kids, and as they dressed, he told the boy exactly what had happened the night before. Alexander was dubious until the NYPD showed up to escort Hood and his son from the hotel. The six officers treated Hood as one of their own, commending him as they led the two through the basement to the garage and a waiting motorcade of three squad cars. The rock-star exit impressed Alexander more than anything he'd experienced in New York.

The Hoods and the other families flew back to Washington, D.C., on an Air Force 737. Sharon had been very quiet during the hour flight. She sat with Harleigh beside her, the young girl's head on her shoulder. Hood had sat across the aisle, watching. Like most of the young musicians, Harleigh had been given a mild sedative to help her sleep. Unlike most of the girls, however, her sleep was punctuated by tiny whines, shouts, and spasms. Maybe the greatest tragedy of all, Hood realized, was that he hadn't saved Harleigh from that damn room. The poor girl was still there in spirit if not in body.

The aircraft landed at Andrews Air Force Base, ostensibly so the military could assure the privacy of the children. But Hood knew better. Andrews was where Op-Center was based. After they taxied, Hood saw Op-Center's white van waiting for him on the tarmac. Lowell Coffey and Bob Herbert were both visible in the open side door.

Sharon didn't see the men until she was on her way

down the steps. Hood acknowledged them with a nod. They remained in the van.

The State Department had provided wheelchairs for anyone who wanted them. They also provided a bus to bring everyone home. An official told the parents that their cars would be collected from the airport later that day.

Sharon and Hood both helped Harleigh into a wheelchair. Alexander manfully took his place behind the chair as Sharon turned to her husband.

"You're not coming with us, are you?" Sharon asked. Her voice was flat and withdrawn, her eyes distant.

"I honestly didn't know they'd be here," he said, jerking a thumb toward the van.

"But you're not surprised."

"No," he admitted. "I did kill someone on foreign soil. There's going to be fallout from that. But you'll be okay. Bob's arranged for round-the-clock police protection at the house."

"I wasn't worried," Sharon said and turned toward the chair. Hood took her hand in his. She stopped.

"Sharon, don't do this."

"Do what?" she asked. "Go home with our children?"

"Don't shut me out," he said.

"I'm not shutting you out, Paul," Sharon said. "Just like you, I'm trying to stay calm and deal with things. What we decide over the next few days is going to affect our daughter for the rest of her life. I want to be emotionally ready to make those decisions."

"We have to be ready to make those decisions," Hood said. "That's *our* job."

"I hope so," Sharon said. "But you've got two families again. I'm not going to waste any more energy fighting for equal time."

"Two families?" Hood said. "Sharon, I didn't ask for this to happen. I was out of Op-Center! If I'm back, it's because I'm in the middle of an international incident. I—*we*—won't be able to handle this alone."

Just then, the State Department official came over. He told them the bus was loaded and waiting. Sharon told Alexander to go ahead. She said she'd be there in a moment. Hood gave his son a wink and told him to keep a careful eye on his sister. Alexander said he would.

Hood looked back at his wife. Sharon was looking up at him. There were tears in her eyes.

"And when this international incident is finished?" Sharon asked. "Will we have you then? Do you really think you'll be happy helping to manage a household instead of running a city or a government agency?"

"I don't know," Hood admitted. "Give me a chance to find out."

"A chance?" Sharon smiled. "Paul, this may not make any sense to you, but last night, when I heard what you did for Harleigh, I was angry at you."

"Angry? Why?"

"Because you risked your life, your reputation, your career, your freedom, to save our daughter," she said.

"And that made you *angry?*" Hood said. "I can't believe that—"

"It did," she said. "All I ever wanted from you were little bits of your life. Time for a violin recital, a soccer game, a vacation once in a while. Dinner as a family. Holidays with my parents. I rarely got any of that. I couldn't even get you to sit with me last night while our baby was in danger."

"I was too busy trying to get her *out*—"

"I know," she said. "And you did. You showed me what you can do when you want to. When you *want* to."

"Are you saying I didn't want to be with my family?" Hood said. "Sharon, you're stressed out—"

"I said you wouldn't understand," she told him. The tears trickled down her cheeks. "I'd better go."

"No, wait," Hood said. "Not like this—"

"Please, they're waiting," Sharon said. She withdrew her hand and ran toward the bus.

Hood watched his wife go. After the accordion door was shut and the bus growled to life, Hood started walking toward Coffey and Herbert.

Now Hood was angry.

He couldn't believe it. Even his wife had found fault with what he'd done in the Security Council chamber. Maybe she and Chatterjee should hold a press conference.

But the anger began to pass as Hood walked toward the van. And just as suddenly, something else began to eat at him. It was a mixture of guilt and doubt, and it started bubbling up the moment Hood saw Bob Herbert stretch out his big, welcoming hand.

The moment Hood realized that he no longer felt so alone.

The moment Paul Hood had to ask himself the honest and very painful question:

What if Sharon was right?

FIFTY-SEVEN

Washington, D.C.
Sunday, 10:00 A.M.

The greetings were warm, and the good wishes were sincere as Hood entered the van. There was no driver. After Herbert shut the door and Hood had settled into the passenger's seat, Coffey drove the short distance to Op-Center. The attorney informed Hood that they'd only be at Op-Center long enough for him to shower, shave, and put on a clean suit Herbert had brought from the house.

"Why?" Hood asked. "Where are we going?"

"To the White House," Coffey said.

"What's waiting for me there, Lowell?" Hood asked.

"I honestly don't know," Coffey admitted. "Secretary-General Chatterjee is flying down with Ambassador Meriwether to see President Lawrence. They're meeting at noon. The president is the one who wants you there."

"Any idea why?"

"I can't imagine the president wants a he-said, she-said thing," Coffey replied. "Anything else I can think of is not good."

"Meaning?" Hood asked.

"Meaning he may want to send you back to New York in the custody of the American ambassador," Coffey said. "To make sure you're around to answer any questions the secretary-general and her associates may have. A gesture of our concern."

Herbert's wheelchair was parked behind and between the seats. "A gesture," he snorted. "Paul saved the friggin' place. What he did took as much guts as I've ever seen. Mike and Brett were also great. But Paul—when I heard that you were the one who took the last guy out, I was never prouder of anyone. Never."

"Unfortunately," Coffey said, "international law does not provide for 'proud' as a defense."

"And I'm telling you, Lowell, if Paul is sent to New York or the goddamned Hague and the International Court of Supposed Justice," Herbert said, "or some other half-assed place where they serve up scapegoat on hot coals, *I'm* gonna take hostages."

The debate was typical Herbert-Coffey and, as usual, the real world was somewhere between the two extremes. There were legal issues, to be sure, but courts also took emotional exigencies into consideration. Hood wasn't as concerned about that as he was about the near future. He wanted to be with his family, helping Harleigh through her recovery. He couldn't do that if he were defending himself in some other country.

Hood also wanted to stay with Op-Center. Maybe resignation had been an overreaction. Maybe he should have taken a leave of absence.

And maybe that's all academic now, he reminded himself. A few days ago, his future was still in his own hands. Now it was in the hands of the president of the United States.

Since no one else knew that Hood was being brought here, none of the primary weekday staff was present.

The weekend team congratulated Hood for his heroism and Harleigh's rescue. They wished him luck and support with whatever came next.

The hot shower felt good on Hood's sore muscles, and the fresh clothes felt even better. Forty-five minutes after arriving at Andrews, Hood was back in the van with Herbert handling security and Coffey at the wheel.

FIFTY-EIGHT

Washington, D.C.
Sunday, 11:45 A.M.

Sitting in the limousine that was taking her to the White House, Mala Chatterjee felt unclean.

It had nothing to do with her physical state, though she could have used a long rest and a bath. She had settled, instead, for a shower in her office and a nap on the flight down.

The feeling she had was the result of watching diplomacy die in a slaughterhouse. Though she hadn't been able to control the bloodshed, she was determined to control the cleanup. And it would be thorough.

Mala Chatterjee had not spoken much with Ambassador Flora Meriwether during the ride up. As cohostess of the Saturday-night event, the fifty-seven-year-old ambassador had been late going to the Security Council, just as Chatterjee had been. Thus, the ambassador and her husband had not been among the hostages. However, the ambassador had not remained with the other delegates after the takeover. She had gone to her office, claiming that this was a matter for Chatterjee and her advisers to handle. That was true, although Meriwether could not have put more distance between herself and the takeover.

The ambassador didn't want to appear to pressure the

UN into allowing American negotiators or SWAT personnel to become involved, Chatterjee knew. Which was ironic, given how the siege turned out.

Mala Chatterjee did not know how the ambassador felt now. Or what the president was thinking. Not that it mattered. The secretary-general had insisted on this meeting because she needed to immediately reestablish the right of the United Nations to settle its own disputes and discipline those nations that broke international law. The United Nations had been quick to condemn Iraq for invading Kuwait. They could be no less quick to bring the United States to justice for interfering in the hostage crisis.

The international press was waiting en masse for the limousine when it passed through the southwest appointment gate. Ambassador Meriwether declined to speak but waited while Chatterjee spoke to the group.

"The events of the past eighteen hours have been difficult ones for the United Nations and its family," she said, "and we mourn the loss of so many of our valued coworkers. While we are gratified that the former hostages have been reunited with their families, we cannot condone the methods that were used to end the crisis. The success of the United Nations and its operations depends upon the forbearance of the host nations. I've asked for this meeting with the president and Ambassador Meriwether so that we can begin to accomplish two very important goals. First, to reconstruct the events that undermined the sovereignty of the United Nations, its charter, and its commitment to diplomacy. And second, to make absolutely certain that its sovereignty is not violated in the future."

Chatterjee thanked the group, ignoring shouted questions and promising she'd have more to say after meeting with the president. She hoped that she conveyed the feeling that she'd felt violated by members of the American military.

The route to the Oval Office is a zigzag that takes a visitor past the office of the press secretary and the Cabinet Room. Beyond the Cabinet Room is the office of the president's executive secretary. This is the only entrance to the Oval Office, and a member of the Secret Service is stationed there at all times.

The president was ready promptly at noon. He personally came out to welcome Mala Chatterjee. Michael Lawrence stood six-foot-four, with a close-cropped head of silvery gray hair and dark, sun-weathered skin. His smile was wide and genuine, his handshake was strong, and his deep voice resonated from somewhere around his knees.

"It's good to see you again, Madam Secretary-General," he said.

"Likewise, Mr. President, though I wish the circumstances were different," she replied.

The president's blue gray eyes shifted to Ambassador Meriwether. He had known her for nearly thirty years. She had been a fellow poly-sci student at NYU, and the president had pulled her from academia to serve in the UN.

"Flora," he said, "would you mind giving us a few minutes?"

"Not at all," she said.

While the president's executive secretary shut the door, the president showed Secretary-General Chatterjee to a seat. Chatterjee's shoulders were straight, her neck tall and stiff. Dressed in a gray suit, no tie, the president was more at ease as he used a remote to click off the TV. The set had been tuned to CNN.

"I heard your remarks to the press," the president said. "When you talked about the events that undermined the sovereignty of the United Nations, were you referring to the terrorist attack?"

Chatterjee sat in a yellow armchair. She folded her hands on her lap and crossed her legs.

"No, Mr. President," the secretary-general said. "That is very much a separate issue. I was referring to the uninvited attack by Mr. Paul Hood of your National Crisis Management Center and two as yet unidentified members of the United States military."

"You're referring to the attack that ended the hostage crisis," he said pleasantly.

"The result is not the issue," Chatterjee countered firmly. "At the moment, I am deeply concerned with the means."

"I see," he said. The president sat behind his desk. "And what would you like to do about it?"

"I would like for Mr. Hood to return to New York and answer questions pertaining to the attack," she said.

"You want him to go right now?" the president asked. "While his daughter's recovering from the attack?"

"He doesn't have to return immediately," she replied. "The middle of the week would be acceptable."

"I see. And these questions," the president said. "What do you hope to accomplish?"

"I need to formally ascertain whether laws were broken and whether boundaries were overstepped," she replied.

"Madam Secretary-General," the president said, "if

I may, you're failing to see the larger picture here."

"And that is?"

"I believe that the New York Police Department, the State Department, the FBI, and U.S. military units in the region acted with extraordinary restraint and respect, given how many young Americans were at risk. When the situation deteriorated and your own security forces were repulsed—yes, three of our people did go into the Security Council. But they did it selflessly and effectively, like U.S. soldiers have always done."

"Their courage is not being questioned," Chatterjee said. "But the law-abiding nature of the many does not outweigh the heroic lawlessness of the few. If laws were broken, then legal remedies may be required. This is not whim on my part, Mr. President. This is our charter. This is our law. And there have already been demands that those laws be upheld."

"Demands made by whom?" the president asked. "By nations whose terrorists were killed in the attack?"

"By the civilized nations of the world," she replied.

"And to satisfy their civilized bloodlust, you'll want to put Paul Hood on trial," the president said.

"Sarcasm noted," Chatterjee said. "And yes, a trial is a possibility. Mr. Hood's actions demand it."

The president sat back. "Madam Secretary-General, last night Paul Hood became a hero to me and about two hundred and fifty million other Americans. We had a few villains in this, including a rogue CIA agent who will probably spend the rest of her life in prison. But there's no way on earth that man is going to stand trial for saving his daughter from a terrorist."

Chatterjee regarded the president for a moment. "You will not turn him over for questioning?"

"I think that pretty much sums up this administration's position," the president said.

"The United States will defy the will of the international community?" she asked.

"Openly and enthusiastically," the president replied. "And frankly, Madam Secretary-General, I don't think the delegates to the United Nations will care for very long."

"We are not the Congress, Mr. President," she said. "Don't misjudge our ability to remain focused."

"Never," the president said. "I'm sure the delegates will be very focused trying to find suitable schools and apartments when this administration supports removing the United Nations from New York to another world capital, say Khartoum or Rangoon."

Chatterjee felt herself flush. *The bastard. The bullying bastard.* "Mr. President, I do not respond to threats."

"But you do," the president said. "You responded to that one, quickly and openly."

It took her a moment to realize that he was right.

"No one likes to be pushed," the president said, "and that's all we're doing here. What we need to do is to find a nonconfrontational, nonthreatening solution to this problem. One that's going to work better for everyone."

"Such as?" she asked. As frustrated as Chatterjee was, she was still a diplomat. She would listen.

"A more productive way of appeasing those irate delegates might be if the United States were to begin paying all of its two billion dollar debt," the president said. "The delegates would have more money for UN programs back home, such as the World Food Council, the Children's Fund, the Institute for Training and Research. And if we work this right, they'll feel as though they've

360

won something. They will have won American capitulation on the debt issue. Your own status will not suffer,'' he pointed out.

Chatterjee looked at him coldly. "Mr. President, I appreciate the thought you've put into this. But there are legal issues that cannot be dismissed.''

The president smiled. "Madam Secretary-General, almost twenty-five years ago, a Russian—Alexander Solzhenitsyn—said something at a commencement address that this lawyer never forgot. 'I have spent all my life under a Communist regime,' he said, 'and I will tell you that a society without any objective legal scale is a terrible one indeed. But a society with no other scale but the legal one is not quite worthy of man either.' ''

Chatterjee regarded the president carefully. This was the first time since she'd entered the Oval Office that she saw anything in his eyes, in his expression, that approached sincerity.

"Madam Secretary-General,'' the president said, "you're exhausted. May I make a suggestion?''

"Please,'' she said.

"Why don't you go back to New York, rest, and think about what I've said,'' the president told her. "Think about how we can work together to establish new moral objectives.''

"Instead of deciding old ones?'' she asked.

"Instead of rehashing divisive ones,'' he replied. "We need to heal the divide, not make it wider.''

Chaterjee sighed and rose. "I believe I can agree to at least that, Mr. President,'' she said.

"I'm glad,'' he replied. "I'm sure the rest will fall into place.''

The president came from behind his desk. He shook her hand and walked her toward the door.

The secretary-general hadn't expected the meeting to unfold like this. She had known the president would resist her demand but thought that she'd be able to use the press to sway him. Now, what could she tell reporters? That the president had been a bastard. Instead of turning over an American father, he'd offered to put the UN back on sturdy financial footing and help thousands of fathers in underdeveloped countries worldwide.

As they crossed the thick blue carpet with the gold presidential seal, Chatterjee thought how ironic it was. Coming to the White House, she'd felt unclean because diplomacy had died. Yet here, in this room, it had just been practiced with skill and intelligence.

Why, then, did she feel even dirtier than before?

FIFTY-NINE

Washington, D.C.
Sunday, 12:08 P.M.

Paul Hood had been in enough politically and emotionally charged situations, both in government and on Wall Street, to know that the outcome of important meetings was often decided before the meetings were called. Key people, often no more than two, spoke or got together beforehand. By the time everyone else arrived, the talk was mostly for show.

This time, there wasn't even a show. Not inside the office, anyway.

Hood had waved to the press on his way in but declined to answer any questions. When he entered the Oval Office, Ambassador Meriwether was chatting with the president's executive secretary, forty-two-year-old Elizabeth Lopez. The two were comparing perspectives on the previous day's activities. They stopped when Hood arrived.

Hood had always found Lopez to be polite but formal. Today she was warm and welcoming. She offered him coffee from the president's private pot of Kona, which he accepted. The usually poker-faced ambassador was also unusually outgoing. Hood thought it was ironic that the only mother who seemed to disapprove of him today was the mother of his own children.

The ambassador told Hood that Mala Chatterjee was inside.

"Let me guess," Hood said. "She's demanding that I appear in front of some ad hoc committee comprised of people who hate the United States."

"You're jaded," the ambassador smiled.

"But not wrong," Hood said.

"The secretary-general is not an unreasonable woman," Ambassador Meriwether said, "just idealistic and still a little green. However, early this morning, the president and I discussed a possible solution to the problem. One which we believe the secretary-general will find acceptable."

Hood sipped his black coffee and was about to sit down when the door to the Oval Office opened. Mala Chatterjee walked out, followed by the president. The secretary-general did not look happy.

Hood put his mug aside as the president offered Ambassador Meriwether his hand.

"Madam Ambassador, thank you for coming down," the president said. "I'm glad to see you're all right."

"Thank you, sir," she said.

"Ambassador Meriwether," the president said, "the secretary-general and I just had a very productive exchange of ideas. Perhaps we can fill you in while we walk you back to the southwest appointment gate."

"Very good," she said.

The president's eyes shifted to Hood. "Paul, it's good to see you," he said, offering his hand. "How's your daughter today?"

"Pretty shaken up," Hood admitted.

"Understandably," said the president. "Our prayers

will be with you. If there's anything we can do, please ask.''

"Thank you, sir.''

"In fact, I think we've got things pretty well under control here,'' the president said. "Why don't you go home to your daughter?''

"Thank you, sir,'' Hood said.

"We'll let you know if there's anything else,'' the president said, "though it would be a good idea if you stayed away from reporters for a few days, let Op-Center's press rep handle this. At least until the secretary-general has had a chance to talk to her people in New York.''

"Of course,'' Hood said.

Hood shook the hands of the president and the ambassador. Then he shook the hand of the secretary-general. It was the first time she looked at him since the night before. Her eyes were dark and tired, her mouth was downturned, and there was gray in her hair he hadn't noticed before. She said nothing. She didn't have to. She hadn't won this battle either.

A security area sat between the end of the main corridor and the west-wing entrance. Lowell Coffey and Bob Herbert were there, chatting with a pair of secret service agents. They had not been invited to the meeting but wanted to be nearby in case Hood needed moral or tactical support or even a lift, depending on where he had to go after the meeting.

They approached Hood as the president, secretary-general, and ambassador went out to meet reporters.

"That was quick,'' Herbert said.

"What happened?'' Coffey asked.

"I don't know," Hood said. "Ambassador Meriwether and I were not in the meeting."

"Did the president say anything to you?" Coffey asked.

Hood smiled weakly. He put a hand on the attorney's shoulder. "He told me to go home to my daughter, which is exactly what I intend to do."

The three of them left the White House. They avoided reporters by heading toward West Executive Avenue and then making their way south toward the Ellipse, where they'd parked.

As they left, Hood couldn't help but feel bad for Chatterjee. She wasn't a bad person. She wasn't even the wrong person for this job. The problem was the institution itself. Nations invaded other nations or committed genocide. Then the United Nations gave them a forum to explain their acts. Just allowing them to be heard had the effect of legitimizing the immoral.

It occurred to Hood then that there might be a way for Op-Center to help rectify those abuses. A way he could use the team's resources to identify international criminals and bring them to justice. Not to trial—to justice. Before they struck, if possible.

It was something to think about. For though he owed his daughter a father, a family, he owed her something else as well. Something very few people could hope to deliver.

A saner world in which she could raise her own family.

SIXTY

Los Angeles, California
Sunday, 3:11 P.M.

He had been to many places in the world. The Arctic. The tropics. Each had their individual charms and beauty. But he had never been anywhere as instantly appealing as this place.

He walked out of the terminal and sucked down the breezy-warm air. The late afternoon sky was clear blue, and he swore he could taste the ocean in it.

He tucked his passport in his sports jacket and looked around. The courtesy buses were stopping along the curb, and he selected one that was going to a brand-name hotel. He didn't have a reservation. But when he went to the desk, he would tell the receptionist he did. He had forgotten the confirmation number; it was *their* job to remember, not his. Even if they couldn't accommodate him they would scurry to find him some place to stay. Brand-name hotels did that.

He sat down in the tram and turned around to look out the window. The spidery off-white control tower flashed by. There was rich greenery by the side of the road. The traffic moved swiftly, not like it did in New York and Paris.

Ivan Georgiev was going to like it here.

He would have liked South America, too. But things

hadn't gone as planned. Sometimes they didn't. Which was why, unlike the others, he had an escape route. If everything went wrong, Annabelle Hampton was supposed to send her floaters to collect him. The plan was for him to meet her later, at the hotel, and arrange for her to be paid either from the ransom or from his own funds.

When she didn't show, he assumed the worst. Later, when the floaters returned to put him on a plane and get him out of the country, he learned that she'd been taken. She would probably plea-bargain her way to fifteen years in prison by telling authorities about the CIA/ UNTAC link, they said. Which was why he had to leave. The CIA planned to deny everything.

Georgiev was supposed to fly on from Los Angeles to New Zealand. But the Bulgarian didn't want to go to New Zealand. He didn't want the CIA to know where he was. Besides, he had money and he had ideas. He also had connections with Eastern European expatriates, especially the Romanians, who had set up film companies in Hollywood.

Georgiev smiled. His associates had told him that the film industry was a ruthless, sexy business. A business where a foreign accent was considered exotic and cultured and was a guaranteed invitation to parties. A business where people didn't stab you in the back in private. They stabbed you in the front, in public, where others could see.

Georgiev smiled. He had the accent and he would be happy to stab people wherever they chose.

He was going to like it here.

He was going to like it very, very much.

In Italy for thirty years under the Borgias they had warfare, terror, murder, bloodshed—they produced Michelangelo, Leonardo da Vinci and the Renaissance. In Switzerland they had brotherly love, five hundred years of democracy and peace, and what did they produce? The cuckoo clock!

—Orson Welles

Tom Clancy's
Op-Centre

Created by
Tom Clancy and Steve Pieczenik

THE INTERNATIONAL BESTSELLER

Situated in Washington, Op-Centre is a beating heart of defence, intelligence and crisis-management technology, run by a crack team of operatives both within its own walls and out in the field. When a job is too dirty, or too dangerous, it is the only place the US government can turn.

But nothing can prepare Director Paul Hood and his Op-Centre crisis-management team for what they are about to uncover – a very real, very frightening power play that could unleash new players in a new world order . . .

A powerful profile of America's defence, intelligence and crisis-management technology, *Tom Clancy's Op-Centre* is the creation of Tom Clancy and Steve Pieczenik – inspiring this novel, as well as the special NBC Television presentation.

ISBN 0 00 649658 X

Tom Clancy's Op-Centre

Mirror Image

Created by
Tom Clancy and Steve Pieczenik

THE INTERNATIONAL BESTSELLER

The Cold War is over. And chaos is setting in. The new President of Russia is trying to create a new democratic regime. But there are strong elements within the country that are trying to stop him: the ruthless Russian Mafia, the right-wing nationalists and those nefarious forces that will do whatever it takes to return Russia back to the days of the Czar.

Op-Centre, the newly founded but highly successful crisis management team, begins a race against the clock and against the hardliners. Their task is made even more difficult by the discovery of a Russian counterpart . . . but this one's controlled by those same repressive hardliners.

Two rival Op-Centres, virtual mirror images of each other. But if this mirror cracks, it'll be much more than seven years' bad luck.

A powerful profile of America's defence, intelligence and crisis management technology, Tom Clancy's Op-Centre *is the creation of Tom Clancy and Steve Pieczenik – inspiring this and other gripping novels.*

ISBN 0 00 649659 8

Tom Clancy's
Op-Centre

Games of State

Created by
Tom Clancy and Steve Pieczenik

THE INTERNATIONAL BESTSELLER

In the newly unified Germany, old horrors are reborn. It is the beginning of Chaos Days, a time when neo-Nazi groups gather to spread violence and resurrect dead dreams. But this year Germany isn't the only target. Plans are afoot to destabilize Europe and cause turmoil throughout the United States.

Paul Hood and his team, already in Germany to buy technology for the new Regional Op-Centre, become entangled in the crisis. They uncover a shocking force behind the chaos – a group that uses cutting-edge technology to promote hate and influence world events.

A powerful profile of America's defence, intelligence and crisis management technology, Tom Clancy's Op-Centre *is the creation of Tom Clancy and Steve Pieczenik – inspiring this and other gripping novels.*

ISBN 0 00 649844 2

Tom Clancy's Op-Centre

Acts of War

Created by
Tom Clancy and Steve Pieczenik

THE INTERNATIONAL BESTSELLER

Syrian terrorists have attacked a dam inside the borders of Turkey, threatening the water supply of their very homeland. It is not insanity, but the first step in a deceptively simple plan: force all-out war in the Middle East. This will draw elite troops out of Damascus, leaving the Syrian president unprotected – and an easy target for assassination.

What the terrorists don't know is that a new Regional Op-Centre is now on-line in Greece. A mobile version of the permanent crisis management facility, the ROC is a cutting-edge surveillance and information mecca. And it can see exactly what the Syrian rebels are trying to do.

But the terrorists are more resourceful than anyone thinks. They also have ways of obtaining classified information. And the Regional Op-Centre – the United States' latest weapon – is a prize not to be passed up . . .

A powerful profile of America's defence, intelligence and crisis management technology, Tom Clancy's Op-Centre *is the creation of Tom Clancy and Steve Pieczenik – inspiring this and other gripping novels.*

ISBN 0 00 649845 0